HOPE WILL ANSWER

Hope Against Hope
Time of Hope

HOPE WILL
ANSWER

Susan B. Kelly

CHARLES SCRIBNER'S SONS
New York

Maxwell Macmillan International
New York   Oxford   Singapore   Sydney

First United States Edition 1993

Charles Scribner's Sons
Macmillan Publishing Company
866 Third Avenue
New York, NY 10022

Macmillan Publishing Company is part of the
Maxwell Communication Group of Companies.

ISBN 0-684-19523-2

Printed in the United States of America

For Marion and Jim Kelly
With Love

Because he cleaves to me in love, I will deliver him;
I will protect him because he knows my name.
When he calls to me, I will answer him;
I will be with him in trouble,
I will rescue him and honour him.

91st Psalm
Verses 14−15

HOPE WILL ANSWER

Prologue

Something is wrong.

There is only blackness in the computer room and Alison Hope dare not switch on the light. Although the room gives on to a City street with its plate glass window, wide as a shop front, the glass is tinted and the night is overcast and the moon is presently overwhelmed by cloud.

She tiptoes across the room, raising each foot only when the other is safely earthed. Under her breath she mutters a half-remembered childhood warble:

Whenever I feel afraid ...

Her foot skids against a box of computer printout and she stops and listens. She hears nothing but her own breath. The room is sound-proofed so that the noise of the printer may not drive workers in the ground-floor offices insane.

I hold my head up high ...

She is nearly there, at the operator's console. From there she will be able to log into the master libraries; see who else is logged in, and why, and from where.

Tonight must be the night, the night she makes the breakthrough. She has thought that on other nights but tonight has got to be the night. Time is running short. She has allowed herself two weeks, has promised to give up after two weeks.

They have been the longest two weeks of her life.

In a few minutes, perhaps, she will know the identity of the master craftsman who is draining money from FIX, destroying the credibility of Orion Software, ruining Philip's livelihood. The master craftsman who may, this morning, have tried to kill her.

Then, thank God, she will be able to go home. Unless he is too clever for her.

Only the printer is in the way now. How she longs for the clatter of the keys, nocturnally clearing the backlog of listings, which has so often jangled her nerves in the past. How she longs for any sound at all.

And whistle a happy tune . . .

Her foot brushes against something large slumped on the floor in front of the printer and her voice rises to shriek —

So no one will suspect I'm afraid . . .

— as her foot makes contact with a form in the shape of a human body but oddly still and quiet and her hand reaches down and chances on a cheek which is already cooling and her fingers slide along, groping for a pulsebeat which they cannot locate, and come back covered in something warm and gummy.

Alison Hope would never scream at a dead body, not like other, feebler, women. Alison Hope is as tall as a man and as fit as a man and as tough as a man any day of the week. She wouldn't panic — not a strong, hard woman like Alison Hope.

But wait. This woman is not, after all, Alison Hope — successful businesswoman, Managing Director of Hope Software, wealthy chatelaine of Hope Cottage in the Hop Valley. This woman is Mary Lewis: freelance computer programmer, poor, mousy, living in a shabby bedsit off the Holloway Road. She has been at great pains to *become* Mary Lewis these past few days.

Outside, the moon frees itself at last, penetrating the tinted glass, glittering on the frosted steps of the area and the broken spectacles on the computer room floor. A few strands of Mary's long mousy hair come loose from their elastic band and fall over the dead face; over eyes fixed in an understanding which had come too late.

Mary Lewis screams.

Chapter One

'So then I thought of you,' Philip Hunter said. 'Please say you'll help me, Alison. I don't know who else to turn to.'
'Nonsense,' Nick said. 'You must call in the police.'
It was half-past two in the afternoon in early November. The three of them were sitting round the dining table at Hope Cottage looking at the leftovers of a superb Sunday dinner. Alison had surpassed herself this time, Nick thought: duck, thinly sliced, on a bed of herb rice with home-made red cabbage and peas; then a choice of lemon soufflé or baked apples. He had chosen both. So had Philip.

Nick felt pleasantly full, pleasantly mellow on half a bottle of burgundy and, until a few minutes ago, very content with life.

Beyond the french windows it was drizzling as it had been for the past week and they had to have the dining room lights on even in the middle of the day. Sunset was not far away.

Alison sat at the head of the table opposite the windows. They had all risen late that day and, with no plans for braving the weather, she had put on a black track suit and her slippers; her normally tamed hair left to float almost to her waist in a fog of red. She was leaning forward in her chair, cradling a cup of coffee to her chest, listening to what Philip was saying. He and Nick sat on either side of her, facing each other.

If Alison was looking at Philip, Nick was looking at Alison with well-disguised lust. Had they been alone he would have suggested a quiet afternoon in bed; as it was he

3

was philosophical. Nevertheless he shifted uncomfortably in his seat and spread his napkin across his lap.

Philip was looking at Nick with mild exasperation. He had consumed a whole bottle of the burgundy without difficulty and his usually pale face was flushed.

'I can't do that. If I call in the police and tell them I'm a victim of computer fraud it'll make Orion Software a laughing stock and all my clients will up sticks and sign on with the opposition.'

Orion Software, Nick thought. Orion the Hunter. Philip wasn't quite the unimaginative bore he appeared to be.

'I don't want a prosecution,' he was saying. 'I just want to find out who's doing it, stop them and plug the gaps in my security.'

'That's right,' Alison said, nodding.

'Besides,' Philip went on, 'it's hard enough to get decent staff at the best of times and morale will hit rock bottom if they all think they're under suspicion.'

'There's no need – ' Nick began but Philip interrupted him rudely.

'So all in all the last thing I want is a load of pig-ignorant coppers clodhopping about the place in bloody great boots.'

'Thank you,' Nick murmured. He contained his anger. He knew Philip's sort: the middle-class liberal who bad-mouthed the police largely because he considered them his social inferiors.

But Philip had the grace to look embarrassed, 'I'm sorry ... I didn't mean ... I keep forgetting. You're not much like the policemen I've met in London. You must admit, surely, that delicacy is not the trademark of the modern urban policeman?'

A vision of Detective Superintendent Ted Seymour, disguised as a grizzly bear, waltzed through Nick's mind and he had to smile. He reined his thoughts in with difficulty to concentrate on what Philip was saying.

'I need to put someone of my own inside to find out what's going on. I racked my brains to think who there was who was both up to the job and whom I could trust. Alison is my last hope. Do say you'll help, Alison.'

4

'More coffee anyone?' Nick asked, getting up, taking his napkin with him. As he went through the door into the kitchen he heard Alison say, 'Of course I'll help, Phil. It sounds like fun.'

'Oh no you won't,' Nick said to himself as he spooned coffee into the filter. 'Fun, is it? Not if I have any say in the matter.'

When he got back to the dining room they were down to details.

'I think you should be a freelance,' Philip was saying. 'We've got Phase Two going live in a few days with much blowing of trumpets. I'll say there's going to be a third phase following straight on – make it all singing and all dancing – '

'Enabling you to charge for an upgrade?' Alison put in.

' – so we'll need some extra hands to get it ready for the spring.' Philip ignored her cynical, and accurate, remark. 'The clients are always suggesting enhancements so it all sounds very plausible.'

'But I know so little about mainframes,' Alison objected. 'They're going to think it very odd when you get in a freelance who doesn't know the software. I'm a micro expert. You'd much better make me a trainee. Then I can hang about asking dumb questions all the time and everyone will treat me like dirt and ignore me and no one will suspect that I'm spying on them.'

'Until they spot you logging into the master libraries one day. If you're freelance no one will think it at all odd if you hang around the place at evenings and weekends. In fact they won't think anything you do is odd. They'll just put it down to the usual freelance's eccentricity.'

'I still think John Hacker's going to be more suspicious of a freelance. But ... if that's the way you want to play it.'

'You'll need an assumed name, of course. Yours is quite well known. Someone at Orion may have heard of you.'

'I might even be recognised.' Alison ran her fingers through her hair and gave what sounded suspiciously like a simper. 'My photo does appear in the trade press sometimes. I think I should be disguised.' Nick groaned. They both looked at him in surprise, having completely forgotten his existence.

'Finished your little fantasy?' he enquired. 'Call in the police, Philip. There's a special squad now which deals exclusively with computer fraud. They operate out of Wood Street in the City. Some of them are FBI trained. They know the ropes and they understand the need for secrecy. They will not "clodhop" around. Alison is not going to look for your hacker and that's an end of it.'

As he began to clear away the dishes with a quite unnecessary amount of noise, Nick could feel Alison's glare boring through to a spot somewhere behind his kidneys. He left the room. He would talk sense into her later, when they were alone together.

'I'll call myself Mary,' Alison said, loudly enough to be sure of his hearing. 'That sounds nice and innocuous.'

Nick examined his conscience. Was it merely jealousy which accounted for his dislike of so many of Alison's friends from her London life? It seemed to him that she did all the giving in these relationships – materially and emotionally – and they did all the taking. Or was that what real friendship was about: giving freely what was needed without keeping a tally?

This weekend was his first meeting with Philip Hunter and he wasn't impressed. He saw a shallow, self-satisfied man in his early forties – although you had to get within wrinkle-sight to spot it, from across the room he could easily pass for thirty. A vain man, then, with a weak and ungenerous mouth.

Nick suspected him of being manipulative. He certainly knew which of Alison's character traits to work on: her intellectual arrogance, her natural sense of superiority, her genuine concern for those she cared for, her unacknowledged need to be needed.

'No one would suspect a meek, mild Mary of any skulduggery,' Philip agreed with enthusiasm. 'I knew I could count on you, Alison.'

'And I can remember to answer to it as it's my middle name so it won't sound too unfamiliar. Mary . . . um, um – ' She thought for a few seconds then yelled triumphantly, 'Mary

6

Lewis.' She sat smiling happily into her empty coffee cup. Mary Lewis. It would be like wearing a cloak of invisibility or Bilbow Baggins' stolen magic ring.

'Just the job!' Philip jumped up and clapped his hands together. He did a little celebratory dance. He was a tall, lean man and looked now like a gangling overgrown child, capering about the room in glee. Alison joined him and they did something which looked like a cross between a tango and the twist round the dining table.

This, Nick thought as the coffee percolator began to spit and splutter, was what the psychologists who came to lecture at Bramshill called *folie à deux*. Take two otherwise sane people, marinate liberally in Givry Domaine Thénard 1985, stir well, then leave the mixture to mature. They will wind each other up to undreamt of heights of idiocy, and crimes which exhaust the imagination. Brady and Hindley were the textbook example. He poured the coffee into a china pot and carried it into the dining room.

'There's one more thing we'd better decide on,' Alison added slyly. 'What rate are you going to pay me for the work I do?'

She laughed at the expression on Philip's face. He hadn't got as rich as he was today by being open-handed.

Gerry Walsh weaved his way gracefully through the crowds at Heathrow's terminal 3, patting the inside pocket of his jacket to reassure himself that his passport was there. He made a mental note never to take a long-haul overnight flight ever again.

Gerry was tired — a tiredness which could not be fully explained by the 'red-eye' flight. Tired and grubby. Tired and broke. And his homecoming had to be in November — his least favourite month, when spring seemed a lifetime away. It had been Indian Summer back in San Francisco, hundreds of miles to the south of London, and the hortensias had still been in bloom in the gardens on Russian Hill.

He had no luggage to wait for at the carousels. All he owned was in the green nylon bag slung over his right shoulder. He had no one to buy coming-home presents for either, and had contented himself with one bottle of duty-free Scotch. So he skirted the scramble for squeaky luggage trolleys and made straight for the Nothing to Declare channel at Customs.

The only official on duty today was a young blonde woman, scratchily smart in her new blue uniform with gold braid. Gerry eased his aching back into a more upright position, sucked his stomach in hard and treated her to his sexiest smile. She smiled back as he cleared the channel unimpeded. Even tired and grubby, the old Walsh charm was still oiled and in working order. The thought put the spring back in his step as he queued through Passport Control and headed for the tube.

Heathrow was the terminus and he had no trouble getting a seat. He would go straight through on the Piccadilly Line to Earls Court. He knew a rooming house there where he could get a cheap bed for the night. Then the agenda was: a cosy launderette for the contents of his nylon bag; a cat-nap while his socks looped round in the drier; back to the lodging house for a shower and a change of clothes; think about shaving off the beard even though a handsome young attorney in Santa Barbara had christened him The Viking because of it; a burger and chips – take-away, that would cost less; then to the Club Copa round the corner in the Earls Court Road for a few hours' cruising. With a bit of luck he might find a bed there for the next few nights which would justify the price of a drink.

Damn it! Today was Sunday. That meant the pubs wouldn't be open until seven, though he'd heard on the grapevine that they could now stay open all afternoon on a weekday. Puritan England was finally being dragged into the twentieth century. Back in the States – the land which had invented prohibition – you could at least get a drink when you wanted one.

Tomorrow he'd have to start looking for a job, ring up a few agencies. There shouldn't be any problem. Computer programming skills like Gerry's were in big demand, even if he hadn't touched a terminal for the last six months, and he still had a few contacts in London despite his two-year absence.

It was his first glimpse of England in those two years:

eighteen months spent making money in Australia had been followed by six months having a bloody good time touring the States and spending it. Now it was time to touch down to earth.

Dear horrid old London. Not many changes. Smoking was now banned everywhere on the tube since last year's fire at King's Cross but they hadn't extended the ban to the litter on the platforms and the carriage floors. Earls Court would still be full of winos and weirdos and people muttering to themselves who might be on drugs or might have come from the Poetry Society in the Square. Or both. Still, it was home or had been since he'd left Liverpool at the age of nineteen. He had kept his vow never to return.

He would be thirty next month – Boxing Day, to be precise, a Christmas baby. Did that explain his lassitude? Was it time to settle down, find some steady work, buy a flat, open a building society account? Then he remembered the smile of the blonde girl at Customs. He wasn't past it yet, wasn't quite ready to take root, although a little bit of money in the bank sounded good.

He jumped out of the train at Earls Court and strode up the escalator at the Warwick Road exit, whistling 'Waltzing Matilda' as he brushed past travellers who were content to let the moving stairs do all the work.

Gerry Walsh was ready to take on the world again.

'Okay, shoot,' Alison said. She settled herself comfortably on the window seat in the small sitting room. Philip took the leather armchair a few feet away.

'Isn't Nick going to join us?' Despite the argument at lunchtime, Philip had been hoping for some free advice from a tame policeman.

'He's curled up with "Songs of Praise",' Alison said in disgust. 'He's washed his hands of us.'

Nick's choice of a television programme which normally sent him screaming from the room when Alison – who enjoyed a good loud hymn – switched it on, had been pointed. She could hear the distant strains of harmony through the wall.

Philip adopted a deliberately glum expression. 'He won't let you come.'

Alison bridled as he had intended. 'I don't need his permission! Now, are you going to give me the details or am I going to be groping around in the dark?'

'Where to start?' Philip stuck his long legs out in front of him and crossed them at the ankles. 'The project's called FICS, Financial Investment Computer System – known as FIX for short.' He spelt the little pun for her.

'It provides a comprehensive bureau package for firms of stockbrokers, enabling them to keep track of clients' accounts and make payments, or demands for payment, on settlement day. It's a stand-alone – doesn't interfere with any of the Stock Exchange computer systems.'

'Known as SEX, for short?' Alison queried. Philip gave her a stony look and went on.

'As I was saying – some of the big firms of stockbrokers have developed their own systems but there was obviously a market for the rest, who'd want a ready-made package and to buy time on an off-site mainframe. So we started work a couple of years ago when people first started panicking about Big Bang and went live in the spring, hardly behind schedule at all.'

'And everything was okay?'

'Everything was wonderful – for one month. We took on new clients by word of mouth, upgraded the computer, doubled the size of the database. I ordered a new BMW ... and then, it started.'

'When exactly?'

'Sometime in May. It's hard to be more specific than that since the customers don't notice anything amiss until after settlement day, if then. Usually they haven't noticed the discrepancy until their next audit. I lie awake at night worrying how many more little time-bombs are just ticking away, waiting to explode in my face. It's a slow bleeding – he's not greedy.'

'He may not be greedy, but he's cocky.'

'That's right,' Philip agreed. 'He's not taken us for several million before disappearing to South America. That means he's confident enough to think he'll get away with

10

it indefinitely and, the way things are at the moment, I'm afraid he may be dead right.'

'His cockiness will be his downfall,' Alison asserted, with considerable self-confidence of her own.

'I'm not a religious man,' Philip said, 'but I'm praying it may be so.' The choir next door, as though in support, launched into 'Through the night of doubt and sorrow' to the *Z Cars* theme tune.

'So what is the scam, exactly?' Alison asked.

'Well, it's genuine computer fraud. You know, of course, that most of the capers that get puffed up as computer fraud aren't the real thing at all?'

Alison nodded. 'The Chief Accountant sends in a few false invoices, authorises them himself and collects the proceeds. The fact that the accounting system is computerised is incidental — he'd have done just the same thing on a manual system.'

'Exactly. In other words, the fraud is usually at input stage, before it gets anywhere near the computer. But our boy is logging into the computer on a dial-up line, finding out clients' names and passwords and creating account records for himself in a variety of different names. He logs himself a nice little sale, worth a few thousand quid. Settlement day comes, out goes the cheque to an accommodation address. There you have it. Childishly simple.'

'What about the accounts the cheques are paid into?'

'I thought of that.' Philip looked pained. 'And so did he. The account is held from another accommodation address and is switched straight into another bank account as soon as it's cleared. There's no tracing him and, of course, there's a limit to how helpful banks are prepared to be to the man in the street.'

'Which is where the police would earn their keep,' Alison pointed out.

'We went through all that at lunch, Alison.'

'I know, and I do understand your reasons. But you're going to start losing customers anyway, scandal or no scandal.'

'So far I've managed to compensate the clients and hush them up. I've told them to be extra careful how they choose their passwords and who they tell them to but you know what people are like about security.'

Alison laughed. 'FRED, PASSWORD, 1234. I've seen them all on live systems. And they think no one can possibly guess that they're using the name of their pet cat.'

'If only they were *that* imaginative. I've also circulated a list of names the hacker has used to date. But it's not hard to think up new ones – all you need is a browse through the telephone directory. He uses straightforward names – William Robinson, Henry Clarke, the sort of thing no one thinks of querying.'

'A real William Robinson may get a bit of a shock then. Do your clients normally use dial-up lines?'

'They have direct lines, but we need dial-ups in case of emergency and for maintenance, engineering work, that sort of thing. Also new clients usually get a dial-up line to try the system out on approval. We don't go to the expense of getting a proper line installed for them until they've signed the contract. I got all the telephone numbers changed at one stage but it didn't help since the clients had to know them in case of emergency.'

'And you can't get British Telecom to monitor the lines, find out where the calls are coming from?'

'Again, not without going public on the problem.'

'Don't you have safeguards, a list of terminals with legitimate access to the live system, or something like that?'

'Everything like that! He's laughing at us. Logging in from God-knows-where and marking the transaction as having been done from a legitimate terminal ID. That's why I'm sure it's an inside job. That, and his finding out the new phone numbers almost at once.'

'It usually is,' Alison remarked. 'So I shall need a complete breakdown of all the suspects.'

'Don't call them that! I hate to think it's any of them. I hate to think that any of them could do this to *me!*' He brought his fist down hard on the stuffed arm of the chair and for a moment Alison thought he was going to cry.

'Cheer up.' She crossed the room to sit next to him and

put her arm around his shoulder. 'Auntie Alison is here. The seventh cavalry has arrived.'

'You think you can do it? Catch my hacker.'

'Let's call a spade a spade, shall we?' Alison said gently. 'And call him a thief.'

'Yes. It makes it easier to think of it that way.' Philip made an effort to pull himself together. 'More impersonal. Look, give me a couple of days to collect my thoughts, Alison. I'll check my files, dig out everyone's CVs and personnel records. Come and see me as soon as you get to London and I'll give you the low-down on the whole lot of them.'

Chapter Two

Gerry arrived late at the aptly named Brief Encounter just north of Trafalgar Square on Wednesday night and found it hard to get through the door. He squeezed his way to the bar, upsetting a couple of drinks en route and defusing the resultant protests and threats by blowing kisses indiscriminately. There were no familiar faces so it looked as if he'd have to buy his own first drink.

He had kept the beard after some reflection. Women complained that it tickled but men seemed to like the rugged look it purportedly gave to his face. After two months in San Francisco, he fancied a woman for a change but in his present state of penury he couldn't afford to date women. Gerry was a realist.

He had made several phone calls in the days since his arrival and had been promised at least half a dozen really exciting jobs by hyper-enthusiastic young men who had no surnames. He had dropped his CV round to several agencies and awaited developments. He was still waiting.

Not that it was anything out of the ordinary: November was a bad time of year to be looking for freelance work – people would wait until New Year to start hiring again. After all, if you took someone on at this time of year they'd spend most of their first month half-cut at office Christmas parties. And he was used to being promised jobs which had never existed outside the hyperbolic advertisements of the agencies.

Nor had his attempt to find a comfortable free billet been wholly successful. An innocent and homesick Aussie called

14

Pete, pleased to find that Gerry had spent eighteen months working in his homeland, had offered him the use of his floor and sleeping bag in Earls Court Gardens and he had spent the last three nights tossing and wriggling on cracked lino.

Gerry had a vague notion that he was getting too old to sleep on floors and an optimistic idea that life must have something better in store for him soon.

He ordered a pint of over-priced lager and surveyed the bar. He took a sip as his eye slid automatically over a plump man in tight blue slacks with a Visible Panty Line and made contact with a tall, muscular red-headed man who was leaning against the far wall, fiddling with the small silver hoop in his left ear. The man smiled at him and Gerry raised his glass to him with a barely perceptible movement. There was something about a red-head . . .

'Some enchanted evening,' Gerry hummed to himself, as his new friend began to make his way nonchalantly towards the bar. 'You may see a stranger, you may see – '

'Gerry? Is it really you?' Gerry spilt some of his lager as a hand clamped down on his shoulder from behind. The red-headed man shrugged and walked off to join Visible Panty Line. Not a man of taste then.

'Gerry Walsh,' the voice repeated happily.

'Philip Hunter.' Gerry's greeting was less enthusiastic. 'Long time no see. You look good.' He brought the compliment out automatically but, pausing to look Philip up and down, he had to concede that he *was* looking good. He was certainly looking rich.

'I thought you were abroad,' Philip was saying. 'Australia, wasn't it?'

'That's right. I just got back. Just this week.'

'Place get too hot to hold you?' Philip asked with forced joviality. 'Ha ha.'

'Ha ha,' Gerry agreed politely.

'Drink up. Let me get you another. What'll you have?'

Not like old Phil to be so generous, Gerry thought. He must indeed be pleased to see him. Obviously the circumstances surrounding their last meeting were to be tactfully forgotten.

15

Nick had come home early that evening and found Alison in the study upstairs, hunched over the book where she detailed her personal expenses. A few strands of red hair came loose from her french pleat and fell over the pages as her face frowned in concentration. She stabbed from time to time at her calculator.

'Did you get a receipt for that petrol you put in the Jag for me the other day?' she asked without looking up.

'I forgot. Sorry.'

'Honestly, Nick, I want to get these cash books straight before I leave for London.'

He sat down on the window seat. 'You've made up your mind then?' he asked, after a pause.

'Yes, of course. I told Phil I'd do it and I shall. He's at his wits' end. Anyway, I could do with a bit of excitement.' She gestured out of the window behind him. 'Little Hopford in a drizzly November is not my idea of the good life. London's always lively in the run-up to Christmas. Parties, bright lights, Christmas shopping. It'll be fun.'

Alison had been a confirmed Londoner before coming to settle in the Hop Valley some two years earlier and, despite her commitment to her new life, she often grew restless.

'And if I ask you not to go?' he said.

She glanced up and smiled at him. 'Don't play the heavy, Nick. It doesn't suit you. Whatever are you so worried about?'

'Firstly ... I don't want you to go for selfish reasons – I admit it freely. Secondly – and this is the important point – I'm afraid for your safety. There's a lot of money going missing – and that's just the thefts Philip knows about. Has it occurred to you that the thief may turn violent if he thinks someone's on to him? You admitted there was a chance of your being recognised.'

'I'm going to dye my hair and wear lenses to change the colour of my eyes.'

Nick jumped up in exasperation and began to pace up and down the room. 'Crime isn't a game, Alison! This hacker is dangerous and clever and probably ruthless. There's nothing the police dislike more than amateurs interfering and getting themselves into trouble – '

16

'The police won't know about it. I shall probably be in and out in two or three weeks. I'm off on Sunday anyway, starting at Orion on Monday.'

'Alison,' Nick said quietly, 'I hoped never to have to remind you of this but you leave me no choice.' He leant on the desk, his dark eyes holding her green ones like a stoat mesmerising a rabbit. 'I want you to think back to the time your life was in danger. I want you to remember the panic and despair you felt that night when you thought you were going to die. Do you remember how it felt?'

'Oh, stop it! Don't be silly.' Alison's head jerked back in alarm, her eyes freeing themselves from his.

'Do you remember the nightmares, Alison, for weeks afterwards? And then again when you had to give evidence at the trial? You used to wake up screaming. Do you remember all the nights you lay trembling in my arms for hours?'

'Stop it, I said.'

Alison's face was white and Nick felt briefly ashamed but he pressed home his advantage as he would have done in the interview room. 'Ask yourself, just for a moment, if you want to feel like that ever again.'

'Of course not. But you're overstating your case like mad.' She met his eye again, regaining some of her composure. 'Phil helped me a lot when I was starting out, Nick. I owe him. He's calling in a debt.'

'Then he should be ashamed of himself — endangering a friend's life. And a woman too.'

'A debt of honour, if you like. A debt of friendship.'

'Oh.' Nick turned away and stared out of the window down onto the muddy rose garden and into the haze of the wood beyond. It was dusk. He had played the best cards he had. 'Where will you stay?' he asked, reluctantly.

Alison, magnanimous in victory if not always in defeat, answered him kindly. 'I'll find a bedsit somewhere. Islington, probably — my old haunts. It's handy for Moorgate where the office is.'

'Can't you stay with Jan and Peter in Ealing?' Then solid sensible Jan could keep an eye on her for him.

'That would *not* be convenient for the office. Besides they're going to Florida, I told you.'

17

'No, you didn't.'

'Didn't I? I thought I did.'

'I thought Jan hated America.'

'She does. But Peter likes it and since she gave up being an autonomous person and became a baby-breeding machine, she has to do as she's told.'

'Cor,' Nick said in awe. 'There was me thinking she was an attractive, intelligent, personable young woman with a loving husband and a delightful baby son − your godson, whom you neglect shamefully − and all the time she was just a baby-breeding machine.'

'Oh, shut up. Peter's got a job in Orlando for a year, starting January.'

'Then they're not leaving yet, surely.'

'In January, Jan will be eight months and the airlines won't fly her,' Alison explained patiently. 'So they're going early and having a holiday first.'

'The new baby will be born in America then? He can run for president.'

'She. It's a girl. Don't you know anything?'

'I don't approve of all these tests to find out the sex of a baby,' Nick grumbled. 'It's like opening your presents before Christmas.'

'What's your point?' Alison, who always sneaked the wrapping off her presents well before Christmas, opened her eyes wide in spurious innocence. 'You might offer me some professional advice, at least.'

Nick hesitated. His advice, professional and personal, was that she should bloody well stay at home. With him. But if she was determined then he must make it as safe for her as possible. 'Well ... I didn't like what you said about not really knowing the software. It's going to look very suspicious.'

'That's what I told Phil. So?'

'So, it might be an idea if you dropped hints that there was something going on between you and Philip, then people would think it was just jobs-for-the-girlfriend time.'

Alison looked amazed. 'Don't be silly, Nick, everybody knows Phil's gay. It's no secret.'

'I didn't know,' he said.

'Couldn't you tell? Call yourself a detective?'

'I hadn't given the matter of Philip's sexual orientation a moment's thought.'

'So that's not much help.'

'All right. Then the only advice I can offer is, don't trust anyone – however nice and friendly they may seem. Don't confide in anyone as to why you're really there even if you've made your mind up that they can't possibly be the hacker. Remember that it might be Jill Hacker just as easily as John Hacker and remember certain times in the past when you've trusted people – '

'Yes,' Alison said quickly. 'Thanks. I'm glad you're taking it seriously at last.'

'I take it very seriously indeed.' Nick sighed. 'Alison?'

'Yes?'

'If anything happens to you . . . no, sod euphemism! If you get yourself killed, I think I shall lose my mind.'

She put her pen down and crossed the room towards him. 'I'll give it two weeks. If I've not sorted everything out by then I'll give up – honour salvaged, debt repaid. How's that?'

'It's better than nothing. Thank you.'

'Give us a smile.'

Nick managed a reluctant smile. 'I'm not sure I like Philip. I don't think he realises what danger he's getting you into. Or if he does realise, he doesn't much care.'

'Pity you haven't got a small part of his dress sense.' Alison pushed her finger through the ragged hole in the elbow of his sweater.

Nick muttered something about fine feathers and fine birds and changed the subject.

'Bill's booked in for his operation at last.' Sergeant Bill Deacon was Nick's deputy and an old friend. 'He's fretting about that half the time. I get the impression that something else is bothering him too but he's not letting on, whatever it is. Goodness knows what I shall do without him.'

'They'll give you someone else, surely.'

'There's a Sergeant Walpole coming from HQ. He'll be arriving in a day or two so Bill can show him the ropes before he goes off. It won't be the same though.'

19

'It won't be for long.' She put her arms round him and nuzzled his neck affectionately. 'None of it will be for long.'

'There's no knowing. It's a stressful life, in CID, and there's plenty of desk jobs available. I might lose him for good.'

'And then I thought of you,' Philip Hunter said, later that night. 'Please say you'll help me, Gerry. I don't know who else to turn to.'

Gerry Walsh helped himself to another glass of Philip's brandy and another smear of his caviar while he pretended to think the matter over. He hid his internal elation and Philip did not suspect it. A job offer, good pay, and a little light detective work to make it interesting! He had been right – his luck was on the turn.

'It'll make a change,' he said at last. 'Give the job some interest for once.'

'I can't believe my luck, just running into you like that,' Philip said. 'I hardly ever go to the Brief Encounter either. I thought you were gone for good.'

'There's only so much Australia a man can take.' Gerry held out a strong brown wrist for inspection. 'And now they say the sun gives you cancer. But then as far as I can make out everything gives you cancer now: eating, drinking, screwing ... breathing. Eat, drink and be merry for tomorrow we die; that's my motto.'

'Very original.' Philip took the proffered wrist and turned Gerry's hand over in his, examining the scarred knuckles and the ingrained dirt on the palms. Black hairs ran back up his arm and into the cuffs of his sweatshirt like wires. Philip remembered that his whole body – even his back – was covered in this shaggy coat, like a huge, warm, furry animal.

'Start Monday then?' he suggested hoarsely.

'Fine by me. Funds are getting low. I came back via the States. It was fun but pricey.'

'Got somewhere to stay?' Philip tried to make the question sound casual.

'Nothing permanent.'

'Only I can put you up for a few days – just until you get something sorted out, of course.'

Gerry glanced round the Barbican penthouse which Philip had recently bought; taking in the original oils on the walls, the pale supple leather sofas, the persian rugs.

'You always knew how to do yourself well, Phil.' He reclaimed his hand and got up. 'Thanks for the offer but I've got a floor to kip on for a night or two.'

Philip went slightly red and said stiffly, 'Whatever you like. I'll see you out.'

At the front door Gerry said, 'Talk to you soon, then.' He turned back and gave Philip a light kiss on the mouth. 'Thanks for supper.' He walked towards the high-speed lift singing, just audibly, 'Nobody loves a fairy when she's forty'.

Philip shut the door quietly then punched his fist hard into the subtly rag-rolled wall.

'Same old Gerry.' There was bitterness in his voice. Same irresistible Irish charm, despite his unkempt hair and his rough hands; that awful beard and his growing beer belly. How did he do it?

Same damned cussed feckless Gerry Walsh. Same bloody whore. Someone would kill that man one day.

Bill Deacon poked his head round Nick's office door the following morning, looking offensively pleased with himself. He said with a perfectly straight face:

'Mr Trevellyan, Sergeant Walpole is here.'

'Fine. Show him in, will you, Bill.'

Bill stood to one side, speaking with exaggerated politeness as if he were the butler. 'This way, Sergeant. This is Detective Inspector Trevellyan.'

'Good morning, sir,' said the young woman who had just walked into the room. 'It's a privilege to be working with you. I know you well by reputation.' She leant across the desk to offer her hand and Nick, startled, shook it only limply.

'I'll leave you two to get to know each other then,' Bill said with a big grin. 'I'll be in the canteen for the next half hour if you want me, sir.' He left the office and Nick could hear him giggling half way along the corridor.

'Sit down, Sergeant Walpole,' Nick said, recovering from

21

his initial shock. He should have been sent her file beforehand but, naturally, it had got mislaid somewhere along the line. Now was his chance to prove his woolly-liberal credentials.

'My name's Shirley, sir.' She sat down.

'Welcome to Hopbridge, Shirley.'

They surveyed each other for a moment – each full of good will but slightly wary. She was about twenty-seven, really rather pretty with tight dark curls and large, intelligent brown eyes. Of medium height and build, she looked fit and active and brimming with youthful confidence. Nick caught a look of shrewd amusement in her eyes and smiled at her.

'No, you're right, you're not what I was expecting. No one told me. Give me a moment to get used to the idea.'

'I've been on the County CID force for three years, sir, as sergeant, working on Detective Superintendent Seymour's team.'

'Bad luck.' The words were out before he could stop them, but somehow she looked trustworthy – someone you could talk to.

Shirley made a rueful face. 'You know Mr Seymour then?'

'Oh, yes. We don't work that way here, you know.'

'Good.' They nodded and smiled, accustomed to brief and rapid partnerships, understanding each other by instinct, liking each other by the same door.

'I know a lot of men don't like working with a woman.' She persevered in her well-rehearsed speech. 'Because they think they may have to protect her at a crucial moment. I'm a judo brown-belt, sir.'

Oh no! was Nick's immediate thought.

'Excellent,' he said easily. 'You can protect me then. I never got the hang of all that unarmed combat myself.'

She was prickly, he realised, used to teasing, used to the dismay which greeted her arrival – which he might, himself, have let slip on first seeing her – but still vulnerable, desperate to prove herself at every turn, ambitious. She would work twice as hard as any male sergeant they could have sent him. In fact she was probably twice as good as any

22

male sergeant to have survived three years in Ted Seymour's crude masculine world.

'Welcome,' he said again. 'Come on, I'll introduce you to the rest of CID.'

Chapter Three

Bill Deacon and Shirley Walpole were waiting to cross the road outside the Police Station at lunchtime that Friday. There was no break in the traffic.

'There's a woman trying to attract your attention, Sergeant,' Shirley said. Bill turned in the direction she was indicating and smiled.

The two sergeants watched as the woman hurried along the pavement towards them, her heavy leather bag slapping against her thigh — scattering more leisurely pedestrians as she went.

Shirley's first impression was of a dauntingly tall woman a few years older than herself. She stood out from the crowd with her heavy features and sweep of carroty hair and she wore with ease such clothes as Shirley, on her public servant's salary, could never hope to afford.

The red hair, strong features and well-cut clothes were too familiar for Sergeant Bill Deacon even to notice. He saw only a young woman he had come, belatedly, to call his friend.

'Hello, Bill,' Alison panted, catching them up at last.

'Hello, Alison.'

'I've been shouting your name out for ages,' she exaggerated. 'You must be going deaf.'

'Going senile, Miss.'

'When do you go into hospital?'

Bill's smile faded and his face clouded. 'First thing.'

'Are you very worried?' She laid her hand on his arm in a small gesture of comfort.

'Terrified. But I've got to get it over with.'

'I'll tell you one thing – Nick's not looking forward to doing without you. He says the criminals of the Hop Valley will have a field-day with you out of action.'

'The valley will be in very good hands, I'm sure,' Bill said hastily. 'I don't think you've met Miss Walpole, have you, Miss? Detective Sergeant Walpole. She's here from County HQ to look after things while I'm away.'

The two women shook hands, each summing the other up swiftly and negatively.

'I didn't mean to cast aspersions,' Alison said politely. 'I just wanted Bill to know how much we shall all miss him. I'm Alison Hope, by the way.'

'Yes, I thought you would be.' Shirley had got the lowdown on Nick's private life – indeed on the private lives of half the valley – from DC Paul Penruan the previous day.

'There, you see,' Bill said. 'She's quite the detective.' The two women laughed dutifully. 'If you're looking for Mr Trevellyan, he's in the Eagle and Child waiting for us.'

'There's nothing I'd like better than a quiet hour in the Bird and Baby, Bill, but I'm meeting my godmother for lunch and I'm late already. Good luck – I'll be thinking about you.'

Bill smiled once more, touched.

'Nice to meet you, Sergeant Walpole,' Alison concluded. Shirley acknowledged the social lie with a brief nod and did not bother to return the compliment. Alison walked off more slowly in the direction of the town centre.

'So that's the woman Nick lives with,' Shirley said when she was sure Alison was out of earshot. 'I was expecting some raving beauty by all accounts, not an overgrown Yuppie.'

'I think Miss Hope always looks very attractive and elegant,' Bill said coolly.

'Elegant! I could look elegant with several hundred pounds worth of clothes on my back. Well, we'd better get across this road or Nick will think we've been kidnapped.'

'Do you mind if I offer you a word of advice, Sergeant?' Bill said, as he followed her Kamikaze dodging through the market-day traffic.

'Of course not.' Shirley Walpole was very ambitious. She

expected to make inspector in a year or two, after which the sky was the limit. She didn't see what advice Bill Deacon, still a sergeant at forty-four, could have to offer her but politeness cost nothing at this stage.

'It doesn't do to get over familiar with senior officers,' he was saying. Shirley looked blank. 'Calling Mr Trevellyan by his Christian name like that.'

'Oh, I see. He asked me to. It's usual at County HQ, you know.' She crossed her fingers mentally; the thought of calling Ted Seymour anything other than 'Sir!' defied her imagination.

'I daresay he did. There's not a more easy-going man in the county than the Inspector but we're old-fashioned here. You lose nothing by sticking to "Sir" and "Ma'am". Otherwise, before you know where you are, you're calling the inspector "Nick" in front of the Superintendent.'

'I'll bear it in mind,' Shirley said briskly.

He wasn't kidding when he said they were old-fashioned round here, she thought. Queen Victoria would probably have found it a shade old-fashioned. The way Bill Deacon called that Hope woman 'Miss', as if he were the old family retainer, was enough to make you sick. She looked stuck-up with that snotty, upper-class voice and expensive gear. 'Ay'm meeting may godmotha,' she mimicked internally, with more spite than accuracy.

What on earth did a nice bloke like Nick Trevellyan see in her?

Nick rang the Deacons' doorbell shortly after eight that night.

'I just thought I'd look in, see if there was anything needed doing,' he said when Susie answered, virtuously using the chain Bill had fitted. 'Anything I can help with while Bill's under the weather.'

'That's good of you, Nick.' Susie Deacon shut the door, released the chain and stood aside to motion him into her warm hallway with its cheerful yellow wallpaper and displays of dried flowers. 'He's in the bath at the moment but he won't be long. He seems to have got the idea that they don't have baths in hospitals.'

'Probably rather icy, bare ones at that Victorian work-house of ours.' Hopbridge Hospital was centred on a stark stone building, grimly functional and surrounded by portacabins. Bill was due in early the next morning. 'Still, at least you'll be there to keep an eye on him.'

'It's not as bad inside as it looks from the outside,' Susie said.

'Thank God for that.'

'Do you mind sitting in the kitchen? It's cosiest. Have a cup of tea. Or maybe you'd prefer a drink.'

'Tea will be fine.'

'It's nice of you to spare the time to come by, Nick.'

'There are few people I'd rather spare it for,' he said. 'Come to think of it, I don't seem to be that short of time at the moment. Things are quiet back at the ranch. Quick! Find me some wood to touch.'

'I hear Alison's going away. Business, is it?'

'In a manner of speaking.' He followed her into the kitchen and settled on a stool at the breakfast bar. 'Actually, Susie, I'm quite glad to get the chance for a quick word with you alone.'

'Oh?' She turned with the teapot in her hand and smiled at him. She was a pleasant-faced woman of forty, motherly rather than glamorous although she had kept her trim figure. She had been a nurse until the eldest of her three daughters had been born and had recently gone back to the hospital part-time since Trudie, the youngest, had started at the Comprehensive. She was warm and cheerful like her house; competent, discreet, loving. Nick considered her an old friend.

'I just get the feeling he's worried about something,' he began. 'Oh, obviously he's nervous about this operation but I've got the idea that there's something else. Something he doesn't want to confide in me.'

'It'll be this business with Sarah,' Susie said, nodding. She poured boiling water into the teapot and set it down in front of them to draw. She laid out a jug of milk and a pair of sturdy china mugs. Hers said 'Susie' on it, his said 'Chrissie'. 'I'm surprised he hasn't mentioned it to you since it's been preying on his mind. I suppose he didn't want to bother you with domestic problems.'

'You have a problem with Sarah?' Nick could hardly keep the disbelief out of his voice. Sarah Deacon, the eldest daughter, now sixteen and in the sixth form at Hopbridge Comprehensive, had always seemed like an advertisement for the pleasures and rewards of parenthood. She had done very well in her GCSEs last summer, as predicted, was in the school tennis team and showed a fair talent for amateur theatricals. She was pretty, popular and good-natured and had, as far as Nick knew, never caused Bill and Susie a moment's lost sleep.

'*Problem*'s overstating it a bit,' Susie agreed. 'It's just that Bill doesn't approve of her new boyfriend.'

'Is that all!' Nick laughed. 'I don't think Prince Edward would. be good enough for Sarah, would he?' Sarah had, before Alison's arrival on the scene, nurtured a one-sided crush on Nick who had often caught his sergeant frowning at him as though weighing up his honourable intentions and finding them wanting. Sarah had long since transferred her interest to boys nearer her own age and there had been a succession of them, none as yet – so Nick immodestly liked to think – inspiring her devotion to the extent or for the length of time that he himself had.

'So who is the lad?' he asked. 'And what's he supposed to have done?'

'His name's Alex Porter – '

'Rings a vague bell.'

'It might. He's got "previous", as you boys say.'

'Ah.'

'I suppose that's Bill's main objection to him.'

'A biggish objection, Susie.'

'It was just boyish stupidity,' she said firmly. 'His father died when he was a child and his mother let him get just a little too independent. He got into a fight with another lad one Guy Fawkes Night when he was seventeen and they'd both had a few more beers than they were used to, to show how big they both were and how they could put one over on the poor old landlord at the Raven that they weren't under age.'

'Sounds familiar.'

'It ended with the other boy needing stitches and Alex

28

spending four months in an approved school for GBH. It was his first Christmas away from home and I think he nearly died of misery and missing his mum. When he got out, he was too disheartened to go back to school and finish his "A" levels; so he screwed his life up, and he knows it and accepts it. He was completely open about it both to Sarah and me and he's never put a foot wrong since. Don't you people believe in rehabilitation at all?'

'Sorry,' Nick said meekly.

'Once a villain, always a villain, is that it? I mean, what's prison for if not to teach boys like Alex a lesson they won't forget?'

'I plead guilty, Your Honour. Please take one thousand other offences into consideration and have me whipped. Anything so long as you stop looking at me like that.'

'Oh, drink your tea, you silly bugger.'

Nick complied then went on more seriously: 'It's just that prison, even at junior level, is often a training ground for a lifetime on the wrong side.'

'I know.' Susie sighed. 'I know all that.'

'Eight out of ten go on to re-offend within two years.'

'Which means that two out of ten don't,' Susie said sharply. 'Honestly, Nick, I'm used to this sort of response from Bill but I expect better of a woolly liberal like you.' Nick winced. He preferred not to be called a woolly liberal by anyone but himself.

'Okay. There are exceptions and your Alex may be allowed to be one of them. So I won't give him a bad name and then hang him. All right?'

'He's not *my* Alex. But I like the boy − he's more than usually polite to wrinklies like me and Bill. I have no objection to him taking Sarah to the pictures after she's finished her homework.'

'But Bill never forgets and never forgives, eh?'

'It is one of his more prominent characteristics,' Susie agreed.

'Pig-headedness?'

'Let's call it single-mindedness, shall we, since we're drinking his tea.'

'And eating his cake?' Nick said hopefully.

Susie conjured a cake tin out of a cupboard. She took out one of her excellent home-made fruit cakes and hacked him a large slice while going on with her explanation.

'Also Alex is twenty-two, which His Lordship says is too old for our baby, and he rides a motorbike. And I don't mean a Honda 50.'

'What's he do?'

'Motor mechanic. That's another sore point. Bill wants Sarah to go to university. She wants to go too, of course. So manual labour, however skilled, is definitely not "good enough". Basically he's worried Alex will spoil all his plans for her . . . shotgun weddings, etc.'

'I won't say it doesn't happen these days,' Nick said, 'because it very obviously still does. But not usually to girls like Sarah who're pretty and popular and have always had loads of boyfriends. It's the plain ones you have to watch, the timid little things who've been starved of affection. The minute a boy takes an interest . . . well, he just doesn't stand a chance.'

Susie laughed as he intended. 'This one is a little more serious, though. He's older, has more money. He is, even I can see, rather good-looking. He earns her lots of Brownie points with her friends – even having been "inside" only increases his appeal in a funny sort of way.'

'Bit of rough?'

'I suppose. And then he's got his own "wheels". Do young people still use that expression?'

'Why ask me? Since when have I been young?'

Her answer was drowned out by a motorcycle roaring out of the night to disrupt the suburban silence of Riverside Close.

'Homework over?' Nick guessed. Susie pulled back the kitchen blind and Nick caught a glimpse of a young man in full bicycle leathers removing his crash helmet and shaking free a tangle of thick blond hair. They heard footsteps clattering down the stairs before he could even ring the bell.

'In by midnight,' Susie called out into the hall. 'And come and say hello to Mr Trevellyan.'

'I won't be late,' Sarah said. 'I've got an important indoor match tomorrow. It's on concrete and that's not my best surface. Hello, Nick.'

'Hi, Sarah.' He was slightly wounded by the indifference with which she greeted him and a little self-conscious at his own attempt to sound youthful by saying 'Hi' rather than returning her own 'Hello'. He could almost feel his joints starting to creak.

'Want some cake?' Susie asked Sarah.

'No, I'm on a diet.' Her mother sighed theatrically. 'Don't let's start that argument again, Mum.'

'No, dear. Both *Mr Trevellyan* and I agree that you are positively obese.'

Sarah laughed happily, hollered 'Bye, Dad' up the stairs and ran out into the driveway. The young man had put his helmet back on and all Nick could make out of his face in the wintry night were regular features and a certain pallor. He was tall and slenderly built and did not look like one of nature's bullies.

They watched as Sarah put on a spare crash helmet, swung her trim young body on to the pillion seat and put her arms tightly round the young man's waist. They pulled out of the driveway and turned towards the town.

'There's nothing you wouldn't do to protect them,' Susie said quietly. 'The people you love the most − your children.'

'I can imagine.' Somehow Nick's chances of fatherhood never seemed to get any closer.

'You'd cheat, lie, steal ... commit murder to protect them. Bill and I don't agree about the best way to handle things, that's all. Deep down, we're in complete agreement − any boy who lays a finger on our little girl ...'

'She'll be all right,' Nick said. 'Look at the start she's had in life.'

'How d'you mean?'

'Having you and Bill as parents. Any chance of another slice of cake before he surfaces from his bath and scoffs the rest?'

'Have it all. He's not allowed cake and the problem with having three teenage daughters is that they're all *always* on diets.'

Chapter Four

It was late by the time Nick and Alison finished dinner at the Pheasant that Saturday night and the Market Square was almost deserted. Alison's car was parked on the far side and Nick put his arm round her as they walked across the corporation flagstones in replete silence.

As they reached the car, a young couple emerged from Sheep Street and stopped under a lamp post. They were quarrelling. As Alison and Nick turned at the disturbance, the man slapped the girl hard across the face knocking her off balance. She tripped on one of her high-heeled shoes and staggered slightly.

'Wait here,' Nick said and set off towards them at a run. The young man turned at the sound of his footsteps and made a threatening gesture.

'Mind your own business, mate.'

'I'm a police officer,' Nick said hastily. 'What's going on here?'

The young man hesitated. 'You don't look much like one.' He moved a step forward. He wasn't a large man, shorter than Nick himself, but stockily built and lit up with beer and aggression. He had an unintelligent face with little black eyes, like rabbit droppings.

'Well, I am.' Nick stood his ground and folded his arms. 'So if you were thinking of assaulting me, *mate*, think again. Unless you want to spend the night in a police cell.'

The girl had resumed her shoe and came forward.

'It's okay,' she said. 'I'm not hurt. Come away, Kevin.'

The boy wavered, desperate not to lose face in front of the

girl but intimidated by Nick's calm confidence. She plucked at his arm.

'We're going,' she said to Nick. 'We don't want any trouble. He's just had a few, that's all.'

'Are you sure you'll be all right?' Nick said 'Because my girlfriend and I will run you home if you like.'

'No, really, I can cope with him.' She gave him an unconvincing gap-toothed grin. She looked about seventeen. She linked her arm with the boy's and led him away. At the kerb she stopped and called, 'Thanks.'

Nick waited until they had turned the corner, then walked slowly back to the Jaguar. Alison was leaning against the driver's door watching the scene.

'I thought he was going to thump you,' she said.

'So did I for a minute. Good job he didn't.'

'I'll say! He looks as if street fighting's his hobby.'

'I'm not worried about that. But I would have had to arrest him after I'd made a point of telling him I was a policeman. Then I'd have spent the next hour down the station charging him and I've got better things to do. Give me the car keys.'

'I'll drive. I've only had a bit of wine.'

'And some brandy. Hand them over.'

She gave them to him without further argument and got into the passenger seat. She reclined the seat and laid her head on the rest.

'Seat belt,' Nick instructed.

'Okay, okay. I thought you handled that really well.'

'I always go to considerable lengths to avoid a rough house.'

'I should think so! That's only common sense. But if it's unavoidable, you're the first one in, aren't you?'

'Mmm. If you stopped to think too long you wouldn't go in at all.' He started the engine and the car slid off smoothly towards the bridge.

'When there is rough stuff, do you worry about the policewomen?' she asked, suddenly curious.

'Yes. I try not to. They wouldn't thank me for it.'

'I mean Carol Halsgrove can't be more than about five foot four.'

'I don't worry about her so much. She grew up in a rough area with three big brothers. She's streetwise. Also she looks so frail that she gets in under their guard while they're debating whether to thump her or not.'

'You like her a lot, don't you?'

'No one I'd rather have guarding my back, except Bill. No, it's women like Shirley who worry me. They know everything about the theory of unarmed combat, top of the class, but in a real fight they suddenly find the other chap isn't fighting by the rules. They haven't always got the sense to walk away from a fight either — they want to prove themselves.' He glanced sidelong at her. 'Like you. Ever walked away from a scrap, Alison?'

'Don't start on that. I'm going to London tomorrow. I shall be quite all right.'

'Is there anything I can say to change your mind?'

'Not without fighting dirty, and you won't do that.'

Nick turned the car in at the gate of Hope Cottage and drew up at the front door. 'Don't you believe it. Just tell me what to say. I don't care how far below the belt it is.'

'Does Carol have a sex life?' Alison asked as they curled up together on the drawing room sofa a few minutes later.

'What questions you ask! How should I know?'

'It can't be easy, being a policewoman.'

'I imagine not. It's bad enough for the men — their wives put up with a hell of a lot. Mind you, I get the suspicion from time to time that there's something going on between her and Penruan but I can't really put my finger on it. If there is something then they're being very discreet.'

'What makes you think so?'

'One thing is that Carol has started calling him Paul whereas she always used to call him either Penruan or "Stupid". Another thing is that a few months back, whenever I saw Penruan off duty, he had a stunning blonde draped round him — a different one every time. I haven't seen him with anyone for a long time.'

'Carol's not exactly a stunning blonde, is she?'

'No. So if my suspicions are correct, it may be serious.'

'But why are they so secretive?'

'Because they know I wouldn't approve, of course.'

34

'What?'

'It affects people's work — I've seen it time and again. You send them out on surveillance and they're too absorbed in each other to keep a proper watch. Then they have a row and suddenly you can't send them out together at all. I don't allow it on my team.'

'What if I'd been posted to your team? WDC Hope? What would you have done then?'

'I'd have told you to get your hair cut for a start.'

'But when you fell in love with me, silly.'

'I'd have had you transferred out again the minute I fell for you.'

'Isn't that a bit hard if someone's made a lot of effort to get into CID?'

'Yes.'

'So what if it's true about Carol and Paul?'

'I'll make one of them transfer. They can choose which but I'd prefer to keep Carol. She's by far the better officer.'

Nick drove Alison into Taunton on Sunday evening so that she could catch the fast train to London and he could bring the Jaguar back to the Hop Valley. He had made no further attempt to stop her going — had not commented on the mousy tint of her hair or the brown contact lenses through which she had been blinking at him intermittently since Friday afternoon.

She passed through the ticket barrier with five minutes to spare and began to make her way up to the front of the train where there was a better chance of finding an empty carriage.

Behind her on the platform a voice called out: 'Mary,' then more loudly as she did not respond.

'Mary!'

She walked on, deep in thought.

'Hey!' The voice was close behind her now. 'Mary Lewis.'

Alison spun round guiltily. Nick stood right behind her, arms folded, unsmiling.

'Shit!' Alison said. 'That's me.'

'I suggest you remember it,' he said.

35

Alison found a first class carriage to herself. She took a window seat facing the engine and put her small suitcase on the seat beside her.

It was dark and she had no interest in the scenery at present. She was keyed-up, excited. The people Philip would reveal to her this evening, just names tonight, would acquire faces and voices tomorrow morning, would come alive. Surely it would be an easy matter to identify the thief. Alison, to whom dissimulation and lies were an alien tongue, could not believe that anyone could hide their true nature so effectively.

Nick could have told her differently.

Alison was kicking her heels, literally, against the door of Philip's penthouse when a faint ping behind her signalled the arrival of the lift. She stopped her assault on the paintwork as the doors slid silently open a few seconds later and Philip stepped out.

'Alison! Forgive me.' He was effortlessly elegant as usual in perfectly cut jeans, white silk shirt and a black leather blouson. 'I got held up.' His face was a little flushed as he fumbled for his door key. 'You didn't have any trouble getting in downstairs?'

'No.' Alison followed him into the flat. 'The doorman got your message and was expecting me. I've only been here about fifteen minutes. My train was held up.'

'Oh, good. Can I take your coat?' The front door opened directly into the sitting room. Philip took his jacket off and flung it carelessly over the back of the nearest sofa. Despite his words he made no move to help Alison off with her coat and she felt the words as automatic politeness. It was as if Philip wasn't really thinking what he was saying at all but had his mind fixed a long way off.

He switched on the rest of the lights and turned back to her. 'Drink? Christ, Alison! What have you done to your hair?'

'I've dyed it, of course,' she said patiently. 'And don't you think you'd better start practising calling me Mary?'

'Have you eaten?' He walked away into the kitchen without waiting for an answer.

'I had something on the train.' Alison followed him. 'But that drink sounds good to me.'

Philip opened the fridge and took out a bottle of Chablis. He scanned the label critically. 'This do?'

'Lovely.' It was obvious that Philip had had a few already.

'Make yourself at home and I'll bring it in.'

Alison returned to the sitting room, took off her coat and, after a moment's reflection, draped it on top of Philip's jacket. She sat down on the other sofa by the fireplace. The room was chilly and she picked up a box of matches from the coffee table and lit the gas log fire without standing on ceremony, reasoning that he had told her to make herself at home.

'I feel a bit jittery tonight for some reason.' Philip brought a tray in with the bottle and two glasses and put it down on the coffee table. He filled one with wine and handed it to her then stood warming himself in front of the fire for a moment before flopping into the armchair on the other side of the hearth. 'Want to share a joint?'

Alison declined. She wanted to keep her wits about her. She watched with a mounting sense of impatience as Philip painstakingly rolled his joint and lit it.

'Can't we get on? I've got to get up to this bedsit in Highbury. I don't want to be wandering the streets late at night.'

'Sorry.' Philip began to relax and sat back in his armchair. 'I'll send you back in a taxi naturally.'

'Who am I going to meet tomorrow? Who are these people?' To her annoyance Alison felt her throat tighten and she emptied her glass quickly and helped herself to a refill.

Philip took a deep drag and held his breath for as long as he could before letting it out in a small puff.

'In no particular order of merit,' he began, 'let's say "Cast in order of appearance", shall we? The first person you're likely to meet is Jilly . . .

'Jilly MacAlistair. She's the Senior Programmer on the project so she's your immediate boss. She must be . . . thirty-five. She's worked for me for six years and been with

37

the FIX project since it started. She's got the know-how —
both technically and of FIX in particular. I can't see her
having the motivation though, somehow, or the guts.'
'What's she like as a person?' Alison wanted to know.
'Bit of a loner really, not strong on social graces. She works
best on her own. As I say, she's supposed to be in charge
of the programming team but she hasn't got the neccessary
authority. Mostly they go their separate ways and muddle
together at the end.'
He paused for another puff and Alison said: 'Go on.'
'She's shy. I think she prefers talking to computers to
talking to people. I find her rather hard work anyway. She
resists any promotion which would take her away from the
terminal and out with the users.'
'Why do you keep her on? She doesn't sound much of a
catch?'
'Come off it, Al — Mary. You know how hard it is to get
decent staff and technically I've got no complaints about her
work at all. She's a perfectionist, drives herself very hard.
She's an amateur violinist — very talented by all accounts —
flogs herself to death at that too. Not quite good enough to
go professional, though. I think that rankles. Playing the
fiddle is the big passion of her life, I should say.'
'She's not married, I take it?'
'Oh, yeah. Didn't I say? Married straight out of university.
She and her husband live in Shepherd's Bush. His name's
Duncan, he lectures in Computer Science at Brunel. Funnily
enough they were at university with Zac — '
'Zac?' Alison queried.
'I'll get to him in a bit. The MacAlistairs are the nearest
thing Zac's got to friends. Jilly is about the one person in
the office he's civil to. It seems that he and Duncan were in
some sense rivals at college, though.'
'For Jilly?' Alison was beginning to feel a little confused.
'God, no! I've never seen Zac take an interest in a woman.
He's hetero though, as far as I know — just an old-fashioned
misogynist. Rivals academically, I meant. Zac's pretty hot
stuff but it was Duncan who finally walked off with the
research grant and the lectureship, leaving Zac to make his

way in the real world.' Philip laughed, not having much time for academics on the grounds that they weren't very well paid and didn't drive BMWs.

'This Zac is beginning to sound intriguing.'

'I'd call both the MacAlistairs unworldly. She drives a rusty 2CV. Their house is furnished with Aunt Mabel's throwouts. They take their holidays walking in the Lake District rather than sunning in the Seychelles. You get the picture?'

'She doesn't sound like the stuff master criminals are made of,' Alison pointed out.

'She wouldn't be in it for the money anyway. They're both active in the local Labour Party – idealists, leftovers from a less cynical age.' Philip poured himself a glass of wine. 'Cheers.'

'So she might disapprove of the City and all it stands for?'

Philip leant slowly forward and flicked ash onto the gas logs. 'I suppose she might at that.'

'Or *he* might,' Alison said.

Chapter Five

Gerry padded quietly around the Earls Court flat in Pete's slippers and dressing gown, gettings things organised for the morning. He liked to have his clothes laid out, his deodorant and toothbrush to hand, and a mug ready primed with Maxwell House, milk, sugar and spoon. That way he could rise at the last possible moment to spend a few minutes drinking coffee and waking his brain up for the day.

Pete, who had no work permit but worked unofficially in a wine bar most nights, was still out. Gerry had met him, not in the Copa, but in the newsagents on the corner and he had not told Pete that he was bisexual on the need-to-know principal. The boy was young and nervous and would probably have been expecting some sort of assault if he'd known the truth. Why did straight blokes imagine that a gay man would inevitably make a pass at them? They didn't go around expecting every woman they met to leap on them. Pete wasn't his type at all.

He'd had a good and boozy lunch out of Philip that day, had played him along for the whole afternoon, flattering him and flirting with him, hoping for dinner too. But Philip had glanced at his watch, suddenly remembered an engagement — whether real or imaginary — and hailed a taxi. Gerry thought complacently that the engagement was real, that Philip would have preferred to stay; that he had seemed genuinely upset at having forgotten it.

But there had been plenty of time for Gerry to have what Philip liked to call his 'briefing' — as if he were a secret service agent. He'd had the low-down on the staff on the

FIX project and there seemed to be no shortage of plausible candidates for the role of hacker.

Gerry was looking forward to his first day at Orion. The element of playacting, the cloak and dagger game, appealed to him. It was fun to pretend to be what you were not, to see how far you could convince. People were very trusting, in his experience. They took you at face value until they caught you out and Gerry very rarely got caught out.

Not that there was as much deception involved at Orion as he would ideally have chosen. He was using his own name and background and was telling the truth about his recent movements. Still, no one but Philip would know why he was really there, not even the hacker. Especially not the hacker.

Gerry was perfectly complacent about his own ability to outsmart the hacker.

'So tell me about this Zac.' Alison kicked off her shoes and stretched herself out along the sofa. 'Funny sort of name. What's it short for? Zachariah?'

Philip shook his head. 'His name's Clive Zacharzewski. Since hardly anyone can remember, pronounce or spell his surname, he just gets called Zac.'

'The English are very snobbish about names.' Alison laughed with the smugness of one who could trace her family line back for centuries in the parish registers of her native Shropshire. 'In the States you can be called Abner B. Cheeseburger the third and no one so much as sniggers.'

'He's the Technical Support Manager,' Philip went on. 'Come to think of it he's the entire Technical Support team. Late thirties, I suppose. He's been with us about eighteen months — came from Mathers and Brown after he'd had some sort of blazing row with Dick Mathers. I considered myself very lucky to get him.'

'A real boffin?'

'He's certainly got the technical know-how and he knows the FIX project inside out. He's a genius in his own way which is why it was odd that it was Duncan MacAlistair who walked off with all the academic honours. I think Zac

41

is just a little too quirky, a little too close to the boundary between eccentricity and dottiness.'

'In other words, he gets up people's noses?'

Philip smiled. 'Dear Alison. Cutting through the crap, as always.'

'He hasn't managed to have a blazing row with you yet?'

'Not yet. But I do quite a bit of tongue-biting. There are days when I come home with a mouth so sore I can hardly eat. He's got a gift for knowing exactly where your weak points are and hitting them unerringly.'

'Sounds like a real charmer. Why do you keep him? Do you really need him that badly?'

'Remind me not to hire you as my personnel manager,' Philip said sarcastically. 'First you wanted to fire Jilly and now Zac. You know what it's like in this business − there are so many incompetents, so many accidents wandering around looking for somewhere to happen − you cling on to the good ones and pamper them like your own baby. I've got a good team at Orion now and not having them resign on me in high dudgeon is one of the reasons I'm not calling in the police. Remember?'

'Sorry. Go on.'

'There's rarely a week goes by when someone doesn't try to headhunt Zac, as it happens, but he stays with Orion. Okay, I pay through the nose for him but I think it's mostly that he likes a challenge and this project has certainly been that.'

'We're looking for someone with the ... what? The motivation and the guts to pull a stunt like this. I like the sound of your Zac.'

'He's a real loner. Got no friends in the office except, I suppose, Jilly. He never comes for a drink after work − always says he's too busy. Single. As I said, he doesn't seem to have much time for women − I've never heard him so much as mention a girlfriend. He's a workaholic. He moans a lot about how overworked he is but he gets bored when things are slack.'

'What about his finances? We may be looking for someone who's genuinely in some sort of financial mess rather than just greedy.' Alison made a mental note to find someone who could check credit records for her. Nick could probably do that.

'I don't see how he can be short of cash,' Philip was saying. 'He's got no dependents. He lives in a small place down by Clapham Common – he's lived there for years, since before it was fashionable. He *complains* about it getting fashionable. He can't have much of a mortgage. I provide him with a car and pick up all the running expenses. I've never known him go away on holiday.'

'Blackmail?' Alison hazarded.

'About what?' Philip enquired witheringly.

'Just thinking aloud.'

'He works an eighty-hour week,' Philip continued. 'Which doesn't leave him much time to spend all that time-and-a-half. If it's him, he must be in it for the love of the chase – to prove he's cleverer than the rest of the world.' He nodded slowly. 'Yes, I can see that.'

'He might resent all the money he sees being paid out to your clients' clients. He might think that they're getting money for nothing, just because they're rich in the first place, while he's working his balls off and not making half as much.'

Alison, despite her own financial success, was not an unqualified supporter of the City of London – perhaps because of the difficulty she'd had getting anyone to finance Hope Software a few years ago. It was a different story now, she reflected wryly, proving that old saw about how banks would only lend you money if you could convince them you didn't need it. She had few investments herself, preferring to plough all her profit back into the company; or spend it.

'It's a point of view with something to recommend it even,' she concluded.

'That's an interesting idea,' Philip murmured, looking mildly shocked. Then he shrugged.

'The possibilities are almost endless.'

'An inferiority complex?' Alison suggested. 'He needs to prove himself to himself. Napoleon complex – little man out to rule the world.'

'I didn't say he was a little man,' Philip pointed out acidly. 'He's about average height and build actually. In fact he's

Mr Average as far as looks and clothes go – brown hair starting to thin.' He raised a complacent hand to his own thick blond crop. 'Specs, grey suit, blue shirt, striped tie. He wouldn't exactly stand out at a conference of systems analysts.' Philip thought for a moment.

'Except ... there's a lot of suppressed anger there somehow. He makes me nervous. Comes into rooms as if he was the SAS. I can see him killing someone because they wished him good morning in the wrong tone of voice.'

'It's WDS Walpole, sir,' Shirley said on the telephone, late that same Sunday night. 'We've got a rape. Fourteen-year-old girl.'

'Shit!' Nick said. 'Where?'

'In Riverside Park. They've taken her straight to hospital. I'm leaving for the park right away.' She gave him the details.

'Get everyone organised. I'll meet you there in fifteen minutes. I'll handle the hospital end.'

He hung up.

Detective Constable Carol Halsgrove crawled off the bed towards the phone which had been ringing for some time.

'Oh no,' she muttered. 'Leave me alone. Stop ringing.' She picked up the receiver.

'Hopbridge 12649.'

'It's Nick. I know you're not on call tonight, Carol, but I need you.'

'Yes, of course, sir.' Carol glanced back at the bed where Detective Constable Paul Penruan was reclining with a smug look on his face. 'Have you been unable to get hold of DC Penruan, sir? Because I might know – '

'It's a rape. Fourteen-year-old girl. Can you get to the hospital?'

'I'll be there in ten minutes.'

'Elizabeth Parrish. Can you wait there until I come?'

'Yes, sir.' Carol hung up and began to dress.

'Thanks for trying to foist it on to me,' Paul said. 'No luck, eh?'

'Nick wants a woman.'

'You should be so lucky.' Carol flung a cushion at his head but he sensed her heart wasn't in the gesture. 'What's up, love?'

'Rape, fourteen-year-old girl.'

'Oh God, Carol! I'm sorry. I had no idea.'

She wriggled into her jeans and started pulling on her socks and shoes. 'If there's one thing I hate it's questioning some little kid about sex crimes. It puts me off for a month. So be a good boy and don't be here when I get back, okay?'

Shirley Walpole was also looking very glum when Nick found her near the north-eastern exit of the park.

'She was just a child,' she said angrily. 'Not one of your fully-grown fourteen year olds. A little kid.'

The SOCOs were doing their best but it was raining again and any evidence was being swiftly washed away into the shallows of the Hop.

'Have to get them into the water,' Nick said. 'For all the good it'll do. Will you tell them or shall I?'

'You tell them.'

'Not afraid of George Cruickshank, are you, Sergeant?'

'Not *afraid*, no.'

'All right.' Nick went off to give his orders. There was a lot of grumbling and a lot of to-ing and fro-ing and fetching of floodlights and waders.

'You go home,' he said to Shirley when he got back. 'I'll go to the hospital and talk to Carol.' Shirley nodded dumbly.

'See you in my office in the morning,' Nick said kindly. 'Early. And preferably bright.'

Carol Halsgrove was in the hospital foyer when Nick got there at about half-past eleven. She was wearing jeans and a sweater and a raincoat and her expression was as dark as the weather. He was about to put a companionable hand on her arm but thought better of it.

'You're wet through,' she said.

'I know, it's pissing down again. Is she all right? I mean I know she isn't all right but is there any permanent damage?'

'Nothing physical, as far as we can make out, but she hasn't been examined yet.'

'What? Why not? Surely the doctors know it takes priority over everything else.'

45

'Because she gets hysterical if anyone touches her. One of the ambulance men put an arm round her to help her in and she screamed the place down. She hasn't said a word either since she stumbled into that corner shop near the park entrance and collapsed.'

'But we're certain she's been raped?'

'Her pants had been torn off, and there was blood still running down her legs.'

'Jesus! What time did she get to the shop?'

'Shortly after ten, according to the owner. She was just closing and came with her in the ambulance.'

'That was nice of her.'

'It's Mrs Morecombe, Riverside Stores. I sent her home and said we'd take her statement tomorrow. Liz has been sedated now and she's asleep. Her parents are with her.' She put her fist up to her mouth. 'She's just a little kid, sir. Body of a twelve year old.' Nick made no move, wanting to comfort his long-time comrade and not liking to.

Damn it! Surely he could comfort the girl without being a sexual threat himself.

'Carol?' He took her other hand and squeezed it.

'I'm all right.' She took the fist away from her mouth and gave him a shaky smile. 'Thanks, Nick.'

'Will you ask her parents if they'll see me?'

Mr and Mrs Parrish were a bewildered, middle-aged couple, Elizabeth their only child. They had obviously developed a rapid emotional dependency on Carol Halsgrove which showed, Nick thought, how good she was at her job.

'This is Detective Inspector Trevellyan,' she said now. 'He's in charge of the case. He'll get the man who did this.'

Nick, wishing he were as confident, shook hands with the Parrishes. Mrs Parrish looked near to breaking point.

'Has your wife seen the doctor, sir?' Nick asked Parrish.

'I don't want to be doped,' she said firmly. 'I want to be here when Liz wakes up. She needs me.'

Nick felt helpless.

Mrs Parrish said hesitantly, 'If you get him, will she have to go through it all in court?'

'We'll make it as painless as we can,' Nick promised.

'She'll be anonymous. The papers won't be allowed to publish her name.' The Parrishes looked at each other in relief and Nick felt a great pity for them, knowing that their ordeal was just beginning, that the shock which was carrying them through for the moment would soon wear off. Experience told him that the chances of keeping Elizabeth's identity secret in a small town like Hopbridge were nil. Nurses would go home to tell their mothers the shocking tale; uniformed constables would frighten their sisters and fiancées with it. They might just as well splash it over the front page and get the agony over with.

'We've never had anything to do with the police before,' Mr Parrish said. 'That little girl, Miss Halsgrove, she was so kind to our Liz.'

'You've been kind too,' Mrs Parrish said tearfully. Her husband put a tender arm round her and they returned to resume their vigil at their daughter's bedside.

Chapter Six

'What can I tell you about Ruth Harper?' Philip gazed moodily into the gas fire. 'She's impenetrable. Affable, even friendly. Always stands her round. Attractive, intelligent, personable – laughs at my jokes. She's about as open and candid as the Sphinx.'

He shuffled uncomfortably on his sofa and gave Alison a weak smile. 'Am I getting paranoid? Six months ago I was the most trusting man in the whole of London. Today when I buy my morning paper and the man behind the counter says, "Good Morning, sir," I say, "Prove it!"'

'No one would blame you for being a bit paranoid, Phil. After all, someone is most definitely plotting against you.'

'I like to think it isn't personal. All the same, it's one of the reasons I'm so grateful to you and . . . to my real friends. I'd got to the point where I can't trust anyone.'

'Where does this Ruth fit in?'

'She's the Systems Analyst. She's freelance but she's been with Orion since FIX started so she's just as much part of the furniture as the rest of the team.'

'Programming background?'

'No. She got into analysis via a business background. She was something in the City herself until about five years ago – worked for a broker. She knows stockbroking inside-out.'

'So she might not have the technical know-how?'

'Possibly not. But the man she lives with has – a bloke called Carl Forster, like the novelist.'

The name seemed familiar. 'Rings a bell.'

'It would. He writes for *Computing Tomorrow*.'

'Ah.' The computer world proliferated with free and not so free magazines, most of which were over-technical and tedious. But *Com Tom* – as it was known – was a compulsive mixture of up-to-the-minute technical briefings spiced with the moral scruples of the *Sun*.

'The most vital thing in this whole business is not to let Carl know about the hacker. It'd be all over the front of *Com Tom* the next day and Orion would be finished.' Philip groaned. 'He's going to be in the office this week as well, when Phase Two of the system goes live, to report on it, and he's as sharp as a needle. We'll have to watch what we say. That means not letting Ruth suspect anything, of course.'

'Noted. But why do you say Forster might have the necessary hacking skills? He's a different sort of hack, surely?'

'A hack with a computing background. *Com Tom* is good technically – they carry conviction. All their people have hands-on experience. Carl was a programmer for three years.'

'If Ruth is a freelance Systems Analyst with a steady contract, she's not going to be exactly hard up, is she? What do you pay her? A thousand a week?' Philip nodded despondently. The ever-rising salaries of his staff were a source of almost physical pain to him.

'More, with the overtime she puts in.'

'And she'll have a good accountant to make sure she keeps as much of it as possible.'

'I see what you mean. But they live pretty high, her and Forster, and largely at her expense, I suspect. He's some years younger than she is and has a bit of a roving eye. She must spend a fortune on clothes, hairdos, trips to the beautician – all the stuff you women do when you're frightened of getting old.' Philip smirked heartlessly although his monthly expenditure on his own appearance would have kept an Indian village in rice for a year. 'They go to nightclubs, theatre first nights, opera, ski-ing trips, the Caribbean . . . high-profile stuff.'

'She sounds interesting. How old is she exactly?'

'Late thirties. Forster must be about thirty-two.'

'And they live where?'

'Kentish Town – the nice bit.'

'Handy for the City. Where are *Com Tom*'s offices?'

'Just off Tottenham Court Road.'

'Who else do I need to know about?'

'The two trainee programmers – William Marks and Jennifer Tatton. We call them Willy and Jenny, the twins.'

Alison frowned. It sounded familiar but for a moment the literary allusion eluded her.

'The Woodentops,' Philip prompted. 'You know: there was Mummy Woodentop and the baby, Daddy Woodentop, Sam who worked in the fields, Willy and Jenny, the twins . . .'

'And the very biggest spotty dog you ever did see,' Alison supplied, enlightened.

'And they all lived together in a little house in the country.'

'Got there. Why do you call them that?'

'Because they're inseparable, of course. I think it was Zac christened them that – he's got a lively wit when he can be bothered.'

'Is that so?'

'They started the same week, about a year ago. So I suppose they're really juniors now rather than trainees. They're under contract – you know, I train them and they promise to work for Orion for two years in return or repay their training costs. Anyway, they both came in for the rough edge of Zac's tongue in the first week and Jilly, as I told you, can be a bit ineffectual, so they just . . . bonded together. Now they stick up for each other, work in tandem, share a flat –'

'Is is sexual?'

'I'm quite sure not. It'd be downright incestuous. Twins isn't quite right, come to think of it but we liked the name so much that it just stuck. In fact, Jennifer is more like a big sister to William. She's the dominant one and the bright one. He tags along and does as he's told.'

'But if they're so junior, is it likely that they'd be able to come up with a fraud like this?'

'Jennifer read Computer Science at Hull. William did it

50

for "A" level but she's streets ahead of him technically. I
know Jennifer has a home computer though I'm not sure
what sort and I don't now like to ask.'
'Probably a Sinclair Spectrum,' Alison said snobbishly.
'That would suffice.'
'Oh, come on!'
'Really. You need a different keyboard but you can hack
into a mainframe with it. That's the trouble: hacking is so
bloody *easy*. Still, you're right, the hacker's almost certainly
using something a little more upmarket. An Apple, say.'
'Two people in it together,' Alison mused aloud, 'egging
each other on. It's an interesting thought. It might seem less
scary that way. More like a game.'
'I don't see Willy and Jenny as serious contenders,' Philip
said. 'They've not been with us long. I can't believe it could
be them. But then I can't really believe it can be any
of them.'

'Who're you trying to get into?' he asked, peering over her
shoulder.
'Davenports.' The FIX logo came up on the screen as she
manipulated a few functions. He admired the way her fingers
seemed to dance over the keyboard.
'One of the big stockbrokers?'
'The biggest we've got. Almost too big for this system –
I can't think how Philip managed to convince them.'
'He's a smooth talker when he needs to be. Very per-
suasive. Anything interesting?'
'I'll let you know when I've cracked one of their passwords.'
'Ah. Nothing obvious, then?'
'I've tried the usual. I've been trying them for weeks.'
'There are plenty of other clients who're not so careful,
surely.'
'None who can be as useful to us as Davenports. They're
brokers for half a dozen pension funds and three or four
big insurance companies. They handle thousands of sales
and purchases every week – transactions carried out by
real professionals. Otherwise I would certainly have given
up by now.'

51

'Any point in me ringing them up tomorrow and saying I'm an engineer and would they mind just giving me a sample password for some tests I'm doing on the line?'

'Too risky. We've come this far. Don't let's blow it now.'

He watched as she tried a series of words — both real and nonsense — one after the other without success. She noted the words she had tried neatly at the end of a formidably long list headed 'DAV163' — the user name by which Davenports was known to FIX.

'Do we know anyone who works there?' he asked. 'After all, it's a big firm. Anyone who knows anyone who works there would do at a pinch. You know, so we can burble on about how *interesting* it must be to be a broker and how much we'd *love* to see their office where all this high-powered brokering goes on. We might get a guided tour and then maybe find a list of passwords stuck up on the terminal.'

She shrugged her tense shoulders. 'You're the one with all the contacts. I think they're too security conscious for that though. No, I shall have to write a password-generating program and leave it to run overnight sometime. I've written them before. It may take days to break it, though. Or maybe they're canny enough to include things like dollar signs and exclamation marks, in which case we'll never do it.'

He made a derisive noise. 'Come on! No one can remember passwords like that. They have to write them down. Either way, we've got them.'

'Do your networking if you like. Charm and smarm. Two approaches can't hurt.'

'I object to "smarm" and it's too late to start now.' He looked at his watch. 'I dunno, though. It's not eleven yet. I'll just give Russell a ring — he's a broker, he knows everyone.'

'Okay, partner.'

'Anything else I can do meanwhile?'

'A cup of tea would be welcome. I shall put in another couple of hours here before bed.' She broke off typing to note the words 'BIGBANG' and 'OLDLADY' down on her list.

'I'll make you one if you take back "smarm",' he said, ruffling her hair affectionately.

'I can put you up for the night, if you like,' Philip said shortly after midnight. 'The spare bed's made up and you won't be cramping my style or anything – sad to say.'

'Thanks, but I want to get into my part tonight. By first thing tomorrow I've got to *be* Mary Lewis.'

To live in her skin and wear her cheap clothes and think her alien thoughts and see the world through her brown eyes.

Philip reached for the telephone. 'I'll call you a cab. Where's it to again?'

'Ronalds Road, N7. It's one of those turnings off the Holloway Road.' Philip made a sour face. 'Yes, it is pretty gruesome but it won't be for long. I may spend some nights at Jake and Simon's flat too. I've got some legal business to sort out with Jake.' Jake Trowerbridge was Hope Software's solicitor and plans were well in hand for the company to go public in 1989.

'Jake and Simon,' Philip said thoughtfully. 'It's ages since I last ran into them. How are they?'

'In the pink, as far as I know.'

'You know, Alison –'

'Mary.'

'Mary. Sorry.'

'You are going to remember to call me that at the office, aren't you? Otherwise I may as well pack up and go home now.'

'I said I was sorry.' Philip put the receiver back on its rest and Alison looked pointedly at her watch but he didn't notice. 'You know ... Mary, when you're in your twenties, you look at established couples and wonder what the hell they're thinking of – tying themselves down when there are so many delicious fish in the sea.'

'Yes, yes,' Alison said briskly. 'About that cab –'

'Then in your thirties, opportunities get a bit less, it's true, but you're still having fun. Then you wake up one day, you're over forty and you begin to wish that you could find someone to settle down with too.'

'I know what you mean,' Alison said. 'But it's a question

of finding the right person, isn't it? What's the number for the minicab firm?'

'I wish someone special would come along for me ...' Philip said glumly. 'Come along and stay.' Alison sighed. She wished Philip wouldn't smoke dope since it always made him maudlin and self-pitying. 'My business is going down the tube,' he continued, 'and nobody loves me.'

He picked up the receiver again and, to Alison's relief, began to press the buttons.

'It's nearly midnight,' Nick said, glancing at his watch. 'I think that's enough for one night. More than enough.'

'I've got my car, sir,' Carol said, when she realised Nick was on foot. 'I'll run you home.'

'No, I'll walk. It'll help me to think.'

'You're not walking three miles to Little Hopford?' she said incredulously. 'In this rain.'

'What? Oh, no. Alison's away for a few days. I'll sleep at my flat.'

'Sure you don't want a lift there? It's still pretty wet.'

He hesitated then, seeing the rain spattering against the window panes, said, 'Okay, thanks.'

'Give me two minutes. I'm dying for a pee. See you back here.'

As Nick stood aimlessly outside the lavatories awaiting her return, a young nurse came bustling in at the front door and hesitated on catching sight of him. Why did nurses always bustle, he wondered, was it the only method of locomotion they knew?

'Hello again,' she said after a pause.

Nick had an excellent memory for faces — it was essential in his job — but he had no recollection of ever seeing this one before, although the voice seemed familiar. It was a nondescript sort of face: neither pretty nor plain. She was an anonymous sort of girl: neither tall nor short, fat nor thin, old nor young. No, that was nonsense, of course she was young. He was sure he had seen that gap-toothed smile quite recently too, but could not place it.

'Sorry,' he said finally. 'You have the advantage of me.'

'Last night? In the square?'

Nick's astonishment almost betrayed itself in a gasp. He could see the girl in his mind's eye, reeling from her boyfriend's slap. He saw her as tall on her stilettos; her black hair falling across her cheek, red where the slap had made contact; glamorous in silver lurex and a black mini-skirt. He had taken her for seventeen. She was, he now saw, more like twenty-five. Her hair was back in a bun from which no wisp escaped. She was shorter in her sensible lace-ups. She wore a blue-striped nurse's uniform under her plain winter coat, a little silver crucifix on a chain her only ornament. She nibbled nervously at ragged nails as he stood there staring at her.

'You didn't recognise me without my glad-rags,' she said. 'I'm Theresa O'Shea – Tessa.'

'Nick Trevellyan.' Nick remembered his manners and they shook hands awkwardly. 'Detective Inspector. Look, Tessa, I know it's none of my business but do yourself a favour and get rid of that boyfriend of yours. He's bad news.'

She smiled and said calmly, 'Kevin O'Shea's not such a bad lad at heart.'

Nick winced. So the young lad, for surely he couldn't be much over twenty, was Tessa's husband. He had really put his foot in it. 'I didn't realise,' he murmured, relieved to hear Carol coming up behind him. She was humming a recent number one hit – 'He ain't heavy, he's my brother' – which told him she was starting to make the trek back to normality after the horrors of the evening.

'I've got to be off,' he said. 'Goodnight, Tessa.'

'Goodnight to you.' She started to turn away then asked, 'Have you the right time on you?'

'Five past twelve.'

'I'm late going on duty. Sister will be fuming and staring at her watch.'

By unspoken agreement neither Nick nor Carol mentioned the case as they drove away. They were tired and stale, they were too close to it, and they both wanted to sleep that night.

'Isn't that Alison's car outside your flat?' Carol said,

as she pulled up in the Market Square a few minutes later.

'She hasn't taken it with her.'

'I thought you hated driving it.'

'I do. Mine's broken down again. Carol ...'

'Yes, sir?'

'Did you have Penruan with you when I rang this evening?'

'... Yes, sir.'

'You know my views.'

'Yes, sir,' miserably.

'Is it serious?'

'I ... think so. I'm fairly sure he hasn't been seeing anyone else – and you know what he's always been like.'

'Promiscuous.'

'It's not entirely his fault,' she said, 'looking the way he does. Women have been chasing after him since he was fifteen.'

'Poor little corrupted innocent! He's not good enough for you, Carol.'

'Ah, don't say that. He may not be very bright, but he's kind and good-natured and ...' She tailed off.

'You love him,' Nick supplied.

'I think so. And at least he's here. He's not always running off to London or New York or bloody Timbuktoo and leaving me on my own,' she added recklessly.

Touché. He thought of something and let out a little laugh.

'What?' Carol asked.

'It just struck me that I seem to have spent the last few minutes giving unsolicited and officious advice to young women about their love lives. Why are women so much nicer than men? Why do they put up with so much from men? Why don't I mind my own business?'

Carol smiled and shook her head. 'Paul's all right, really. He's not such a bad lad at heart.'

'But that's exactly what she said!'

'Who?'

'The other unwilling recipient of my agony-aunting.'

'What? That nurse you were talking to?'

56

'Yeah. How long has it been going on? You and Paul?'

'It started when that poor girl was strangled – Frisco.'

'All this time,' Nick said in self-disgust. 'Right under my nose, and I'm supposed to be a detective. Well make sure I don't find out about it, okay?'

Carol beamed. 'Oh, Nick, you really are the most ...' She flung her arms round his neck and kissed him.

'Hey! That's enough of that.' He disentangled himself. 'You'll incur Alison's wrath, which is awe-inspiring.'

'Is it?'

'You've never seen her in a temper, have you? It's quite a sight.'

'I shall warn Shirley, then,' she said slyly.

'What?'

'Watch out for her, Nick, she's got her eye on you.'

'Don't be silly.'

'It's true. Almost the first thing she asked me about you was whether you were married.'

'I trust you told her I was.'

'No. Well you're not, are you?'

'Unfortunately.

'I imagine Alison's not the easiest person in the world to live with,' Carol ventured.

'No, but it has its compensations and it's never boring. Thanks for the warning. I shall take any necessary steps to defend my virtue.' He laughed. 'Goodnight, Carol.'

'See you tomorrow. Thanks, Nick, I –'

'I know. You did a great job this evening.'

He started to get out of the car but she leant across and put her hand on his arm. 'It is really all right? You and Alison?'

'Yes, certainly.'

'You haven't quarrelled?'

'No. Really. She's gone to London against my better judgement and advice but we haven't quarrelled about it. I'm expecting her home for the weekend. Goodnight, Carol.'

He walked wearily up the two flights of stairs to his flat, still smiling at the ridiculous idea that Shirley Walpole had designs on him.

After Alison had gone, Philip's conscience began to trouble him slightly. Should he have told her that he'd got Gerry in to investigate the fraud as well? Should he have told Gerry about Alison? He'd been so anxious to have Gerry working for him, so he – Philip – would be able to see him almost daily, that he'd half forgotten that there was already one private detective on the case.

Better to let sleeping dogs lie, he decided finally. If he told them, they'd just put their heads together and he'd only get one lot of detective work done while paying for two. Anyway, who could you trust these days?

Philip closed his conscience down for the night – it was never very alert at the best of times – and went to bed.

Chapter Seven

Monday mornings were usually bad, but they weren't usually this bad.

'The girl went to visit her grandmother every Sunday –' Nick began.

'The girl?' Shirley interrupted.

'Sorry. Elizabeth ... Liz. She went to visit her grandmother every Sunday for her tea. Then she'd spend the evening with the old lady – just watching TV and keeping her company until it was time for her to go home to bed.'

'Where does the grandmother live?' Shirley asked.

'In a council flat in West Hopbridge.' Shirley wrinkled her nose; she'd been in the valley long enough to work out the social geography. 'She's very independent, it seems,' Nick went on, reading the grimace. 'The Parrishes have asked her often to come and live with them but she prefers to keep her own place.'

'Liz wasn't left to walk back from West Hopbridge all by herself late at night, surely.' Shirley's voice was indignant.

'She wasn't raped in West Hopbridge,' Nick pointed out. Liz Parrish had been attacked in Riverside Park: a pretty oasis of gentle undulating greenery where the residents of the valley came to play with their children, walk their dogs, row and even swim in the Hop, stroll hand in hand in the summer sun. The Riverside Estate was the most 'sought after' residential area in town.

'Usually her dad came by and picked her up in the car at about ten,' Nick explained. 'But the car had been in the garage for a few days – it needed an MOT and there was a

59

part they couldn't get hold of. So Liz said she'd get the last bus into Hopbridge then walk home from the bus station. She'd done it before. Riverside Park is a shortcut − it cuts off a good five minutes.'

'What filthy luck. The wrong place at the wrong time! And all to save five minutes.'

'Isn't it always the way?'

'Where do you want me first?' Shirley asked briskly.

'At the grandmother's, I think. It's faintly possible that the rapist followed her from there.' He consulted the scribble on the notepad in front of him. 'Mrs Elsie Parrish, 14 Galsworthy House. Ask around outside ... any kids who might have been hanging about when Liz left. See if they noticed anyone following her.'

Shirley was already on her feet with the air of a grandmother being offered a free egg-sucking lesson. 'Anything else you want me to organise?'

Nick thought for a moment then shook his head. 'Carol is staying at the hospital waiting for the victim ...' he caught Shirley's eye again, 'I mean waiting for Liz to wake up and give us a description of the man. Penruan is coordinating house to house with the uniformed branch round the Riverside Estate. Then he's going to see Mrs Morecombe − the shopkeeper who called us.'

'And what will you be doing?' The question sounded abruptly rude but Nick took it in the spirit of simple enquiry in which it was intended.

'I'm going to go through the records with Dave Appleby − see if any known sex offenders have been let out recently. When I've done that I shall probably go round to the hospital and see how Carol's getting on.'

Shirley was already half way out of the office, anxious to be on her way and doing something.

'See you later then.'

It was usual to make an effort on your first day, Alison thought as she watched the other newcomer out of the corner of her eye. They had been left in some sort of waiting room on the ground floor of a 1960s concrete office block just off Moorgate. They had duly been waiting for fifteen minutes.

It was usual to wear your interview suit on the first day. If she had to sum her unwanted companion up in one word, it would have been 'shaggy'.

Alison herself was in a chain-store brown suit which had no lining and so hung rather badly, and an over-fussy blouse which tied at the neck and was already itching. After the first day you could descend rapidly – assuming you didn't have to go out to meet clients – via casual skirts or trousers to jeans and teeshirt. Her companion, a tousled man of about thirty, was starting at the bottom. He sat slouched in a too-low chair, his long legs stretched way out before him, reading an old copy of *Computing*. His beard needed trimming – or, even better, shaving off – and his belly needed a break from beer. As she watched him, he yawned, tossed the paper back on to the table and looked at her in a way which suggested he had been aware of her scrutiny.

'First day?' she asked primly. He nodded. 'Me too.'

'Better stick together then.' He gave her the suspicion of a wink.

'My name's Mary Lewis.'

'Gerry Walsh.' He did not offer his hand but looked her up and down without disguise. 'You fairly new to contracting, Mary?'

'No. It's been five years now.'

'Only I know most of the people on the circuit. Where did you work last?'

'I've been abroad a lot,' Alison said hastily. 'Papua New Guinea.'

'Yeah? You must have run into George Bantam –' Alison cursed inwardly. Surely PNG was far enough away to avoid the You-Must-Know syndrome. ' – he was working for the police force out there in Port Moresby.' He laughed. 'In full uniform – they don't have civilian staff so even the cleaners have a rank. The idea of old George in a police uniform is enough to make a cat laugh – assuming it was acquainted with George, as you must be.'

'Never heard of him,' Alison said. It had to be easier than bluffing. Old George? The tall-short, fat-thin black-white chap with the blue-brown-green eyes? Twenty-five going on fifty? My best friend.

'Surely all the ex-pats know each other in a place like that,' Gerry persisted.

'It's a huge country. I didn't go out much. There was a curfew a lot of the time, you know. It's not Guildford.'

'All the same —'

The door opened and Alison stifled a sigh of relief.

'Mary? Gerard?' They both stood up. 'Sorry to keep you waiting. I'm Jilly MacAlistair, your team leader.' She shook hands with both of them. 'Would you like some coffee before I take you up and introduce you to everyone?'

'That's all right,' Alison said as Gerry said, 'I could murder a cup.' They all laughed and Alison admitted that she would like some coffee. She was thanking God silently that she didn't have to endure this sort of thing in her real working life any more.

Jilly led them into a ground-floor kitchenette.

'Only we're on the top, that is the fourth, floor,' she explained, 'and the lift is out of action half the time so you grab your coffee when you've got the chance.'

The smell of over-boiled coffee filled the room from two steaming percolators and they helped themselves. Alison stood sipping her coffee which was too hot and black for enjoyment and took in what she could of Jilly.

Face to face she did not look sinister. She looked comfortable — solid and plain with no effort at adornment. You saw her sort waiting at the school gates in their hundreds every day, somebody's mum. Only she wasn't anybody's mum, Alison remembered, and she had to be a lot less bovine than she looked. And she wasn't much older than Alison herself, despite her acquired air of middle-age. She looked harmless, that was the only word for her.

Nick's voice whispered in her ear: 'Don't trust anyone, anyone at all. Remember the times in the past when you have trusted people ...'

'Shall we get going then?' Jilly derailed Alison's train of thought, led the way to the solitary lift and pressed the button which lit up. 'Working today. Make the most of it.' She pointed. 'That room opposite is where the computer is kept, by the way, and the printer is in there too. There are no operators. We load discs and tapes and collect listings

62

ourselves. You need a cardkey to get in. Actually you need a cardkey to get in the front door, as you probably noticed. Remind me to give you both one. You need to enter a code number for the computer room as well as the key. It's 1234. Think you can remember that?'

'Just about,' Gerry said.

The lift arrived and Gerry entered first without any time-wasting after-youing. He certainly knew how to make himself at home, Alison thought, as he pressed the button for the fourth floor.

'Philip's not in this morning,' Jilly told them as they ascended jerkily. 'He's gone to see a client with Ruth — that's Ruth Harper, our Systems Analyst. Apparently it's quite an important client and he has some interesting ideas for enhancements. Ruth's gone along to see how feasible they are.' Gerry merely grunted. 'It all makes work for the working man, or woman, to do,' Jilly concluded with a laugh.

'And Phil gets to charge for a new upgrade,' Gerry remarked. Alison looked at him with respect — she was beginning to like Gerry.

The office of Orion Software covered the whole of the top floor and was open-plan except for a small room at the front of the building which was, Alison deduced, Philip's own bolt hole.

The occupants of the room glanced up as she and Gerry followed Jilly in. All except for an intense-looking man in red-rimmed spectacles who was typing with three fingers faster than Alison had ever seen anyone type in her life. He had taken off his suit jacket, rolled up the sleeves of his blue shirt and his unknotted tie drooped on the keyboard. She half expected to see beads of sweat forming on his forehead. As she watched, he stopped typing for a few seconds and smiled to himself, satisfied about something.

She looked nervously round and nodded greetings to anyone who met her eye. It felt strange knowing so much about these people in advance; it was as if she had been reading their private diaries or love letters.

Apart from the intense man, who had to be Zac, there were two young people who could only be William and Jennifer —

63

their twin brown heads bent over a computer manual. Each wore a grey suit, a white shirt with a narrow silvery stripe, and while William wore a blue and red striped tie, Jennifer had knotted a similarly-patterned scarf round her neck. As Jennifer glanced up, Alison saw that her eyes were bulbous and her cheeks crimson with little broken veins, which was all that prevented her from being pretty.

Gerry put his hands in his pockets and surveyed his audience with apparent indifference.

'This is Mary and Gerard, everybody,' Jilly said. 'I won't tell you who people are at this stage, you'll only get confused. This is your desk, Mary.' She pointed to an empty table by the window. 'With Gerard opposite.'

'Gerry,' he said, and sat down.

'Oh good, a window seat,' Alison said.

'You'll find out why,' Jilly told her. Alison looked puzzled. Seats by the window were usually much coveted and jealously guarded. Jilly laughed and explained. 'It's right by the radiator which is always much too hot; if you open the window everyone else complains of the draught. Oh, and the flat roof above the window lets in water into the back of your terminal – and often down the back of your neck – when it rains. Are you surprised it's not popular?'

'If we get short of space, someone can sit on the windowsill,' Gerry remarked. The wooden sill was at least three feet wide, marked where hot coffee cups had been left on it and streaked where the rain had leaked in. Alison put her bag down on it and peered out. It gave on to the rear of the building into a claustrophobic courtyard or atrium with concrete paving slabs and empty flower tubs.

'The Garden of Eden.' Gerry put his hands behind his head and smiled up at Alison. He seemed entirely at his ease which was more than she could say of herself. She took her coat off and put it down on top of the bag. There were still acres of bare windowsill. She felt a little helpless. Detecting was already less fun than she had expected. She sat down on the edge of her chair.

'Zac,' Jilly said. 'Zac.' The intense man took no notice.

'ZAC!'

'What!'

'These are Mary Lewis and Gerard, I mean, Gerry Walsh.'

'So I gathered, woman.'

'This is Clive Zacharzewski, Zac for short. Our technical support guru.'

'Welcome to the madhouse,' he said grudgingly. He stopped typing again and surveyed them both without a smile. 'I usually do the interviewing round here. I give people a bit of a technical going-over. But apparently Philip thinks he can manage to hire people without my help now.'

He resumed typing, dismissing them both. William and Jennifer began to giggle in their corner and William caught Alison's eye and winked. Zac glared at them and muttered, 'Children!'

Jilly shrugged apologetically and mouthed, 'You'll get used to him.'

Alison remembered what Philip had said, that Jilly was the one person in the office Zac was civil to. If that was civility . . .

Mrs Morecombe was serving a garrulous customer when Paul Penruan arrived to see her that morning. He waited, standing out of the way near a display of crisps where he had a good view of her. She was still attractive at about fifty, with her hair neatly set, the grey shaded out, the whole tinted a reddish brown. Middle-aged women always dyed their hair red, he knew. His mother did. She said it looked softer on an older face than a dark colour.

Paul's mother had been widowed when he was twelve and had never remarried. He had two younger sisters. Of course lately he'd been spending a lot of time at Carol's flat and he'd told his mother not to expect him home last night, although Carol wouldn't let him move in altogether, insisting that Nick would go spare. Last night, as she'd seemed so upset, he had obediently gone home to Mum who had hugged him, made him some comforting cocoa and swallowed her questions.

Paul, as the only male in the family, knew how to talk to women. They liked him and not just for his pretty face. Nick, knowing all this, had sent him to charm Mrs Morecombe and coax her memory. Bill Deacon liked to make out that

Penruan was useless, but Nick found him invaluable for dealing with middle-aged ladies. They were always eager to please him.

The customer, an elderly woman, had already heard of the rape and was offering various theories as to what was wrong with the modern world. Mrs Morecombe was answering her as briefly as she could and Paul admired the way she was making no attempt to cash in on her role of Good Samaritan. The old woman obviously had no idea that she was talking to the discoverer of the crime.

When she was finally free he came forward, introduced himself and showed her his warrant card. She looked at him in surprise — she had not been expecting such a tall, handsome and personable young man.

'Come through the back.' She patted her hair into place as she put a notice saying 'Back Soon' on the door, slipped the bolt and led him into a small store room with two stools. 'I sit here when I've no customers — just for a little rest. Like some tea?'

He declined with thanks. 'It's a hard job you've got here, Mrs Morecombe.'

'Bette, please.'

'Bette. Do you run the place on your own?'

'Since my husband died last year. My daughter lends a hand but I don't like to ask too much of her. She's got three kiddies to look after.'

'Never! You're never old enough to be a grandmother.' Mrs Morecombe bristled with pleasure — everyone agreed she didn't look fifty-three.

'You work a very long day,' he said, 'if you're open until ten at night.'

'No, dear. I shut at six.'

'But last night ...'

'I was still here but the shop was long shut. I was stocktaking. The little girl came banging on the door — gave me quite a turn. I suppose she saw the light on. How is she? I rang the hospital this morning but they wouldn't tell me anything as I wasn't family. And I realised I didn't even know her name.'

'I'm not sure how she is.'

66

'Only she couldn't seem to speak. But then she didn't need to. I could see what had happened right enough.'

'Didn't she say anything at all?'

'A sort of whimper, maybe. "Help me." I took one look and called an ambulance and your lot. Then I ran out into the street to see if there was any sign of the man.'

'That was very brave of you.'

'It's just what anyone would have done. But there was no one else in sight.'

'Can you see the park gates from the shop?' Paul asked.

'You can. But, as I say, I was stocktaking so I wasn't looking.'

'Had you any impression of anyone running past shortly before the girl got here?'

She shook her head. 'I'd like to help, love, but people walk past all the time — that's why they built a shop here, because people have to pass it. I didn't hear any running. If I had, I'd just have thought it was kids. There are so many entrances to the park, aren't there? He might have run away to the main entrance, or slipped out by the water meadows.'

Paul took out an official statement form and asked her to fill it in.

'What, now?' Outside in the street, someone began to hammer on the locked door. She peered out. 'That's Mrs Wilkinson, wanting her bread.'

'I'll call back for it this afternoon, if you like.' Paul got up.

'That'll be fine, dear. I'll do it lunchtime. My daughter takes over for an hour then.'

'I'll see myself out.' He handed her a card. 'Here's the number where you can reach me if anything comes to you. See you later.'

Paul walked off to check up on the house-to-house team, knowing that he'd made an old woman's day and that if anything came to her, the smallest detail, she'd call him.

Chapter Eight

'I blame myself.' Elsie Parrish plonked herself down in an armchair and motioned Shirley to follow suit. She lit a cigarette and inhaled.

The one-bedroomed flat was tidy and clean but not obsessively so. Elsie, unlike so many pensioners worried about their household bills, had her heating turned well up and the little sitting room was welcoming. The furniture was not new but not shabby either. There was a TV and video, a stereo with large speakers and a pile of magazines on the coffee table. How strange it must be, Shirley thought, to be retired and have almost unlimited leisure. She could not imagine it.

Elsie Parrish was in her late sixties, comfortably plump and obviously still took trouble with her clothes. Despite her present distress she had made the effort to powder her face, belonging to the generation which liked to put a good front on things – especially to official strangers.

Shirley herself wore no make-up, no jewellery except the heavy gold watch which had once been her father's, nothing superfluous to her neatly-tailored brown trousers and jacket and cream shirt.

Elsie did not in the least remind Shirley of her own grandmother who had brought her up; who had cleaned from attic to front doorstep every day; and who had not allowed smoking or television in the house. Her childhood had had an air not so much of genteel poverty as of genteel stinginess.

'Sorry,' Mrs Parrish went on. 'I'm forgetting my manners. I should offer you some tea, Miss Walpole.'

'Let me make it.' Shirley jumped up again. The flat was small and there was no doubt which door led to the kitchen. She went in, not giving Mrs Parrish time to protest, and filled the kettle with fresh water from the tap.

Mrs Parrish had followed her in and stubbed out her cigarette, half-smoked, in a saucer on the draining board. 'I'm supposed to have given up,' she explained, 'but what with the shock ...' She watched in approval as Shirley made the tea with the economy of fuss and movement she brought to every task.

'It's traditional, I suppose,' she said. 'A "nice cup of hot, sweet tea" as a palliative for all traumas.'

'You have nothing to reproach yourself with, you know,' Shirley said gently.

'Guilt isn't rational,' Mrs Parrish told her. 'If I hadn't been so stubborn, if I'd taken Tony and Barbara's offer to move in with them and Liz ... well, she wouldn't have been there, would she, last night?'

And if Mr and Mrs Hitler hadn't hit it off when they met, Shirley thought, we wouldn't have had Auschwitz.

'You have a right to lead your own life,' she said.

'I've lived on my own for ten years − since Albert died. I couldn't face the thought of sharing a house with anyone but him, of having people under my feet all the time. Living alone makes you selfish.'

'No. It makes you independent.' Shirley poured boiling water into the kettle and Mrs Parrish took two china cups and saucers down from a shelf and picked up a bottle of milk from the worktop.

'Never fancied mugs,' she said. 'Come on. Let's make ourselves comfortable.'

'I called by a little earlier,' Shirley said, following her back into the sitting room. 'But you were out.'

'I was at the hospital.'

'You didn't want to stay there?'

'I agreed with Tony and Barbara that we'd work a sort of rota so that one of us will always be there when she needs us. I'm taking the evening shift today.'

'She won't be left alone, I promise you.'

'But it's not the same, is it, waking up to find a policeman by the bed?'

'No,' Shirley admitted. 'Though it'll always be a police-woman.'

'We had such plans for her,' Elsie Parrish said. 'Tony's my only child. I tried to have more but I just kept miscarrying. No reason for it, the doctors said, just Nature's way. Then Liz turned out to be an only child too. All our hopes rested on her. There wasn't much money about when Tony was young and he had to settle for being an accounts clerk. But Liz wanted to be a vet, you know.' Shirley murmured something.

'Yes. Loves animals, she does. And she worked so hard at school. You need better "A" levels to be a vet than to be a doctor, did you know that?' Shirley shook her head although she had been dimly aware of the fact. 'And now she's lying there in that hospital and she won't even speak. Not even to her old Nanna.'

Mrs Parrish sat for a moment with tears forming in her eyes. Shirley sipped her tea in silence, realising instinctively that an excessive show of sympathy would cause the old woman to break down completely and that she needed to be in control at present. After a moment she recovered her spirits enough to ask, 'Did you roll up outside in a police car?'

'I'm CID,' Shirley said. 'Plain clothes, plain cars.'

'I bet that disappointed them.' Mrs Parrish gestured towards the window. 'They'd be hoping for a siren and flashing lights. They think it's better than the telly.'

'Your neighbours were kind enough to come out and tell me you'd gone out,' Shirley said ironically. They had stopped short only of taking photographs. Except for one bossy woman at Number 13 who had mistaken her for a reporter and had almost thrown her down the stairs before Shirley had managed to get her warrant card out. She told Mrs Parrish this story to cheer her up.

Elsie smiled faintly. 'That'd be Joyce, next door. She's a proper friend – left me in peace. The rest of them have been round offering to do things – shopping, housework. All they really want is to see how I'm taking it and have a look at a place which is not even the scene of the crime. I bet the park's crowded this morning, isn't it? Hundreds of people who've suddenly decided the dog needs a good walk?'

'The relevant area's been sealed off,' Shirley said. 'But there will certainly be an audience behind the barriers.'

'Nosey bastards!'

'Human nature, I'm afraid.'

'You'll be searching the place then, like on the telly?'

'Fingertip search,' Shirley agreed. 'There were a few bushes around — the chances are he's left a thread from his sweater or his coat on a handy thorn. A hair, perhaps. It'll be vital in getting a conviction.'

'That won't help Liz, though, will it? It can't be undone.'

'It will stop him ruining the lives of other little girls. I know that's not much consolation now.'

Elsie Parrish got up and took a photograph from the top of the television set. She handed it to Shirley. 'Albert,' she explained. 'Mr Parrish. We had a good married life. I know you young people think you invented sex, and it's certainly true that we were a lot more ignorant in those days, but we learnt together and it made us happy. Albert used to say it was the only pleasure you could still get for free.'

Shirley was touched at this token of the old lady's trust. She examined Albert, stiffly buttoned-up for the formal portrait. Now she came to look for it, there was a twinkle in his eye. Her own grandfather in a similar photograph, worshipped on the mantelpiece like a heathen god, had worn no such twinkle. Her grandmother would rather have died than discuss sex with Shirley. She would rather have died than serve milk from the bottle. She would have made no great distinction in impropriety between the two.

'Can I ask you a few questions?' she asked, relinquishing the photograph.

'Of course.' Mrs Parrish had been fiddling with her cigarette packet for some time and now admitted defeat. She took one out and lit it as Shirley began.

'Do you know exactly what time Liz left last night?'

'It must have been a quarter to ten. The news was just starting on ITV. There's a bus at about ten to. Supposedly.'

'Did you see her down the stairs? Or to the bus stop even?'

Elsie shook her head. 'I get a touch of rheumatism in the winter. I try to stay out of the wind and damp. Liz would never hear of me going down with her. No, I just saw her to the door, put the chain and bolts on to make sure *I'd* be quite safe for the night, then I went into the kitchen to make my cocoa before bed.'

'You didn't happen to look out of the window?'

'The kitchen's at the back, as you saw.'

'Would you say that Liz confided in you?'

'We sometimes talked about things girls find hard to discuss with their mums, but mostly in general terms. I've no way of knowing what else she kept back.'

'She never mentioned a boyfriend?'

'Never. She was young for her age. Still keen on netball and the Girl Guides. She only started her periods about six months ago – late these days. We talked about that. Some of the other girls at school had been laughing at her because she hadn't started yet, so it was a relief to her.' An unpleasant thought struck her. 'He could have made her pregnant.'

'She's been given what they call a Morning-After pill,' Shirley explained. The old lady nodded briskly – she read her women's magazines. 'With her parents' knowledge and consent, of course.'

'Small mercies.'

'That's all really,' Shirley said, aware that the questions seemed somehow inadequate to the event. 'You mustn't blame yourself,' she repeated. 'You're not omniscient.'

'Nor omnipotent,' Mrs Parrish agreed. 'Allow me my little bit of wallowing, dear. I shall survive. I always have.'

'I must get on.' Shirley got up. 'I've got to talk to all those nosey neighbours, I'm afraid. Or listen to them, rather. I shan't tell them anything they don't need to know, don't worry.'

'It'll be all over the papers anyhow,' Mrs Parrish said philosophically. 'Oh, I know they won't be allowed to give her name but everyone'll know who she is all the same.' She gestured out of the window again. 'They all knew by first light.'

It was sadly true, Shirley knew. If you sneezed at breakfast in a small town like this, complete strangers would be asking you by lunchtime how your cold was.

'I'll come and see you again,' Shirley said. 'If I may.'

'You'll be welcome, my dear.' The old lady held out her hand for Shirley to shake and Shirley, after the briefest of hesitations, leant forward and kissed her powdered cheek.

There had been moves over the years to close Riverside Park at night, to patrol it with dogs, to put street lighting along the pathways. All had foundered on the rocks of local pig-headedness – why should they be deprived of their public facility at night? – or parsimony. Alsatians and electric lamps didn't come cheap.

So it was that Riverside Park, several acres bordering the Hop River, as its name implied, remained accessible round the clock. At this time of year people still walked their dogs there after dusk. Gardeners, who worked from eight until four, were the sole figures of authority.

On the whole the people of the valley took pride in their municipal park and it suffered remarkably little from litter or vandalism. Until now, Nick would have described it as a peaceful place – the sort of place where a weary Detective Inspector could go for a walk to refresh his spirits and think.

This morning there was no shortage of things for the weary DI to think about. Nick had deviated from the timetable he had given Shirley but salved his conscience by ensuring at regular intervals that the hated bleeper device in his pocket was switched on.

He followed the path from the main gate, through the more formal part of the gardens. The north-eastern part, bordering the Riverside housing estate, had deliberately been left as a wilderness of ball games and hide-and-seek.

Since Nick was a fast walker, he soon left behind the well-trimmed lawns and the topiary and, plunging through dense shrubbery and unmutilated hedges, tried to put himself in the shoes of the rapist, to imagine the deviant thought processes of an unbalanced mind. He was more than a little relieved that the task proved beyond him.

73

The SOCOs had found the place where the man had hidden. Had he heard Liz's approach and slipped into the bushes ahead of her? The evidence suggested not. The blades of grass behind the bush had been systematically uprooted and torn into pieces about an inch long. He had apparently been there for some time. Waiting for a stray woman? A stray girl child? Had he waited in the same place every night for days, in the damp, for the opportunity he longed for? Should he be looking for a man with a head cold?

The torn blades of grass were like another man's doodle — they were dealing with a nervous, fidgety character. And yet at the same time the footprints had scarcely moved, indicating stealthy stillness. The uniform length of the torn pieces suggested an obsessive personality to Nick. He would have gone home with soil beneath his fingernails but his compulsive nature would have sent him heading straight for the nailbrush. His wife might have noticed, though, or his doting old mum.

The footprints were size nine, a commonplace sort of studded sole, indicating a boot rather than a shoe. They had found little in the way of threads. Perhaps he had worn a Mackintosh or a leather jacket — something without fibres.

There had been a couple of greyish threads on the bush — pure new wool from a sweater or jacket. Or they might have been there for weeks, months, left by a child playing hide-and-seek that summer.

And hundreds of men wore jackets like that — grey tweed. Nick had one hanging on a hook behind his own front door. He had bought it to celebrate his promotion to Inspector and his return to his home town. That had been five years ago. Perhaps it was time he thought about buying a new one.

If he had a suspect, he could check his clothing and shoes against the samples and check his blood against the sperm samples they would get from Liz Parrish when she had recovered sufficiently to be examined.

But he had no obvious suspect. There were no convicted sex-offenders currently living in the Hop Valley. All he could do was to question men with a known history of violence. But the rape of an under-aged girl was a very specialised form of violence. The most brutal criminals – men who could cut a security guard down with a sawn-off shotgun for the sake of a few pounds, then go home to a peaceful night's sleep – would turn in prison on a child sex offender; force him into solitary for his own protection.

The park proper gave way to meadows, dropping gently to the east bank of the Hop as it strolled the last few miles to the sea at Hopmouth. The meadows grew long every summer and were popular with young couples since the grass could be flattened to make a comfortable *al fresco* bed.

In autumn the grass was cut. As a small child in the late fifties, Nick had delighted in watching the council workers mow it with an old-fashioned scythe; now they used a motor mower. The old hay shed still stood there though, and the grass was still collected to dry until it could be sold to the local riding stables.

He stood looking moodily across the meadows until disturbed by a uniformed constable who had come up unheard behind him.

'Hey, mate!' Nick jerked round, surprised by this instrusion on his reverie. The young man recognised him, reddened and backed away saying, 'Sorry, sir. I didn't realise it was you. Only we were told to keep a look out for loiterers.'

'Quite right, Dunn.' Nick had given the order to the Relief Sergeant himself that morning. 'The criminal famously returning to the scene of the crime.' He looked at his watch. 'Time I stopped loitering.' PC Dunn turned away and Nick called after him, 'Oh, and Dunn ...'

'Sir?'

'"Hey, mate!" is not how we address members of the public while they're still presumed innocent.'

'Sorry, sir,' Dunn repeated.

Chapter Nine

Alison was sitting at her desk, noting down suitable error messages for the new program she'd been given. People got very upset if computers asked them to do anything without saying 'Please'.

'Your listings, love,' Gerry bent low over Alison's desk and opened out the top one, speaking very quietly.

'Look, I hope you don't mind me telling you, but I think you've got hold of the wrong end of the stick here. This database navigation you've gone for isn't the most efficient way of going about it. In fact, not to put too fine a point on it, it won't do.'

Alison coloured. She took her glasses off and blinked up at him. The contact lenses had proved so uncomfortable that she had been unable to bear the thought of re-inserting them that morning. She had resorted to a pair of over-the-counter spectacles hurriedly purchased on her way to the office that day. She was confident that no one would notice the change in her eye colour – people were so unobservant.

'I'm not really used to hierarchical databases,' she murmured in apology. 'Only relational ones.'

'Don't worry about it.' He perched on the edge of the desk and explained quickly, quietly and comprehensibly where she had gone wrong. Alison scribbled notes on the listings, nodding and muttering her thanks.

She was finding things more difficult than she had anticipated. After eight years of running Hope Software she had expected to be able to cope with one hand tied behind her back. But life on a big mainframe project was

76

very different from the world of micro-computers where she had made her name and her fortune, and she was painfully aware that if it hadn't been for Gerry she would have made quite a few gaffes already and had the other staff wondering what the hell she was doing there. He didn't seem like a man with a wing to spare for sheltering lame ducks though.

'Thanks,' she muttered again.

Gerry smiled down at her. 'You can buy me a drink this lunchtime if you really want to thank me.'

'I'd like that,' Alison said, meaning it. After all, Gerry was the one person here she could trust — the one person who couldn't possibly be the hacker. He'd been safely in Australia until six months ago and touring around America ever since. No one could set up such a skilful fraud while travelling round a vast continent — you needed your own computer, modems, safe phone lines.

Deceit was alien to Alison's nature and living a lie — with a false name, false brown hair, glasses with plain lenses, weighing up every word before she spoke, trusting nobody — could easily become an unbearable strain.

So when Gerry rose at twelve-thirty, shrugged his jacket on and raised his eyebrows at her, she followed him eagerly out into the City of London.

'Where do you live, Mary?' Gerry asked as they carried their drinks carefully to a corner seat upstairs in the Globe, five minutes later.

'In a bedsit just off the Holloway Road.' Alison had had to find somewhere at short notice, somewhere to suit the part she was playing of a single, rootless, young woman. Bedsit life was very different from the luxury of Hope Cottage. She wasn't eighteen any more: there was nothing picturesque about having to share a bathroom, one and a half flights down, with four strangers. 'It's a bit squalid but it's handy for the office and you know what the housing situation is like in London.'

'I know all right.'

'How about you?'

'I'm kipping on a friend's floor in Earls Court at the moment. I might take up the offer of a bed from a rather

77

more affluent friend though. I haven't decided. It's not as if I shall be long in London either way.'

'Where will you go?'

'Anywhere. Nowhere. South Africa, New Zealand, Canada ... Hell. Anywhere, so long as it stops my feet itching.'

'What are you running away from?' Alison wondered aloud.

Gerry laughed but did not answer. Instead he said, 'Perhaps I shall go back to Australia. You can find most things there – sea, mountains, desert. Did you ever go out into the desert in Papua? It gave me such a shock the first time I went out there and saw camels. I had no idea they were found in Australasia.'

'Yes, I was a bit taken aback too.'

Gerry changed the subject. 'And where's home? Your real home?'

'The West Country, I suppose.' She was on safe ground here. 'I've no family. My parents are both dead. I'm an only child.' The pleasure of being able to tell four truths without pausing for breath was almost dizzying.

'You're not married, then?'

'No. I've never been married.' Five!

'Me neither.' There was a brief silence while they sipped their drinks and Alison eyed the food bar lasciviously.

'Boyfriend?' Gerry asked casually.

Alison hesitated. Gerry's motives for being so helpful were becoming increasingly obvious and there was something strangely attractive about him despite, or because of, his scruffiness, his devil-may-care attitude, his footloose way of life. Besides, he might prove useful to her. She wanted to put him off gently.

'I broke up with someone recently. I don't want to talk about it. I'm steering clear of all that sort of thing just now.'

'It's like riding a horse,' Gerry said. 'You should get straight back on as soon as you fall off.'

'It isn't anything like riding a horse,' Alison said firmly. 'Unless you've been used to a very peculiar sex life.'

'Versatile rather than peculiar,' Gerry said with a grin.

78

'Food, I think.' It was time to change the subject. She got up and made a beeline for the seafood lasagne.

Gerry watched her push her way through the crowd – meek mousy Mary Lewis who worked away all day at her terminal, who watched and listened a lot but spoke little, who didn't sneak off ten minutes early in the evening or come back twenty minutes late from lunch. Who worked late every night, in fact.

Mary Mouse, who wore a cheap shiny brown suit. Were those the only clothes she possessed? Even he, Gerry, had a change of jeans. And she was wearing that most detumescent of garments – a woolly cardi. She didn't make the best of herself although, when she took those ugly glasses off, those green eyes could knock you for six.

Good Little Mary Mouse.

Only she didn't walk like Little Mary Mouse, that was the odd thing. She walked like a woman who knew where she was going and what she was doing. In fact, she walked like a man. Not many women did that. And now she was getting served ahead of that bloke in the violent purple and green striped tie who had been there before her.

Gerry didn't like mousy-meek women – they clung. But his hormones were responding to Mary Lewis all right, and Gerry always listened to his hormones. What he liked most about her was the luminous intelligence he saw in her eyes: those green eyes which had, unaccountably, been brown the first time he met her – just last Monday.

Mary Lewis had to be the most obviously suspicious person in the office. He'd put her top of his list of suspects except that she'd only just started, like himself, and Philip had been so sure it was an inside job. Presumably that was why Philip hadn't told him about her in his 'briefing'. Odd that she hadn't known old George out in PNG though – he knew from experience how the ex-pat communities clung together. Odd that she didn't seem very wised up on the topography and fauna of New Guinea either.

He got up and followed her to the food bar.

*

79

Ruth Harper had finally made an appearance when Alison got back just after two. Gerry had lagged behind to buy a *Standard* in the hope that there might be some cheap flatshares in it.

Ruth was using a word processor at her desk in the far corner of the office but came forward to greet the newcomer. It was the first normal human welcome Alison had had at Orion.

Ruth was a glossy woman: her hair artfully cut, her body pushed and pummelled into submission and a Ralph Lauren suit. She had a winter tan which Alison regarded with envy − being obliged with her own red-head's colouring to stay out of the sun.

'I'm sorry I wasn't here when you arrived,' Ruth said, shaking hands. 'Glad to have you aboard. We need some extra help since Philip's suddenly started running us ragged with Phase Three deadlines. A week ago, no one even knew for sure there was going to be a Phase Three.'

'The project seems to be a great success,' Alison ventured. Ruth's expression was polite but indifferent − her eyes already straying back to the text on the green glare of her word processor. What had she expected? Alison asked herself suddenly. That the hacker would walk around looking furtive and clutching a bag marked 'Swag'?

'The clients love it,' Ruth agreed. 'It makes such a change to have your work appreciated, doesn't it?'

'Usually it's all brickbats and no bouquets,' Alison said.

'I gather you're a friend of Philip's.' She hit a key and stored the files she had been working on.

'Well, you know,' Alison said cautiously. 'More acquaintances really. I just ran into him a couple of weeks back and he offered me a job on the spot.'

'He did that with Gerry, too. It's not like him − '

'Gerry is a friend of Phil's too?' Alison interrupted in surprise.

'Apparently. As I say, it's not like Philip. Caution is usually his middle name − that and Economy. Odd sort of chap, by all accounts.'

'Phil?'

'Gerry.' Alison, who thought Gerry was easily the sanest

person she had met at Orion, didn't reply and Ruth went on: 'You're new in town, then?'

'Just back from three years in Papua New Guinea,' Alison agreed. Dear God, please don't let Ruth know anyone in Papua New Guinea. I promise to be good.

'Never heard of it,' Ruth said obligingly. 'When Gerry gets here, I'll take you through an overview of the system. Jilly's given you something to be getting on with meanwhile?' Alison said that she had and Ruth sat down again and began to move the cursor over a long list of files. Alison resigned herself to a boring afternoon and went back to her desk. 'You know we've got Phase Two going live tomorrow?' Ruth called after her.

'I knew it was some time this week.'

'There'll be a bit of a reception here for the press. Drinks, canapés − you've picked a good time to arrive.'

As though by arrangement, shortly after six-thirty that evening, they all left the office together − everyone except Zac who muttered something about taking security copies if only people would push off and leave him to it. At the corner of the street, William and Jennifer chorused 'Goodnight' and turned south towards Bank station on the Central Line. Alison knew that they shared a flat somewhere near the Mile End Road.

Gerry called, 'See you tomorrow,' and disappeared into Moorgate station. He was going to look at a flatshare in Balham. Jilly pulled a plastic carrier bag out of her briefcase and made for the nearest supermarket. Ruth, with a motion of the hand barely perceptible to Alison, brought a black cab whining to a halt at the kerbside. Alison heard her say 'Queen Elizabeth Hall' in a commanding tone before climbing into the back seat. She rode off with a wave of her umbrella.

Alison started to follow Gerry's example but was seized with a sudden desire to walk all the way home − if you could call that bedsit 'home'. There had been a time when she'd enjoyed riding on trains in the rush hour, observing the other passengers, relishing the spontaneous hostilities which broke out as people fought over a seat. Now she couldn't face the noise, the bustle, the too cold or overheated carriages, the mess. She had slowed down since leaving London, changed her priorities, and now wondered how London commuters kept a hold on their sanity.

It had stopped raining and walking home would delay the moment of her arrival at the depressing assortment of flats and studios which made up the Victorian slum in Ronalds Road. She could get something to eat on the way, then, with a bit of luck, she'd find an old-fashioned telephone box where she could call Nick without being exposed to wind and prying ears. The pay-phone outside her bedsit was too public.

It would give her a good forty minutes' thinking time too – she found walking conducive to thinking.

The rain had been replaced by a sharp wind. She buttoned her brown duffel coat up and wrapped her beige scarf round her neck. Alison favoured blacks and greens for her own clothes but Mary Lewis had struck her as a beigy-brown sort of woman. She had no gloves so she slung her bag over her shoulder and put her hands in her pockets as she turned into Finsbury Pavement and up into the City Road.

She hastened through the spooky underpass at Old Street with her head down, passing the metal-boarded shops with their elaborate graffiti. Outside the grubby public toilets a young woman asked her if she could spare any loose change. Alison shook her head and took the steps two at a time to re-emerge gratefully into the cold air.

The road to Angel seemed interminable and it struck her too late that she could have cut off the corner by weaving through the network of roads to the south and west of City Road. She was very tempted to jump on a 43 bus which, she now realised, would take her most of the way home. But she persevered. This grey thoroughfare had once been a street of tall, gracious Georgian townhouses; now they leant tipsily together as if only the fact that they were terraced kept them from falling over.

At Angel, she turned into Upper Street. This area was familiar to her as she had lived in Islington before her migration to the Hop Valley. She could have taken a detour to see her old house in Colebrooke Row. No, she'd save that for a rainy day – a day when she really needed cheering up. She also resisted the urge to stop at the York, her old local — it would be too depressing to find it full of strangers.

Most of the shops were unchanged since she had last walked up this road two and a half years ago, and she stopped outside her favourite bookshop — closed for the night but with a dim interior light still illuminating a patch of pavement. There were notices inviting people to join a local writer's group, a calligraphy class, an alternative medicine workshop. A poster — 'Owing to unforseen circumstances the light at the end of the tunnel has been extinguished until further notice' — made her smile.

Avoiding the swirling cars at Highbury Corner, she was on the last leg. She glanced at her watch. Forty minutes so far — it was further than she'd thought. British Rail would have had her home half an hour ago. She carried on north up the Holloway Road. There were quite a few pedestrians about — huddled young women in cheap coats, rushing home to lonely bare rooms and makeshift meals.

Women very like Mary Lewis.

Near the turning to her bedsit she stopped and bought some fried chicken and chips to take away, unable to face the formica tables, overflowing ashtrays and bulging plastic ketchup bottles shaped like tomatoes which were the alternative. She realised too late that her bedroom would stink of fried food all night.

It occurred to her as she walked in at the open front door of the house that she hadn't done any thinking at all on her walk — not about the case anyway. There was no post for her, nor was she expecting any. There was just a pile of letters for people who had long since left this address and whose whereabouts were unknown. She trudged up two flights of stairs and unlocked the door of the stale room overlooking the wilderness of rear garden.

After her greasy meal and a cup of instant coffee prepared in the curtained-off 'kitchenette' in the corner, Alison went out in search of a telephone box. She soon gave up hope of the old-fashioned type and started hoping for one in working order. Finally she found one which had a long queue and took only phone cards. She shuffled off to find somewhere which sold them.

83

So it was late when she rang Hope Cottage. She got only her own voice on her own answering machine. She rang Nick's flat instead but there was no reply. She swore gently. There were so many things she wanted Nick to check for her — the credit-worthiness of all the staff for starters; and whether any of them had criminal records. She had also wanted to ask him if there was any way he could check that Gerry had indeed been in America for the last six months — to ensure that Shaggy Gerry wasn't telling her shaggy dog stories.

Where was Nick? It wasn't as if he'd got any special case on at the moment — just the usual round of petty theft. Unless something had cropped up in the few days since her departure.

A man in a track suit demanded aggressively if she was going to be much longer and she banged the receiver down and hurried off tearfully into the night.

Chapter Ten

To answer Alison's question: Nick was in the quietest corner of the Eagle and Child. He was sipping tomato juice, eating cheese and onion crisps in the absence of any better supper, and arguing with Shirley Walpole as to whether it was worth trying to reconstruct the crime.

'It was pouring down,' Shirley said. 'You're not going to get any passers-by turning up.'

'It's always worth it. Carol's so small she can pass for a young girl at a distance. It may just jog someone's memory.'

'You're the boss.'

'I want to do it one night when it's raining again, though, and it seems to have dried up all of a sudden.'

'Feeling is running high in the valley,' Shirley said. 'The incident room's been snowed under with people wanting to help.'

'None of them has any actual information though. It's just been a case of "Anything I can do. Anything."'

'I think some of them just want to form a lynch mob,' Shirley agreed. 'And there's a sort of prurience about it all too. Excitement. Elsie Parrish had had the same sort of thing from her neighbours. It makes me want to throw up.'

She stared glumly into her glass. The words were barely out of her mouth before she realised that she meant them literally. She did feel sick, or at least faint.

'Shirley?' Nick's voice came to her across a great distance. 'Are you okay?'

*

'Feeling better now?' Nick asked twenty minutes later.

'Much better. Thanks.' Shirley put her empty mug down on the coffee table next to a plate with some crumbs of bread and cheese and an apple core on it.

'Want some more coffee? Or I think Alison left a bottle of brandy here somewhere. A drop of that might help.'

'No. I'll be fine in another minute. I'm so ashamed.'

'Don't be. No one thinks any the less of you for it, least of all me. I expect it was just going without supper that did it.'

'I'm used to that. I'm not usually affected like this, but this sort of rape . . .'

'Yes. I know.'

'Sex should be a good thing, a happy thing. That little kid, how will she ever be able to form a loving relationship now?'

'I feel the same, you know.' Nick patted her on the arm. 'Sex between two people who love each other is something beautiful, unique. Even couples who are not in love can share enjoyment, mutual pleasure and comfort. Then at the other end there's prostitution, incest, pornography and rape.'

Shirley shuddered and tried to bury herself more surely in the cushions of the sofa. For a long time neither of them spoke, then Shirley said: 'Do you want to go to bed, Nick?'

'I'm fine. You just sit here until you're feeling better, I don't mind. I'm not really tired.'

'That wasn't what I meant.' Shirley took a deep breath. 'I meant what you said just now. Mutual enjoyment, mutual comfort.'

Nick stared at her in disbelief. 'No! I mean . . . no thanks.' Shirley flushed. 'I wasn't . . . I hope you didn't think I said that as some sort of come on.' He got up from the sofa and walked to the window, placing a safe physical gulf between them.

'Forget it,' she said.

'I'm a happily married man, you see.'

'You're not married at all.' Shirley turned the temperature down several degrees. 'If you were, you wouldn't be in such a hurry to turn down a bit on the side.'

'I resent that slur on the male sex.' Nick tried to keep the

86

tone light-hearted. 'Look, Shirley, I'm flattered. You're an attractive woman. But it's what I was saying just now about sex between two people who love each other. There's no place there for infidelity. I love Alison, you see, and nothing on earth would tempt me to be unfaithful to her.'

'Someone said she was away.'

'Yes, she is. That doesn't give me a licence to start sleeping around.'

'Someone said you'd quarrelled.'

'*Someone* is mistaken.'

'Just an uncomplicated fuck, Nick. No strings. I won't tell her if you won't.' She stood up and joined him at the window.

'Stop it, please. You'll hate yourself in the morning.'

Since Nick's flat was on the second floor, he often didn't bother to pull the blinds. They were both silent for a few minutes, staring out of the window over the empty town. Nick wished she would go. Then she spoke again.

'Someone said she goes away a lot.'

'Someone has been busy,' Nick said sharply. He would have a few words with Paul Penruan in the morning. 'Yes, she has to go away on business – to New York or Los Angeles sometimes, to London often. The business – Hope Software – just grows and grows. Sometimes she's away for as much as a month.'

'I'd better go.' She turned away.

'I'll see you safely back to your car.'

'That isn't necessary. I can take care of myself.'

'Ah yes, the judo. I'll come with you anyway.' He took his coat from the hook inside the door and put it on to pre-empt further argument.

'Thanks,' Shirley said. 'Will you be even kinder than you already have been and forget the things I said this evening?'

'What things?'

Shirley laughed for the first time that day.

The next morning, Carol Halsgrove reported in before going off duty. She had spent all night at Liz Parrish's bedside.

'She's still not speaking. We've tried everything.'

'Damn and blast!' Nick said.

Liz Parrish was his only hope of any sort of description of the rapist and she had been shocked into an impenetrable muteness. Reg Grey, the superintendent, was asking why no progress had been made and talking of appealing to higher authority in the shape of Detective Superintendent Ted Seymour from Headquarters. Shirley Walpole was avoiding his eye. Alison was two hundred miles away. He wished he'd stayed in bed with the duvet over his head.

'Her mother and grandmother have tried everything,' Carol was saying. 'She's got her favourite books, tapes, family photos. We even persuaded the Charge Nurse to let us bring her pet cat, Daisy, in. She stroked it and hugged it and wouldn't say so much as a word.'

'So what's happening now?'

'The therapist is with her. The one who deals with child abuse cases. She's got the dolls with the full working parts but so far she won't even use those to show us what happened.'

'Have we been able to examine her yet? Get the samples?' Shirley asked.

'She just becomes hysterical. It's the only time she makes any sound, screaming and struggling 'til you think your heart will break. All we've got so far is that the blood on her legs was almost certainly her own – so that's no help.'

'Sedation?' Nick asked.

'It's got to be a last resort, sir. The doctors won't hear of it at the moment. Think about it. Imagine her waking up and realising she's been messed about with down there yet again without her consent.'

'We must think of his other potential victims. But it is, as you say, a last resort. What does the psychiatrist say?'

'The usual sort of stuff. Time the great healer ... a sudden breakthrough when we least expect it ... patience.'

'Who've you left there?'

'WPC Greenslade. With instructions to reach you, me or Miss Walpole if she utters so much as a syllable. There was just one odd thing. I don't know that it'll be much help ...'

'Well?' Nick asked.

'The Charge Nurse looked in shortly after I arrived at ten

88

o'clock. He was just going off duty and had forgotten to tell the nurse something – '

'What is a Charge Nurse, anyway?' Shirley asked.

'It's a sort of male Sister,' Carol said, annoyed at the interruption. 'You can't go round calling a bloke "Sister", can you? As I was saying, the late shift was just finishing and he'd put on a sort of woolly balaclava. Only when Liz saw him she became hysterical again. He had to leave the room very quickly.'

'So you think the rapist may have worn a balaclava?' Nick said. 'As issued to the SAS, the IRA, and anyone else who happens to want to heep his head warm or his face concealed.'

'I said it wasn't going to be much help,' Carol pointed out. 'And it might have been a different sort of head covering – a crash helmet, say. It was very dark that night.'

'All the same . . .' Nick thought for a moment. 'What does he look like, this Charge Nurse? If Liz mistook him for the rapist, even for a second, it may be that he's similar in appearance or build.'

'He's about five foot seven.' Carol closed her eyes to aid her visualisation. 'About thirty-five. Quite thick round the chest and middle, but it's muscle rather than fat. He keeps himself fit – he asked me to come up and see his boxing trophies some time.'

'So we may be looking for a shortish, stocky man.'

'He'll be on duty again today,' Carol said, 'if you want to see him for yourself. He's on lates all week. His name's Dave Edwards.'

'I want to go to the hospital this afternoon, in any case,' Nick said. 'Have a word with someone in the psychiatric unit – Dr Frobisher, preferably. He doesn't talk to me as if I were mentally deficient.' Shirley tutted. 'What?' Nick asked, relieved that communication was being re-established.

'Psychological profiling?' Shirley asked.

'It's been very useful at times, very accurate. You know that as well as I do.'

'I can save you the trip. He'll tell you we're looking for a man who hates women and has a very dominating wife or mother. Remember the Yorkshire Ripper? Then they blamed

89

the wife. Or Michael Ryan – the Hungerford massacre, just last year? There it was the mother. One thing you can be sure of is that it'll not be the man's fault. Adam would still be in Paradise if it wasn't for Eve.'

'I thought I was supposed to be the Luddite,' Nick said kindly. 'I'll give Frobisher a ring and if he can see me today, then you can come along and take notes.'

Alison came out of the ladies' lavatory on the third floor landing at twelve-thirty and started on her way downstairs. Looking down into the stairwell, she noticed Gerry padding at high speed out of the front door and quickened her pace to catch him up. He was the most interesting person to have lunch with. She felt a little guilty, though. She ought to be concentrating on her suspects; having lunch with Jilly or Ruth or the twins or, God help her, Zac.

She let herself out of the front door, holding it open – against all the rules – for a respectable-looking stranger who was just coming in and who smiled his thanks. She hurried to the street corner and glanced down Moorgate. Gerry was nearly at the next corner, by the Globe. She was just about to call out to him when Philip appeared out of a shop doorway. Alison shrank back into the entrance to the chemists as the two men embraced. They walked off together in the direction of the Barbican.

Alison made a face at herself in the chemist's display window. 'He wasn't kidding when he said "versatile",' she said under her breath. 'You've been living in monogamous bliss too long, Alison Hope, if you can't recognise an AC/DC any more.'

But the woman who looked back at her, the woman to whom she was speaking, was not Alison Hope. At least it didn't look like her. Alison had always had a strong sense of her own identity. A much-loved only child, a little spoilt and selfish, she had grown up strong-willed, dominant, sure of herself.

But the woman in the plate glass was a meek-looking creature with mousy hair scraped back into an unflattering pony tail and spectacles which made her face long and severe. She wore a brown viscose suit from one of the less expensive

chain stores and a white nylon blouse beneath which her bra
was unacceptably outlined. She looked, perhaps, slightly
older than her thirty-one years; she looked a little care-worn,
a little unloved. She looked tired too, which wasn't surprising
since the sofa bed in her rented room was lumpy and sagged
in the middle.

Alison would have passed her in the street without recognising her.

A horrible thought came to her. Was Alison Hope, then,
only the sum of a collection of objects? Was she just a
wardrobe full of expensive clothes and hand-made shoes,
some good pieces of jewellery, a business card with 'Managing Director' printed on it in italics, a convertible Jaguar,
a big house in the country, a yard of red hair cosseted by a
Mayfair hairdresser?

Dr Frobisher — head of the hospital's psychiatric unit —
pulled a thermos of coffee from his desk drawer and offered
some to Nick and Shirley. They declined politely and Dr
Frobisher poured himself a cup.

Richard Frobisher, who was tall, spare and well-groomed
without quite being handsome, had attained his present
eminence young and saw himself as just passing through on
the way to his rightful place at a more prestigious hospital.
He had a thin, elegant wife, a son and daughter at private
schools, and a high opinion of himself which he called 'good
self-esteem'.

He had a lot of time for Nick, considering him no more
than averagely neurotic. He found him an interesting subject:
he sensed Nick Trevellyan to be an introverted man and
introverts did not usually join the police force. He also
knew Nick to be good at his job while still being liked and
respected by everyone in the valley that he hadn't actually
put inside at some point. Frobisher was happy to talk to him
professional to professional. The same could not be said of
some of Nick's colleagues.

His new sergeant looked all right too: young, quite pretty,
sensible, neat, with a no-nonsense set to the mouth. More
up-to-date than solid old Bill Deacon, no doubt. Body lan-
guage a little tense, though. Another introvert — the police

force was certainly changing. She seemed to be avoiding her boss's eye, as if she didn't like him much or they had fallen out over something important.

'Sure?' he queried, pointing to the thermos again.' It's the real thing, not instant. I grind the beans myself.'

'Thanks,' Nick said again.' But we had some in the canteen on our way in.'

'You call that stuff coffee?' Frobisher made a face and switched to the subject of their visit without warning. 'I've got a ten-year-old daughter myself, Nick. I'll give you all the help I can. So, you want to know what sort of man rapes a child?'

'That's it.'

'I could say any sort of man. You. Me. Given the time and the place and the right frame of mind. "The mass of men lead lives of quiet desperation." Thoreau.'

'I understand that.' Nick was beginning to feel a bit desperate himself. 'But if you could offer some practical help, I should be most grateful.'

'I can tell you the sort of man you're looking for nine times out of ten. If he turns out to be the tenth man, don't come blaming me.'

'Understood.'

'Broadly speaking he's like any other rapist, only more so – if you see what I mean.'

'Not exactly.'

'Rapists – the sort who attack women in the park, that is, not the sort who think they're entitled to a quick jump as payment for dinner – are unable to relate to women. They're frightened of women. They don't know what to say to them, how to chat them up, how to flirt with them. Somehow they missed out on the learning process.'

Frobisher smiled at Shirley and fingered his tie. He had never had any trouble relating to women.

'They may misread the signals as a result,' he went on. 'Take a little harmless flirting from a woman as a green light. The chances are he's not very intelligent – a bit below average, probably. He once read in some pornographic magazine that when a woman says "No" she means "Yes" and he believed it.'

92

'Or maybe he heard some judge say it?' Shirley suggested.

Frobisher looked amused. 'As you say, Sergeant.'

'And the ones who rape children, you said, are more so?' Nick asked.

'They're so frightened of women that they daren't even attack a full-grown woman. They have to choose a child as victim.'

'So what sort of family background are we looking at?'

'Only child, perhaps, isolated. No other children of his own age anyway, no young sisters to rough and tumble with, to tease and torment, to play doctors and nurses with. Domineering mother − or mother-figure.'

Nick avoided looking at Shirley who was writing in her note book, pressing her pen so hard on the paper that it threatened to snap in two at any moment.

'Father absent or ineffectual,' the doctor went on, unaware of the hostility he was arousing. 'No girlfriends, and no friends who are girls either.'

'Could he possibly be married?'

'Almost certainly not.'

'The Yorkshire Ripper was married,' Shirley objected.

'He wasn't a rapist − let alone a child rapist. The nearest he got to sexual contact with any of his victims was masturbating over one of them. No, the serial killer's a different kettle of psychological fish to the rapist. I should be very surprised indeed if your rapist turns out to be a married man, or even to have a regular girlfriend. Or any real friends at all, come to that. He's socially inept, inarticulate, unable to make small talk with anyone.'

Frobisher paused for breath and took a sip of his tepid coffee.

'He may engage in macho sports − shooting, boxing, that sort of thing. He's got the idea that women secretly like the rough approach − are waiting for it, wanting sex while at the same time wanting to avoid taking responsibility themselves for their own libido.' He smiled apologetically. 'I don't mean that he'd rationalise it that way to himself, of course. He wouldn't have the vocabulary.'

'Women are desperate for it but try to pretend they're

not because they've been told that Nice Girls Don't,' Nick paraphrased. 'So they're all just waiting for a big strong bloke to come along and force them to do what they really want to do all along.'

'Nicely put,' Frobisher agreed.

'He doesn't differ that much from a lot of non-rapists, then,' Shirley interrupted, 'except in degree. It sounds like the sort of opinion I hear in the staff canteen every day. He's Mr Average.'

'In a sense,' Frobisher said. He was beginning to revise his view of the new sergeant. Her feminism sounded a little hard-line for his taste. And she was an attractive girl too, shouldn't have any difficulty finding herself a boyfriend — she didn't need to bother with all that Women's Lib cant.

'He may be involved in all-male activities like rugby clubs,' he continued. 'He'll find it easier to talk to the other men there about something specific: the range of a new handgun, who's going to win the four-nations cup this year. They'll consider him a decent sort of bloke, if a bit quiet.'

'That's very helpful,' Nick said. There was no shooting club in the valley but there was one just outside Taunton which would be within reach. Boxing was quite popular in the local youth clubs. Here was useful material for his troops to work on.

'Or he may be a complete loner. He'll try to deny the feminine side of his personality, appearing very much as a man's man. He may be violent in other ways. He may ride an enormous motorbike or drive a very souped-up car. Alternatively he may appear to the outside world as a meek little mother's boy, hugging himself all the time with the knowledge that underneath it all he's a real man, a man who knows how to deal with uppity women.'

'So what you're saying is that he's going to appear at one or other end of the spectrum,' Nick said. 'Either he's Rambo or he's the hen-pecked little man in the seaside post-card.'

'That's right. Or, as I said earlier, he's the man next door with a lovely wife, two kids, a wide circle of friends and a job with prospects. And Liz Parrish just happened to be in the wrong place at the wrong time. It's only happened once, so far. He might not break out and do it again for another ten years.'

'If that's the case we shall never catch him, so I have to work on your more likely theories.'

'Fair enough. But Miss ...' He pretended to think hard although he had registered her name perfectly well when Nick had made the introductions. 'Miss ... Walpole, is it? ... mentioned the Yorkshire Ripper. Remember that the main reason the police took so long to catch him was that he didn't fit the profile. He was just an "ordinary bloke".'

'Age?' Nick asked.

'You've got me there. Who knows when a dormant volcano is going to erupt?'

The socially inept did sometimes marry, Nick reflected, as a group of nurses anxious for their lunch break hurried, chattering, past them near the front desk. Look at Kevin O'Shea – violent, belligerent, he'd found himself a sensible, caring woman like Tessa to look after him.

Women. Were they forgiving angels, or were they crazy?

He would make the time to pay short, stocky O'Shea a visit, Profile or no Profile.

Chapter Eleven

'I'm not sure which of us was the more terrified,' Dave Edwards, the Charge Nurse, said when Nick caught up with him later that afternoon. 'I'd not been tending her much myself, I thought it'd be best to leave her solely in the hands of female nurses.'

'Very wise,' Nick said. 'I've only got policewomen sitting with her too.'

'Exactly. Anyway, I was just going off duty and I'd already changed out of my uniform and put my balaclava and crash helmet on.' He ran a hand over his thinning hair. 'Gets a bit cold on top these nights. Then I realised I'd forgotten to tell Nurse Purvis something. I took off the crash helmet – thinking I'd look a bit silly wandering round the wards like that – but I left the woolly hat on. They told me on Princess Margaret Ward that Purvis had looked in on Liz Parrish so I just stuck my head round the door to give her the message and . . . all hell broke loose.'

'When you say stuck your head round, do you mean that literally?' Nick asked.

The little man understood the question at once. 'No, I went right into the room. It's just a figure of speech. She got a clear look at me.'

'Well, thanks for your help.' Nick got up. 'What sort of bike d'you ride?' he asked casually.

'More like a little scooter,' Edwards said with a laugh. 'It's just that I can't run to a car on a nurse's salary with an ex-wife to support.'

Edwards was a likeable little man, Nick realised. You

96

wouldn't notice him in the street but, when you came to look closely, there was a rough commonsense in his face, complemented by a smile of genuine warmth. He wondered if Carol planned to accept the invitation to go and inspect his boxing trophies sometime.

'Gather you do a bit of boxing?' he said, as Edwards got up to see his visitor safely to the front door. Boxing was one of the 'macho sports' which Frobisher had mentioned and Edwards might know the valley clubs.

But he shook his head.'Used to. It's a young man's game. Took it up in the army, was quite good at it. Fly weight.' He patted his thickening midriff. 'Wouldn't make the weight now. Anyway, I've seen too many people get hurt by it – one of the corporals in my unit took a real bang over the ears. He just wasn't the same person after that. Most of the time he was the nicest bloke you could wish to meet – then, suddenly, he'd blow his top for no reason at all.'

'You think he suffered some sort of brain damage?'

'I've seen in this job what a blow on the head can do to people. The rational part of me, the medical part, says they ought to ban it. The part that used to be a carefree young lad remembers the exhilaration of proving you were a better man than the other guy.'

'See much action in the army?' Nick asked.

'Nah. Usual tour of Germany. Otherwise I spent most of my time in Aldershot. I didn't even go to Northern Ireland. Don't get me wrong, I'm not complaining. Only an idiot wants to go out and fight wars or drop dead under a sniper's bullet.'

'Were you here the night Liz was brought in?' Nick asked.

'No. I've been on lates all week but I was owed an hour by a colleague. I got off at about ten past nine that night, so I missed her.'

'It's awkward finishing work at that time of night,' Nick said sympathetically. 'I should know – I did my share of shift work when I was in uniform. Too late for the pictures, too early for bed. Nothing but the pubs left.'

'Oh, I went straight home with a Chinese takeaway and a

97

video – they're a real godsend to shift workers. You should get one.'

'There's an idea. Anything good?'

'Rocky 3.' He laughed at Nick's expression. 'Okay, so it's crap but I like to watch the boxing scenes. It takes me back. Stallone's not as bad as people make out, anyway. I like the Rambo films too – plenty of action. You don't want something to make you think after eight hours on duty here. You just want to relax.'

They reached the front desk. 'Here we are.' He held out his hand and Nick shook it. 'Nice to meet you, Inspector. Shame it wasn't under more pleasant circumstances. I fancied being a copper myself, you know, when I came out of the army, but I couldn't quite make the height.'

'Pity,' Nick said sincerely. 'But you're doing just as much good here.'

'Let's hope so.'

To anyone in the know, Orion's Phase Two launch party for FIX had an air of bravado about it. Philip, determined to put a good face on things, had pushed the boat out. True, they weren't actually drinking champagne but only the most demanding gourmet could distinguish the *méthode champenoise* wine he had ordered from the real thing. Alison, who enjoyed a good party, settled down to get better acquainted with her suspects, get very mildly drunk, eat lots of canapés, and have fun.

Word had obviously got round in computer journalist circles that no expense had been spared. The offices of Orion Software were crowded with eager young women with notebooks, blasé young men with dictaphones, and hangers-on of both sexes who were only there for the drink.

It was the first time Philip had been into the office since her briefing a few nights ago and he was too busy for her to get a quiet word with him now. He was splendid in an Armani suit: a suave and charming host. She had to admire him – a man dancing as the *Titanic* sank and the band played on.

There was no sign of Zac who had announced that he had better things to do than talk to a lot of idiots and had shut himself away in the computer room. Alison was keeping an eye on Carl Forster who had arrived a few minutes earlier. Philip had greeted him rapturously by name which, she realised, had been for her benefit.

Forster had neither notebook nor tape recorder but accepted a press handout from Philip, folded it up without reading it and tucked it into his inside pocket. He accepted a glass of wine with more enthusiasm.

As he glanced round the room his eyes slid over Alison without pausing. Alison wasn't put out. She knew his type: if a woman didn't appeal to him physically, she might as well not exist. Ruth Harper was petite, blond, glamorous. Tall, bespectacled Mary Lewis, so beige that she almost disappeared into the carpet, didn't exist for Carl Forster, nor did Jenny with her bulging eyes and wind-blown complexion. She understood now why Ruth worked so hard at looking good.

Forster reminded Alison of Gareth Dalston, who had shared her life and her house in Islington for nearly two years. He had had the same way with women he considered unappealing: avoiding them whenever possible, smiling politely if trapped into conversation with one, glancing around for escape routes.

If challenged, Gareth would insist: 'Women? I love them.' In his heart he disliked and feared women and could not have conceived of having a woman as a friend. Women fell into two categories: those he wanted to sleep with and those he didn't. He could see no point to the latter.

It occurred to Alison that Carl Forster was being found guilty and condemned without a trial. Speaking to him would be difficult, however, since he would be able to see no point in her. After a brief exchange with Ruth, he had attached himself to a pouting hanger-on called Debbie and they were laughing and maintaining eye contact near the makeshift bar. Ruth's eyes were following his every gesture. Alison felt sorry for her: she remembered so many evenings when she had done the same thing with Gareth.

She would go over and talk to Ruth. With luck, it

would kill two birds since Forster would be bound to come over and join Ruth eventually. Wouldn't he? Casting her mind back a few years, she felt herself to be on shifting ground.

Nick went down to the canteen at six that evening. There seemed no point in wasting time going home and cooking just for himself. Shirley had slipped home though, pleading the need to get right away from the case for half an hour. He noticed Paul Penruan sitting at a table in the corner with a new recruit – a blonde, gamine WPC of about nineteen. She was a pretty creature called Sally Ferris.

He knew that she'd scraped into the force by the skin of her teeth since her father was a small-time antique dealer who had sailed very close to the wind while managing to avoid a police record. The girl herself was not overly bright and he suspected that she was looking for a husband in this closed world where men outnumbered women by something like ten to one. It wasn't a good place to look for a mate, though, he thought cynically. The casualty rate among police marriages was high.

Paul was in full flow, making the girl giggle often. That old CID glamour, Nick thought, the new girls always fell for it. Paul was busy hinting at dark secrets and inner knowledge. He'd done it himself – long ago, in another lifetime.

'Late shift today, Sally?' Paul was saying.

'Yes,' she sighed. 'On until ten.'

'I'll be quite late myself. How about you get off on time and meet me for a drink after?'

Sally giggled. 'I can't tonight.'

'Okay. Just thought I'd ask.'

'I can manage Saturday, though,' she said quickly.

'It's a date.' Paul got up. 'Well, must get back to this big case. Ten o'clock, outside, Saturday. Don't go making any last minute arrests, will you?'

'You work with DI Trevellyan, don't you?' Sally said in her breathless, little-girl voice.

100

'Nick? Sure, I'm his right hand man.'

Sally looked doubtful. 'Isn't WDS Walpole that?'

'She's his right hand woman.' Sally giggled again. Paul turned away with a cheerful: 'See you Saturday.'

Nick, catching this last sentence, looked the other way and chose not to hear.

Ruth watched Alison's approach warily, unwilling to be interrupted in her solitary vice of surveillance. Alison, realising this, had armed herself with a platter of food by way of propitiation.

'Good do,' she remarked. Ruth merely nodded and Alison held the platter out towards her. 'Have one of these seafood vol-au-vents – they're scrumptious.'

Ruth shook her head disdainfully and patted her perfectly flat stomach. 'I never touch pastry.'

Alison, who was tall and naturally lean and had never dieted in her life, gazed at her uncomprehendingly. She put the platter down within easy reach and helped herself to a vol-au-vent. She noticed that Ruth was drinking mineral water. There were limits to how far you should take this health thing.

She examined Ruth carefully and with admiration. Alison did not view other females as potential rivals and was able to appreciate Ruth's calculated beauty while preferring a more lived-in look for herself.

She noticed that Ruth had brown eyes, hinting that she was not a natural blonde but, if this were so, her hair was so cunningly bleached as to give no other clue to the artifice. Alison wondered uneasily when her own red roots would start to show. She'd have to keep an eye on that – no one dyed perfectly good red hair to mouse without a damn good reason.

'That's your boyfriend over there, isn't it?' she asked, following the path of Ruth's hungry eyes.

'My lover,' Ruth corrected. Then, realising she might have sounded a little abrupt, explained: 'Once you're past your teens, "boyfriend" seems a bit inappropriate somehow. Not that any other term is more appropriate.'

'I think that's why people get married,' Alison agreed.

'So they know how to refer to each other in public.' She wondered how best to pursue her aim of getting a few minutes' conversation with Forster. 'Is he ... er ... here in an official capacity?' she asked. 'Or just as your guest?'

'Carl? He's a journalist.' Ruth seemed to swell with vicarious pride. 'He's the top man on *Computing Tomorrow*.'

'Goodness.' Alison contrived to sound impressed. 'I'd love to meet him.'

'Let me introduce you.' Ruth seized the opportunity of breaking up Carl's *tête-à-tête* without a second's delay. She took Alison by the arm and almost frogmarched her over to the bar. Alison managed to stuff the last of her vol-au-vent into her mouth before the pastry disintegrated all over the carpet.

'Melts in the mouth,' she said incoherently.

'Carl, dear.' Ruth insinuated herself between Carl and Debbie. 'I'd like you to meet Mary Lewis who's just come to work on the project. Mary, this is Carl Forster.'

Carl nodded briefly at Alison and said insincerely, 'Nice to meet you.' To her surprise he addressed her in a pronounced London accent. He was a bit out of date, she thought, if he was still relying on that to give him street cred. Could it possibly be real?

She was rather relieved than otherwise that Forster didn't bother to examine her closely. It occurred to her belatedly that her photograph had often appeared in *Com Tom* and Forster, of all people, might recognise her.

He did not trouble to introduce Debbie and she made an excuse and wandered away. Forster looked at Ruth and Alison without enthusiasm. Like Ruth, he had a winter tan. His hair was more obviously dyed since the blond was only on the top, spiky, layer giving an odd piebald effect with his natural brown. He wore a black leather jacket despite the overheated room. In fact all his clothes were black. He might as well have been wearing a badge, Alison thought, saying 'Poseur'.

She noticed Gerry making his way over towards the small group, as if he too was anxious to scrape Forster's acquaintance. Now, here was a man who really *liked* women. She was glad to see him since conversation seemed to have lapsed. Gerry soon remedied that.

'Don't you find it difficult following all the technicalities of the business?' he asked Forster after Ruth had introduced them.

'I had a programming background,' Forster explained briefly. 'Three years behind one of those desks – ' he gestured at the anonymous office furniture with dislike ' – I was the second best DEC programmer in London.'

'Who was the best?' Gerry asked, startled.

'I don't know of anyone better. I was just being modest.' Forster rocked with laughter at his own wit and Ruth smiled with affection. 'I gave it up as soon as the opportunity at *Com Tom* came up, though,' he concluded. 'I'd always wanted to be a writer.'

'And do you think you'll ever become one?' Alison asked with exaggerated politeness. To her surprise, Forster took the snub on the chin. She felt a quickening in his interest as he scrutinised her more carefully and laughed with unforced good nature.

'I suppose some people don't see journalism as real writing,' he admitted, and Alison felt some of her instinctive dislike evaporating.

'You couldn't become a novelist,' Gerry pointed out. 'People would get you mixed up with the other Forster.'

'Edwin Morgan? Good point. Now, why have we never thought of that, Ruth? The perfect excuse for not getting beyond Chapter Three.'

'It doesn't seem to have bothered Margaret Forster,' Ruth said rather waspishly. Alison suspected that she was sick of hearing about this putative novel.

Carl turned to accept some more sham champagne from William and changed the subject, obviously feeling that there had been enough jokes at his expense.

'FIX seems to be a big money-spinner,' he remarked, letting the sharp fizziness wash through his teeth. He and Ruth looked at each other and smiled. Was he speaking ironically? Alison wondered. Was that the smile of complicity of two criminals who planned to bleed Philip dry

103

before disappearing to work full-time on their tans on some Caribbean island?

'John James Turner.' Shirley read out a name from a pile of cards she had on the desk in front of her. 'Two charges: aggravated robbery and actual bodily harm. Asked for two other offences to be considered.'

'Mmmm ... still inside,' Nick said.

'You sure? He was sent down for a two stretch almost eighteen months ago.'

'He didn't make parole — got involved in that prison riot last summer, of all the stupid things. He can never stay out of a fight.'

Shirley put the card to the bottom. 'Alexander John Porter. GBH — six months youth custody. Served four. It was five years ago and he's been clean since.'

'Ah, yes,' Nick said thoughtfully. 'Worth a quick look.'

'That's the last of them. None of them look like real possibles. None with a history of sexual violence.'

'He's new. I was afraid of that. The chances are he's never been in trouble with the police. He's some young lad — somebody's son, husband, kid brother.' Nick rubbed his eyes tiredly. 'We've got nothing to go on: no description, no sightings. No obvious suspects. If only there'd been skin scrapings beneath Liz's nails or something — he must have held her down with her arms under her. And even if I could get sperm samples from her, I might end up having to do DNA testing on every man in the valley.'

'Jesus Christ!'

'It wouldn't be the first time. Remember the Dawn Ashworth case, a couple of years back? That was the first big success for DNA fingerprinting. They took blood samples from over five thousand men in the surrounding area and compared them with the genetic print on the sperm. Even then they nearly missed the killer — he conned a thick friend into providing blood on his behalf.'

'How many men are there of raping age in the valley?' Shirley asked.

'Good question. Where do we set the limits, anyway? The law says a boy under fourteen is physically incapable of rape

104

and you and I both know what dangerous nonsense that is. If the population of Hopbridge is around twenty thousand and the same again in the rest of the valley, we're testing an awful lot of men. I might not even be able to justify the cost to the Super. The Dawn Ashworth case was murder and not just rape.'

'Are we calling it a night, then?' Shirley asked, too tired even to pick up this gauntlet.

'I think so. Make a note to call the army in Aldershot tomorrow. I want to check the service record of a chap called Dave Edwards.'

'What am I checking for?'

'Any blots on his copybook, especially ones dealt with by a military court so they wouldn't appear on the police computer. Any violent incidents. Any head injuries too.'

The telephone rang. Shirley picked it up and said, 'CID. WDS Walpole speaking' She listened for a couple of minutes then said, 'I'll be right there.' She hung up. 'There's a girl at the front desk asking for CID.' Nick got up. Shirley waved him back down again. 'She insists on speaking to a woman.'

'Oh.' Nick was briefly at a loss. 'I'll wait here then.'

Chapter Twelve

As William approached her with another tray of drinks, Alison took one and seized the opportunity to engage him in conversation.

'So they've turned you into a waiter for the evening?'

'The perils of being the office junior, I suppose.' He was a handsome boy, she realised, about twenty-four years old. He was tall and fair with pleasant, regular features, nice manners and a slightly over-done public school voice which she suspected was not wholly genuine. He was wearing the same grey suit he had worn all week but today his tie was blue with little yellow dots. Jennifer, she had earlier noticed, was wearing a blue scarf with yellow horseshoes.

'What about Jenny?' she asked. 'Isn't she the office junior too?'

William laughed. 'You wouldn't catch Jennifer doing anything menial. We may have started at the same time but she's got a degree in Computer Science and I just did the "A" level a few years ago. No, I'm the tea-boy, all right.'

'It took you a while to get into computing then?'

'I tried banking for a few years — I was at the Credit Bank of Mexico — but it was too boring.'

'More boring than computing?'

'At least computing provides challenges — puzzles to solve. Sometimes I think it must be a bit like breaking a cypher. You know, like in the war.'

He was one of those sort of programmers, Alison thought, an overgrown schoolboy; playing games. How dangerous were the games he was willing to play?

'And Philip has been generous with our training,' William said. 'We're off doing a systems design course next week. We're contracted to work for Orion for two years after our training finishes. Otherwise we have to pay back the costs.'

'So he told me.'

Alison plucked an imaginary thread from his sleeve and smiled up at him. He took a step back. Obviously flirtation was not the route to his confidence. She could see Jennifer making her way purposefully over to them through the crush and something told her that William would clam up once she arrived.

'We must have a drink together one lunchtime,' she said quickly. 'And you can tell me all about yourself.'

'Oh!' He looked panic-stricken. He must have concluded she was after his body. Then he relaxed and said, 'Sure. We'll arrange something with Jennifer one day after we get back from this course.'

So they were Siamese twins, Alison thought. And Jennifer protected him from predatory older women.

'What do you think of FIX?' she asked.

'It's very popular. I still know quite a few people in the City and it's highly thought of. People have usually heard of Orion.'

'That's good. Software houses come and go so quickly, it must be nice to know you're not working for a fly-by-night.'

'Mary!' Jennifer came up beside them at last and Alison was pleased to find herself responding to the name without delay. 'How are you enjoying the party?'

'Lovely.'

'William dear, I think Philip wanted you to circulate with those drinks. You look as if you've taken root.' She took a glass from the tray and William padded obediently off across the room. Jennifer turned to Alison and smiled her close-mouthed smile. 'You must think me very stand-offish as I've hardly had a chance to speak to you since you arrived, but I've got a program I simply have to finish by tomorrow.'

'What with being away on this course next week?'

'That's right. Did William mention that? So this is the

first chance I've had to snatch a moment for a chat. How are you liking Orion?' She had fixed her protruding eyes on Alison's face and Alison realised that she had yet to see her blink. It was slightly unnerving.

'Oh, you know. When you're freelance, you get so used to starting a new job every few months that they all merge into one.'

'I thought you'd been abroad, though.'

'Papua New Guinea.'

'So that must have been very different.'

'Not once I was sitting at my terminal. I gather you and William share a flat?'

'That's right. What was the climate like out there?'

'Tropical,' Alison hazarded, glad that Gerry wasn't about to hear this guess — 'Old George' had probably written to tell him it was snowing there. 'Hot with a rainy season. You have a degree in Computer Science, I gather. Where did you do that?'

'Hull. Did you —'

'Do you come from up that way? Is that a slight Geordie accent I can detect?'

'I thought I'd got rid of it. What a disappointment. Are you back in London for good now?'

It was like a joust, Alison thought with amusement. Each of them trying to ask questions without answering any; to extract information without giving any.

She knew her own reasons for not answering too many personal questions. But what were Jennifer's?

'I want to report a rape.'

The girl's voice was so quiet that Shirley had to strain to hear her.

'Can you say that again?'

She was fractionally more audible. 'I want to report a rape.'

Shirley looked at her in surprise. She was a girl of about sixteen, puppy-fattish with straggly brown hair and small dark eyes which were almost swallowed up in her plump cheeks. She was neatly dressed in a way which was both slightly old-fashioned and a little too young for her; in a

108

pleated skirt, white knee socks and Clark's sandals rather than the ubiquitous jeans and trainers. No make-up. She was not muddy, dishevelled or out of breath.

'When did this rape happen?' Shirley asked.

'About two months ago.'

Shirley let out an involuntary expression of annoyance and the girl shrank back as if she had been struck. Shirley, penitent, came round the desk, perched on the front of it and took the girl's hand reassuringly in her own.

'You were afraid to report it?' she prompted.

'I was ashamed.'

'You must never feel that. Never!'

'I thought it must be my fault.'

Shirley eyed her sadly. She was going to take a lot of convincing and it was not really Shirley's job. She would put her on to the Rape Crisis Line as soon as she had got the details. 'What's your name, dear?'

'Pauline.'

'Pauline what?'

The girl looked up at her in fear. 'You won't tell my parents!'

'Pauline, you're just a child. I must – '

'You can't tell them.' She was on the brink of tears. 'They'd be so ashamed. I wouldn't have come if I'd thought you'd tell them.'

'They won't be ashamed, Pauline. They will be sad and angry ... not angry with you,' she added hastily.

'They will be ashamed,' Pauline said stubbornly, 'and they will be angry. With me. You must promise never to tell them.'

Shirley searched the air for inspiration. There was none. Finally she said quietly, 'I promise I won't speak to them without your permission.'

'Pauline Taylor.' The girl answered her question willingly enough now.

Shirley went back behind the desk and picked up her note pad. Pauline gave her address without further argument and gave her age as sixteen. 'And the date of the rape?' Shirley asked.

'September the fifteenth, a Thursday.' Pauline shuddered.

It was a date, an anniversary, which would haunt her all her life, Shirley thought, unless she got the help and understanding and love she needed. And it didn't sound as if she was going to get it from the Ashamed and Angry Taylors.

'And this was where?'

'In the park. That's why I came. Because he's done it again. It must be the same man. I wouldn't have come otherwise. I thought it was just me, you see, my fault for being there, after dark. But now he's done it again. To someone else.'

'It certainly sounds like the same man. Thank you for coming forward.'

'I thought if he could treat me like that, as if I was worthless, then I must *be* worthless. But now he's done it to someone else and everyone says what a nice girl she is — good and quiet and clever and not worthless at all.'

She stopped and Shirley looked at her for a while, impressed by her fluency and saddened by her muddled self-hating reasoning.

'What sort of time was this?' she asked finally.

'Just after eight. I was walking home from Guides.'

'And did you get a good look at the man? Can you describe him?'

'He was tall — about six feet tall. Not heavy, though, quite slim. Dressed all in dark colours — black or grey. He seemed quite young ... twenties, thirties.'

'Did you get a look at his face?'

The question seemed to startle Pauline. She thought about it then said, 'He wore some sort of hat or helmet which hid his face. It was dark. And I closed my eyes while he was ... so I wouldn't have to see the sky and the trees.'

'A white man?' So few black people lived in the valley that any other option was unlikely. But you sometimes got left with egg on your face by forgetting to ask the most obvious questions.

'White. I saw his hands.'

'Were you a virgin, Pauline?' She nodded. 'But you understand what I mean by vaginal penetration?' She nodded again, embarrassed. 'Was that what took place?'

110

'Yes,' she whispered.

'And what did he do after that?'

'Left me there. Ran away. Towards the meadows.'

'Did he speak?' The girl shook her head. 'Not a word?'

'Nothing. He didn't say anything from start to finish.'

Pauline fell silent. Reliving the ordeal, Shirley supposed. One of the principal gifts she had brought to policing was the empathy she was able to feel for the victims of crime. But it became personally painful at times — overwhelmingly so when, as now, she was feeling exhausted and hungry and rejected.

She began to relive Pauline's anguish with her, almost feeling the leaves and the cloying slime beneath her supine body; the dirty hands tearing at her clothes. Had there been no sound except the eerie rustling of the trees, the man's quickening breath and, a long way off perhaps, a dog yapping?

She gave herself a mental shake. This wasn't helping anyone, least of all the victim. She bent over her notebook again. 'What did you do next, Pauline?'

'I went home, sneaked in the back way. It was raining so I called out that I was a bit wet and was going to get straight into a hot bath. That's what I did. I washed all the ... dirtiness ... away.'

'And your parents never suspected a thing? Never noticed your distress?'

'I got such a row for the mud on my Guides uniform. I said I'd fallen over, slipped on some damp ground. And my knickers were torn. I burnt them in the grate the next time my parents went out.'

'And the uniform?'

'It went to the cleaners. It cost a lot. They took it out of my pocket money.'

'Have you seen anyone? Your doctor?'

She shook her head vehemently. 'He'd tell my father.'

'You've had a period since then, I hope?' To Shirley's dismay, Pauline shook her head. 'Then you must see a doctor. If you won't go to your own, I'll fix up for you to see one here. But Pauline ... if he has made you pregnant, then your parents are going to have to find out. You'll have to decide together what to do about it. You have to face the facts.'

'Can't it just be got rid of?' Pauline asked, sobbing.

'That's not possible, not for a minor. Your parents must be consulted.'

Pauline seemed to resign herself to the worse. 'Would someone come with me when I tell them? Tell them for me?'

'Most certainly. In fact, I'll come with you myself.' Apart from anything else, Shirley wanted to see the Taylors, wanted to meet these people who could inspire such fear in their daughter that she was terrified to tell them — the two people she should most naturally turn to in time of crisis — the horrific thing which had been done to her.

Shirley sat leaning forward at the desk, her fists pressed to her cheeks, collecting her thoughts before she sent for a doctor. They'd got nothing much new from this unexpected victim: the vaguest description, conflicting with Liz's reaction to the short stocky Charge Nurse; no bodily fluids, no soiled clothes. Nothing but two months of investigation lost. But she couldn't reproach the girl, even to herself. She understood her reluctance to report the matter only too well.

And she might not be the only one. There could be other silent victims.

'I shall have to take a signed statement,' she explained. Pauline nodded. 'And I'll find you a doctor. Tomorrow we'll talk to your parents. Look, if I make an appointment for you to see someone — ' Pauline shied away at the words ' — a stranger, a woman, someone used to counselling people in your situation . . . if I arrange it, will you go?'

'I just wanted to forget about it. I'd tried to put it out of my mind and then it happened again and I knew I had to come.'

'And I understand what courage that took. Believe me. Now will you have just a little more courage, Pauline? Because until you talk about it, you never will forget it. You can bury it, perhaps for years, but your subconscious will dig it up when you least expect it.'

*

112

'He really knows how to choose his victims!' Nick speed-read Pauline Taylor's statement after listening to Shirley's account of the interview. 'Schoolgirls; Guides uniforms. At least when we get the bastard in court, I won't have to listen to some defence brief telling the jury they must have "asked for it". Not even the most callous barrister's going to try that one with either of these pathetic kids in the witness box.'

'And neither of them with any previous sexual experience to be irrelevantly dragged into the case,' Shirley agreed.

'I'm going to send this one down for a long, long time,' Nick said. There was a loud rat-tat on the glass panel of his door. 'Come in!'

The door had opened even before this invitation could be issued and a tall comfortable-looking man in early middle age walked confidently in and made himself at home.

'Hello, Mike,' Nick said, greeting his old friend, Mike Brewster, the regular police doctor. 'Have you met Shirley Walpole, my temporary DS?'

'No.' Mike nodded a greeting. 'Welcome. They seem to have thrown you in at the deep end, Shirley.'

'That's where I like it,' she replied, slightly wounded at Nick's stressing of her temporary status. 'You can't swim properly in the shallows.'

'Keen, eh? Well, Nick, I've examined your girl, Pauline. I've done a test to be certain but I've been a doctor for a very long time and I know the signs of pregnancy when I see them.'

'Thanks, Mike. It's what we feared.'

'If she wants a termination, best to get it over with as soon as possible. You know the date of conception, I gather.'

'September the fifteenth.'

'Nine weeks.' He nodded. 'That's about what I'd have said. Try to get the abortion over in the next month — the sooner the better. I can't imagine she'll want to keep it?'

'She'll have to talk it over with her family and sleep on it for a bit before she makes an irrevocable decision. If the parents stick by her, she might just decide to keep it. It's not completely unheard of.'

'I don't think that's very likely somehow,' Shirley said. 'That they'll stick by her, I mean.'

Nick planned to sleep at his flat again that night, preferring it to the empty vastness of Hope Cottage without Alison. But first he drove out to Little Hopford and let himself into the house, ostensibly to make sure that all was well although he knew that Alison's cleaning lady would contact him at once if there were any problems beyond her own capable control.

All he found, apart from the regular letter from his sister in Australia, was a message from Alison on the answering machine.

'I shan't be able to make it back this weekend,' she said, to Nick's dismay. 'I'm staying at Jake's — to make some arrangements about the business. Sorry you weren't in. I'll talk to you soon. Love ... and all that.'

Why the hell hadn't she called him at his flat? Nick thought unfairly. She had probably tried and got no reply while he was still mulling over the Parrish case with Shirley or getting heartburn in the canteen. He felt very low.

He could not sleep that night, turning restlessly — never comfortable. The video screen in his head played repeats all through the small hours: the view across Riverside Park on a moonless November night; the thin, speechless figure huddled in the hospital bed; the pain on Mrs Parrish's face as Carol made rash promises that they would catch the criminal who had destroyed her child's peace of mind. Then it played scenes of the birth to Pauline Taylor of a monstrous green baby with claws and a tail.

And all the time there he was — in the background, yes, but nonetheless dominant: the silhouette of a powerful young man in dark clothing — with no features.

Chapter Thirteen

Dial the number. The computer answers on the second ring. Place the receiver on the rubber cups of the acoustic coupler. Up comes the logo on the screen — very tasteful.

'Welcome to FIX — Your Financial Investment Computer System. Please Enter Company Identification and Press <SEND>'

'RLI142'

That's Rogers, Lloyd and Inglis, Stockbrokers, 142 Long Wall. They've been targeted for some time.

'Rogers, Lloyd and Inglis — Access Confirmed. Please Enter Name and Password and Press <SEND>.'

'Rogers. Annette.'

'Paul Rogers Esquire — Confirmed.'

You pompous ass — entering your name on the database with an 'Esquire' after it. Paul Rogers Esquire, senior partner of Rogers, Lloyd and Inglis, Stockbrokers, you'll find yourself a few pounds lighter next settlement day — much quicker than that expensive health club you subscribe to, hoping to keep old-age and spreading waistline at bay. I shall leave you ten thousand pounds lighter. You won't feel the effect immediately though, probably not until your next audit. I am careful and I am not greedy.

I've been monitoring computer accesses from your firm for weeks, Paul Rogers Esquire. I notice you make very few accesses yourself after one o'clock — you lazy so and so, you lazy, rich so and so.

I know who your typical customer is and what his average settlement is in each account.

At first your password was 'SEX' — an all-time favourite among men devoid of imagination, like 'PASSWORD' and 'FRED'. Then Philip put a discreet word round the clients that unguessable passwords must be used and you sighed impatiently and changed it to something perfectly secure.

A simple phone call to that same prestigious City gym elicited the information that Mrs Rogers is called Annette.

'Hello, City Gym? Is Mrs Rogers there at the moment? Mrs Paul Rogers, you know, of Rogers, Lloyd and Inglis? I'm afraid I've temporarily forgotten her Christian name. Annette? Of course, how stupid of me. Not until eight o'clock? No, no message. Well, you can just tell her Hilary called.'

That should give her something to think about.

I can see her, I think — the second Mrs Rogers, surely? She is slim and firm and blonde and has been twenty-nine for three years now. She has her hair done by someone called Toni or someone called Guy so that it looks as if she just washes it and runs her fingers through it; she wears a lot of expensive make-up designed to look like no make-up at all.

Annette is rather a common name, surely, although she's worked hard at her vowels and doesn't show her husband up at City functions. I think she may once have been his secretary.

Will they never learn?

Some of them keep lists of passwords up by the terminal — not that that's much help to me but it shows their mentality, their complacency.

If Annette hadn't done the trick, a little more snooping would have been required to find out what Rogers' kids are called, then his pet cat, his cleaning lady, his old mother in the nursing home in Worthing. But none of that was necessary. The wife's name: the oldest password in the book after Fred and Password and Sex.

Now, who am I today? Mr William Kemp, I think — I haven't been him for a while. No, make that William Kemp Esquire. Sold, fifteen thousand 'A' shares in BPT Holdings PLC at 69.5 pence, that's ten thousand, four hundred and twenty-five pounds — less dealing costs, of course.

Very nice, Bill. You've made a killing. You've been

doing nicely lately — bucking the bear market. You clever
old thing.

There's a surprising amount of activity in the machine
at night, and from some surprising places. Still, I won't
interfere with their fun if they don't interfere with mine.

At least ... not yet.

'Darling, what *do* you look like?' Simon Jarvis shook his
head mournfully over Alison's hair and clothes. Alison, who
had been co-opted to chop onions, did not feel equal to one
of her usual harsh retorts. She wiped an onion-tear away,
making her eyes sting.

'Ow! Ow!' she yelped, reaching for a damp J-cloth and
dabbing at her eyes. She had left off her glasses now that
she was safe with her old friends.

They were standing in the tiny kitchen of Jake and Simon's
flat in Covent Garden while Simon made a start on dinner.
He was a portly man in his early forties. As he had been a
barrister since giving up juvenile hopes of an acting career
at the age of twenty five and had spent his years at the Bar
dining not wisely but too well, it was a bit of a squeeze and
Alison was thankful that Jake hadn't tried to join them. He
was next door opening bottles of wine and interrupting the
conversation through the archway as the mood took him.

'Hurry up with that wine,' Simon shouted out to him. 'I
can't create without a glass of claret in my hand.'

Jake appeared in the archway and handed a bottle through.
'It won't have had time to breathe,' he objected.

'Well, if you'd remembered to open the bottles at four
o'clock as I said, there'd be no problem.' Simon retorted.
Jake, a boyish, handsome man of Alison's own age (they had
been friends since Cambridge), winked at her as he handed
her a spotless crystal glass.

'I got stuck at the office, I told you. We don't all keep
Bar hours.'

'Your office is just round the corner, Jacob,' Simon
pointed out. 'What you mean is that you forgot.'

'It's only Alison we're entertaining,' Jake said, 'not
Princess Anne.'

Simon took a big gulp of wine and said, 'Doesn't taste

117

too bad actually. I can leave this to simmer for a bit.' He
took the lid off the casserole dish and threw half a glass in.
'That'll make all the difference.'

'That cost £6.99 a bottle,' Jake pointed out.

'I've had a good year, so my accountant tells me.' Simon
and Alison left the kitchen in single file and joined Jake in
the sitting room. She winced slightly as she settled on the
well-stuffed Chesterfield.

'I've got backache,' she explained. 'Bloody backache!
Me! It's that sofa bed in my bedsit − I don't think I've slept
a wink since I got there.'

'Well, of course, darling, we'd love to have you here full
time − ' Simon began smoothly.

'You tell lies very badly for a barrister,' Alison told him.
'You know the very idea appals you. I'm too loud and too
bossy and I take up too much space.'

'The flat is what estate agents call "Compact",' Jake
agreed. 'But you really are welcome, Alison, if you can't
stand that place any more.'

'It's sweet of you.' Alison, who was sitting between them,
bestowed a sisterly kiss on each of her friends. 'But I'll get by.
But after this I don't owe Phil Hunter anything anymore. I've
paid my debts in full.'

'How is Philip?' Simon asked. 'One doesn't see much of
him these days.'

'He's been keeping a low profile since that business a
couple of years back,' Jake added.

'What business?' Alison asked.

'He became infatuated with some scruffy northerner,'
Simon said. 'I couldn't see the attraction myself − '

'He had a certain louche charm,' Jake put in.

'Anyway, this chap took him for a ride then dumped him,
swanned off to South America or somewhere, broke Philip's
heart.' Simon looked unconcerned at the prospect. 'Funny.
Up to that point, I didn't know he had one. More wine,
anyone?'

Shirley was feeling more and more uncomfortable in the cold,
joyless sitting room of the Taylor's house. Mrs Taylor had
been banished from the room almost as soon as she had

arrived — Mr Taylor obviously considered that dealing with strangers, especially the police, was man's work. But he had then followed his wife to the kitchen and she could hear lowered voices down the hall. She examined her surroundings as she wondered how to begin.

The room was indefinably old-fashioned — reflecting Pauline's little schoolgirl look and white ankle socks. It wasn't that the furniture differed greatly from that of many other poor families reliant on hand-me-downs but it was ill-assorted, with no attempt at harmony of shape or colour.

Shirley herself had been allotted a chair with an upholstered seat and short wooden legs — a piece of furniture which she remembered her grandmother referring to dismissively as a 'television chair'. It was covered in slippery brown mock-leather and was rendered incongruous by the notable lack of a television or any other instrument of entertainment. The low, teak-veneered table in front of her held some copies of the *People's Friend* — the only reading matter visible in the room.

Shirley straightened her back as she heard Mr Taylor returning and prepared for battle.

The Taylors, like the Parrishes, had come late to parenthood but not, unlike the Parrishes, with any sign of joy in the state. Taylor was in his mid-fifties, an unnaturally thin and meagre-looking man. He spoke first.

'All right. What's she done?'

'I beg your pardon?' Shirley said, bewildered.

'What's the girl done? Shoplifting, I suppose. They're all at it these days — kids of six or seven even. I can promise you, Miss ... whatever your name is ... she won't do it again. I'll see to that. I'll soon knock some sense into her.'

'My name's Sergeant Walpole,' she reminded him. 'But you can call me Shirley.' Mr Taylor looked surprised at the invitation and she did not imagine he would avail himself of it. 'You've got hold of quite the wrong end of the stick, Mr Taylor. Pauline's done nothing. On the contrary, she's been the victim of a particularly nasty crime and will be in need of all your sympathy and ...' she faltered, losing heart, '... love at the moment.'

119

Mr Taylor looked at her narrowly, then sat down on the grey cloth television chair at the other side of the empty hearth.

'It would be better if Mrs Taylor joined us,' Shirley suggested.

'I handle the business in this house.'

Shirley gave up and launched in. 'I wonder if you've heard of the rape which took place in Riverside Park on Sunday night?'

'I heard of it. So? What's that got to do with my girl? Girls who go wandering about in parks at the dead of night deserve everything they get, if you ask me.'

Shirley bit back the retort that no one had asked him. He was about to get enough of a shock. 'Mr Taylor,' she said gently, 'we now know that it wasn't the first time the Riverside Rapist has struck. It was just the first rape which had been reported to us. Women are often too terrified, too ashamed, to report these attacks. Do you remember a day in September when Pauline came home with her Guides uniform torn and muddy?'

Mr Taylor had understood at last. He threw her a look of unalloyed disgust, stood up, walked out into the hall and bellowed:

'Pauline!'

Shirley heard movement upstairs. She had agreed with Pauline that she would speak to her parents alone first, break the news to them gently. They had arranged a time when Pauline would be in but shut away in her room with her homework.

'Pauline! Get down here!'

There was a clatter of shoes on the uncarpeted stairs and Pauline edged into the room a moment later, her face speaking fear. The shouting had also summoned Mrs Taylor who stood in the doorway, alarmed at the anger in her husband's voice. He was too preoccupied to tell her to leave. She was a defeated-looking woman, with dowdy clothes and limp white hair which nothing more elaborate than a comb ever tended. Shirley did not expect much support from that quarter.

'This woman,' Taylor addressed Pauline, pointing rudely

120

to Shirley, 'says you've been raped.' Mrs Taylor let out a gasp of horror.

'It's true,' Pauline muttered, looking desperately at Shirley for support. Shirley rose and went to stand between her and her father.

'Mr Taylor! Your daughter has been the victim – the *victim*, do you hear me? – of a cruel and vicious crime. I will not stand here and let you talk to her as if she was herself a criminal.'

Taylor shouted her down. 'I'll talk any way I want to my own daughter in my own home, you interfering cow!' He turned on Pauline again. 'Not content with disgracing me and your mother, you have to go bleating about it to strangers, to the police. We've never had anything to do with the police in this family, my girl. We've always been respectable.'

'Pauline did her duty in coming forward,' Shirley told him. 'She was able to give us a description of the man which Liz ... which the other victim has not yet been able to do. It's not a matter which could be ignored in any case.' She took a deep breath. 'She has become pregnant as a result of the rape. And all your shouting and bullying isn't going to make the problem go away, Mr Taylor.'

Taylor, punctured, collapsed back in his chair as Mrs Taylor began to sob loudly.

'Don't go,' Pauline whispered. 'Don't leave me.'

'Don't worry, Pauline, I'm not going anywhere,' Shirley assured her. 'If I can't make your father see sense, then I'll call Social Services and they'll take you into care for a few days until he does. Now –' she took Mrs Taylor by the arm with a firm grip ' – why don't you go and make us some tea. And then, when we've all calmed down, we'll talk over the options.'

The O'Sheas lived in a small terraced house in a nebulous borderland between the centre of Hopbridge and the Riverside Estate. Tessa opened the door to Nick and greeted him by name.

'May I come in?' he asked. 'We're making enquiries in this area.'

'About Liz Parrish? Poor little thing. I've been looking after her.' Tessa stood to one side. He was prepared for the house to be mean — nurses were not exactly overpaid. Come to think of it, what did her husband do for a living?

The house was shabby but clean as he had anticipated. It was a two-up, two-down Edwardian construction and the young couple, unlike most of their neighbours, had kept the two downstairs rooms separate. Maybe they didn't have the money to knock through. Tessa led him into the back room and he sat down on an upright chair at a wooden table.

'Is Kevin in?' he asked.

'Just finishing his tea in the kitchen,' Tessa replied. 'You won't mind waiting a minute? Would you like a brew of something?'

'Thank you, no. As I said, we're making house to house enquiries in this neighbourhood. Were you and Kevin here on Sunday evening? Around ten o'clock, ten-fifteen?'

Tessa thought about it. 'We both were,' she said finally.

'Sure?'

'Sure. I was working a night shift and was due in at the hospital later. You saw me arriving as you were leaving.'

'Of course.'

'I'd been asleep until about five, as I was on nights all week. Then Kevin and me were both in all evening. We watched TV.'

'Can anyone else corroborate this?' Nick asked gently. Alibis from next of kin were always treated with suspicion. 'Did any neighbours pop in? Anyone knock on the door?'

Tessa shook her head. 'We keep ourselves to ourselves.' Nick believed her. If he was married to a lout like O'Shea, he'd keep him out of decent people's way, too.

'What's all this!' The boy, Kevin, had appeared at the door and was glaring at Nick. Nick started slightly. It was rare indeed that anyone could creep up on him unheard.

'You!' O'Shea said, recognising him. 'What the hell do you want?'

'I'm a police officer, as I believe I've had occasion to tell you before.' Nick stood up, feeling at a disadvantage with the belligerent youth standing over him. 'I'm the officer in charge of the Riverside rape case. I'm asking all young men in the valley to account for their movements last Sunday night at around ten o'clock.'

He remembered as he stood facing O'Shea that the boy was shorter than himself, not above five foot seven or eight. Certainly nowhere near Pauline Taylor's six foot rapist.

'I was here, with her.' He nodded in Tessa's direction. 'All evening, watching the telly.'

'You didn't go out at all?'

'You nipped out to the off-licence, didn't you, Kev?' Tessa put in 'About half-nine, wasn't it? But that only took ten minutes.'

'Oh, yeah. Course.'

He wouldn't have had time to get to the park and back in ten minutes, Nick knew. And the rape had taken place shortly after ten o'clock.

'Well, I won't disturb you any more,' he said politely. 'Goodnight.'

'Did I mention I won't be in for dinner tomorrow night?' Alison asked as they finished their chicken chasseur.

'No, you didn't!' Simon said sharply. 'I've bought some fillet steak.'

'Only I've been invited out to supper with Jilly MacAlistair and her husband. I didn't know until today, Si, honestly. She asked me out of the blue. It's too good an opportunity to miss — catch them on their home ground.'

'In that case, I forgive you.' Simon reached down and put his plate in front of an oversized Persian tom cat which had been waiting silently and patiently — confident that he would not be overlooked. He licked the plate quite clean and then patted Alison's leg with his paw to prompt her to copy Simon. Alison tried to ignore him.

'Won't nasty Auntie Alison give you her plate, then?' Simon crooned.

'Oh, all right.' Alison handed the plate down. 'Anything to stop your baby talk. But I'm sure it's unhygienic.'

'The dishwasher will remove all known germs,' Jake said. 'Where do these people live?'

'White City. Near the BBC somewhere.'

'Bit of a trek. Bit rough at night too by all accounts. You'd better take a taxi.'

'It doesn't fit the image,' Alison said. 'Mary Lewis isn't a taxi-taking woman. She watches the meter anxiously and doesn't know how much to tip.'

Simon gave her a slightly odd look. 'You'd better walk up to Holborn and get the Central Line straight through then. Can Mary Lewis manage that, d'you think?'

'She's arranged to meet Gerry in advance,' Alison explained. 'I mean, I have. He's invited too. We wanted to arrive together so we're meeting in a wine bar in the Aldwych.'

'Another colleague?' Simon asked, taking the satisfied cat on to his lap. He stroked it with long hard movements which made it arch its back in glee. Alison could have sworn it was smiling.

'Another contractor,' she said. 'Gerry Walsh.'

'Walsh!' Jake echoed. 'That was him. That was the name.'

'Him? Who?' Alison asked, puzzled, and Jake answered impatiently:

'The scruffy Herbert who gave Philip the run around two years ago, of course.'

The owner of the off-licence on the corner of the O'Sheas' road had confirmed seeing Kevin at about nine-thirty on Sunday night.

'You can't miss him,' he said. 'Surly. Never got a smile or a civil word for anyone. It was a bit after nine-thirty as I'd just closed. He banged on the door and I let him in rather than risk an argy-bargy. He bought a six-pack of beer and twenty Bensons. He's not exactly a big spender.'

Nick's next call was at the home of Alex Porter — a neat semi in a quiet street. Mrs Porter answered the door — a cheerful motherly woman — and said that Alex was out. This time he accepted the offer of a cup of tea. Mrs Porter seemed to welcome the company.'

'Friday night,' she explained, gliding efficiently round the kitchen. 'He's out with his girlfriend. I expect they'll go to the disco. They both love to dance.'

'Sarah, is it?' Nick queried.

'That's right. Of course, you would know her, her dad being one of your lot. Lovely girl, isn't she? Just what I'd have chosen for him myself. Got her head screwed on too. I've been telling him how lucky he is and that he'd better treat her right.'

'Is he in the habit of not treating women right?' Nick picked the remark up sharply.

'Bless you, no, love. Inspector, I mean. Not that he isn't a proper boy, my Alex, but he's never rough. He had that knocked out of him the one time he stepped out of line.' She looked at Nick shrewdly. 'That's why you're here, isn't it? It's about that rape. Because he's got a conviction for violence?'

She did not protest that her son was being victimised or ask why the police couldn't leave him alone after he'd paid his debt to society. Alex had let his temper get the better of him once and she was realistic enough to know that he would probably go on paying for it for the rest of his life. Nick respected her clearsightedness.

'Just elimination,' he told her honestly. 'But if you could tell me where he was on Sunday at around ten o'clock, I'd be grateful.'

'He was here, with me.' Nick groaned inwardly. What was the matter with these boys that none of them could fix up a disinterested alibi for himself? 'Sarah had a lot of homework to finish,' Mrs Porter went on, 'and a tennis match the next day so she wanted an early night.' She chuckled.

'He's dead struck on her, you know. Normally if a girl couldn't see him, he'd be off down the pub with his mates, but if Sarah's too busy to come out he moons about the place with a face like a wet weekend in Woolacombe. He spent most of the evening out in the garage, stripping down his motorbike.'

'So you didn't actually see him all the time?' Nick said eagerly.

'No. But I could hear him. And I took him out a cup of tea just after the ITV news — just about ten o'clock. The bike was in pieces then.'

Nick gave up. There was no way Alex could have got to

the park in five minutes with his bike in pieces. Even so, it was the next of kin providing the alibi again. It couldn't be relied on a hundred percent, however much he might like Mrs Porter.

'Make sure you catch up with him,' she said as she showed him out. 'Just think, it could be little Sarah next time.'

Nick preferred not to think about that.

Chapter Fourteen

Nick rang Jake's flat on Saturday afternoon in the hope of speaking to Alison. He got Simon instead.

Nick was fond of Simon. He admired the breezy way he carried off his gay 'marriage' in the conservative world of the English Bar – his Head of Chambers was more inclined to chide him for excessive fraternisation with a member of the 'junior' branch of the legal profession than for any other solecism. Nick liked his enormous Persian Blue, Omar Khayyam – so sleek and plump and conceited that it was hard to tell which of them was parodying the other. He liked his tendency suddenly to burst out quoting that same author while holding out his glass for a tenth refill:

'Ah, my Beloved, fill the cup that clears
Today of past regrets and future fears.'

Most of all he liked the way Simon and Jake had come running to the Hop Valley the moment they heard that Alison had taken into her home the policeman who had investigated her cousin's murder, the policeman who had come within a heartbeat of arresting her for that same crime, the policeman who had saved her life. They had come, expecting to meet a vulgar, bucolic Dixon of Dock Green and, faced with Nick, had retreated in confusion and friendship.

He loved them for caring.

Jake and Simon, like Jan Baxter in Ealing, were exempted from Nick's misgivings about Alison's London friends.

'She's out with Jacob meeting some merchant bankers,'

Simon was saying, 'Not rhyming slang, whatever you might think.'

'On a Saturday?' Nick said incredulously.

'Haven't you heard about the Big Bang down in Back-Of-Beyond-On-Sea?' Simon asked. 'Nowadays they don't recognise evenings and weekends in case Tokyo crashes overnight and they have to send the second Porsche back. Merchant bankers have about as much regard for weekends as policemen do. It'll be a cold day in hell before we barristers forget what a Saturday looks like.'

'I'd have thought Jake knew a Saturday when he saw one,' Nick said.

Simon laughed. 'Indeed he does. But not when She Who Must Be Obeyed has her hands over his eyes. He even tried the not-working-on-the-Sabbath routine, if you please. Said his old mother would turn in her grave. As if Alison didn't know that Jacob's mother lives in Stamford Hill — where she terrorises the bridge club.'

'Well, will you tell her I called,' Nick said, 'and ask her to ring me at my flat tonight?'

'She's going out to dinner with one of her "suspects" tonight,' Simon said importantly. 'She might be late.'

'Tomorrow?' Nick suggested feebly.

'Sure thing, Nicholas. Look, since we've both been abandoned by our beloveds, why don't you come up and see me sometime? It's only a couple of hours on the train.'

'Thanks, but no thanks.'

'Still incurably hetero?'

'That's right.'

'You don't know what you're missing.'

'Have to keep it that way. Make sure she rings me, will you, Rumpole? Don't forget.'

'I shan't forget. Shall I tell you something, Nicholas?'

'What's this? Free advice from a barrister? Hang on while I pinch myself.'

'Not to be taken as a precedent, dear boy. Don't let them know how much you care. Take me and Jacob: I think the sun shines out of his whatsit. I know that and now you know that, but he don't know that. There! I would normally charge fifty guineas for that.' Simon laughed and put the phone down.

'I think it's a bit late for me to start playing hard to get,' Nick said out loud. He hung up. Simon had a point. There was no reason why he shouldn't get the train up to London one night. The mountain might go to Mohamet.

'Stands the church clock at five to ten?' Gerry murmured, 'And is there supper? And if so when?'

'Shh. They'll hear you,' Alison said. 'It was nice of Jilly to invite us. It's the thought that counts.'

'Ah yes, the two poor orphaned lambs.' Gerry sighed noisily and put his feet up on the coffee table. 'Adrift on the cruel sea of the Wicked Metropolis.'

Alison began to giggle tipsily. 'How can lambs be adrift on a sea, for God's sake?' She sagged sideways on the sofa until she was half leaning against him. 'Is that what they call Irish Bull?'

Gerry considered this. 'In an open boat, maybe, following an attempted mutiny.' His arm wandered casually round her shoulder. 'I had you down as a woman who could hold her drink, Mary Lewis.'

'Normally. But we've been here two and a half hours and I have an empty stomach. In fact I don't think it's ever been this empty.'

'I know this trick,' Gerry said. 'My sister used to pull this one. She was a terrible cook so she used to keep guests waiting so long and get them so drunk that by the time the burnt offerings were served up they wouldn't have known if they were eating cardboard *à la provençale*, or what.'

They sat in silence for a moment, contemplating the polished oak table in the corner on which no knives, forks or plates had yet appeared but which was already home to three empty wine bottles.

'Have you sorted out your accommodation problems yet?' Alison asked him.

'I didn't fancy that flatshare in Balham. There was something intolerably dreary about the whole street and my prospective flatmates weren't much better. Pete's floor's getting a bit hard though, and it's not very handy for the office. I shall have to take up another friend's offer to stay at his place ... Unless you have any spare space, that is.'

'None at all,' Alison said firmly.

'Not even room for a little one — making due allowances for modesty, of course.'

'I just have the one room.'

'I don't mind sharing. I'm easy.'

'Evidently. But I'm not.' She heaved herself off him and attempted to sit up straight.

'Okay, Virgin Mary.'

Jilly came back into the room at that moment, red with the heat from the kitchen and flustered apologies, and offered to top up their glasses.

'Sorry I'm late.' Paul Penruan slid noiselessly up behind WPC Sally Ferris who was stamping her feet on the ground to keep warm. 'I got held up on this rape case — we're doing house to house round Riverside Park.'

He had hoped to make it sound important but house to house was a very routine matter and Sally was unimpressed.

'I've been waiting half an hour and I've already got a cold coming on.' She sneezed in support of this claim. 'I was just going to give up and go home.' She had changed out of her uniform and was wearing a short skirt and low-cut top under her mac. She knew she looked good. On her way out, one of the uniformed sergeants had suggested a quiet drink but she'd been forced to put him off for another time. CID might have glamour but a stripe was a stripe.

No wonder she was cold in that get-up, Paul thought.

'Don't do that.' He took her arm. Carol had been treating him like a leper since this Liz Parrish business had started. What was he supposed to say or do? He wasn't a rapist — had never had any trouble finding girlfriends, had frequently had to fight them off. If Carol wanted to give him the cold shoulder it wouldn't hurt her to see that plenty of other women were eager for his company, women younger and more attractive than she was too.

'It's nearly ten-thirty,' Sally was saying. 'Everything's closed by now. Everything in this dump.' She assumed an air of weary discontent, imagining that it was a sophisticated thing to do, unaware how plain and commonplace it made her look.

'It's Saturday. The pubs don't close until eleven – a good bit later in some places I know of.' He spoke cheerily. She struck him suddenly as a spoilt brat. Carol made him laugh, never took anything seriously, never complained. 'It could be worse,' was her motto. But Sally was very pretty, slim yet with curves where there ought to be curves, blonde – just the way he'd always liked them, until Carol. Not too clever either – a man liked to think he was the brains of the outfit.

He steered her down the road, glancing over his shoulder. Not the Eagle – there was always a danger of running into colleagues there.

'I've got my car round the corner,' he said. 'Let's take a quick run out to the Crow's Nest by the sea at Hopcliff. It's only three miles and I can tell you about one of my finest cases – the Great Hopcliff Drugs Raid.'

He had really better take up Philip's offer of a bed, Gerry thought as he accepted a second helping of something Jilly claimed was *Boeuf en daube*. Which meant his bed, needless to say. Not that he had any objection to that but it would mean giving up on Mary and he'd taken a fancy to her.

People thought if you swung both ways you must like your women boyish and flat-chested. It didn't seem to occur to them that if that was what you were after, you might as well stick with a boy. When he was in the mood for a woman, Gerry liked his women to look and feel and smell like women. And speaking of smells, surely that was Elizabeth Taylor's 'Passion' Mary was wearing – another piece of her jigsaw which didn't quite fit.

Still, Philip was the man with the cash – tight-fisted bastard though he was – the man with the Chablis and the caviar and the black silk sheets. Gerry was a bit short of the readies at the moment. He'd go straight to Philip's place tonight, give him a nice surprise, remind him he was now owed a week's pay.

Mary seemed pretty hard up too for someone who'd spent five years in the lucrative freelance market, by her own account. She had nothing to show for it but a rented bedsit off the Holloway Road and a cheap brown suit — it was beginning to look as if those really were the only clothes she owned.

There was one thing, though. At least she couldn't be Philip's hacker, being a newcomer to the company like himself, just back from a long stint abroad like himself and with no visible signs of wealth — like himself.

But how much did 'Passion' cost again?

Not that Gerry was in much doubt as to the identity of his quarry but there was plenty of time — he wanted to be quite certain before he made any move. And a shred of evidence wouldn't hurt.

He brought his mind back with an effort of will to the conversation going on around him. Mary was listening to Duncan talking about his work which seemed to involve micro-computers — a subject on which Mary was apparently quite knowledgeable. Gerry himself had been making all the right noises without taking anything in and now threw in another 'Uh huh' and a few vigorous nods to show that he was well up with the game. But as he listened, he became more and more absorbed in what Duncan was saying.

Jilly was clearly desperate to change the subject.

'I hear enough about computers from nine 'til five every day,' she complained, 'or eight 'til seven, I should say. I don't want them rammed down my throat in the evening too. Anyone fancy a game of Trivial Pursuit?'

She got up and began to clear the table. Alison helped, leaving Duncan and Gerry engrossed in details of Duncan's research. After a moment Duncan called through to the kitchen that he was taking Gerry up to his study for a few minutes to play with his Apple II.

Gerry steered Alison down the road, through a dark underpass beneath the Western Avenue and towards the tube station.

'It's such a bloody long way home,' Alison complained. 'Wish I'd got my car.'

'I didn't know you had a car.'

' . . . Oh, no. That's right.'

'And you don't seriously imagine I would have let you drive it in this condition, do you?'

'If I had been driving,' Alison said with dignity, 'I would not have been drinking and I would not be looking forward to a bloody awful stinking hangover in the morning. *Boeuf en daube*, my foot!'

'At least it's Sunday tomorrow. You can have a lie-in. Got your ticket? Show it to the nice man.' Gerry hustled her down the few stairs to the Central Line eastbound platform. 'What do you make of the MacAlistairs, anyway?'

'She's all right. He's all right. They're all right.'

'God! You're a great conversationalist when you're like this. I rather liked him, Duncan. He's quiet but pretty brainy.'

'Even if he didn't know who the lead guitarist with "The Shadows" was?' Alison and Jilly had had no difficulty in beating Duncan and Gerry at Trivial Pursuit. Alison had noticed in the past that alcohol seemed to open up her subconscious to regurgitate facts she'd had no idea she had stored there.

Gerry ignored the remark. A player was only as good as his partner which was why he preferred singles matches. 'What he was telling us about his new research project − I'd say he's on to something big.'

'Artificial intelligence? There's little enough of the human variety around.'

'You're a cheery little thing this evening, aren't you?'

'I'll believe it when I see it.'

'Duncan's a real boffin, I'd say. Likes the thrill of pitting his wits, pushing back the barriers, testing the limits of the possible. Here's our train.'

'Yes.' Alison, a little sobered by the night air, stepped forward as the train drew into the station. She sat slumped in a corner seat, thinking about what Gerry had just said and trying to think of a way to explain why she was getting off the tube at Holborn when Mary Lewis lived in Highbury and had no friends in London.

Come to that, why wasn't Gerry taking the train to Earls Court?

133

Chapter Fifteen

In fact Alison didn't get much of a lie-in the next morning. She had things to do. Besides, she was awake shortly after seven with a raging thirst. She slipped out of the spare bedroom and into the kitchen and began to heat up mugs of filtered coffee in the microwave as quietly as she could.

'Shh!' she said to the microwave every time it pinged. 'Not so loud.'

After three milky mugs, she felt well enough to go to the bathroom in search of some aspirin and after three aspirin tablets and another hour's lie-down, she was ready for the next stage of Project Hacker.

She banged on Jake and Simon's bedroom door. After a moment Simon's voice yelled sleepily, 'What?'

'It's me. Alison.'

'I didn't think it was the Vice Squad.' She heard Simon heave himself, grumbling, out of bed and he soon opened the door and stood there, leaning against the door frame in his paisley silk dressing gown. 'We're both over twenty-one, officer.'

'I want to borrow your car, Simon.'

'Do you know what time it is? No way.'

'Half-past eight. Be a sport.'

Simon put his glasses on and looked at her more closely. 'God! I hope I don't look as rough as you do.'

'You look worse,' Alison told him unkindly. 'I think you should stay in bed all day. So you won't be needing your car.'

'I don't *need* the car today as it happens. Which is not the same thing as saying you can borrow it.' Simon's car was a beautifully-restored 1967 Jaguar E-Type Roadster and he didn't let anyone drive it, not even Jake. In fact he hardly drove it himself and it spent most of its life in the garage being polished and quietly beating inflation.

'All right then. I just thought I'd ask.' Alison gave in with suspicious ease.

'Okay?' Simon didn't believe a word of it.

'I'll give you five minutes to get dressed.'

'What?'

'If you won't lend me your car, you'll have to drive me.'

'Just do it, Simon,' Jake called out from under the duvet. 'You'll get no peace otherwise.' He turned over and went back to sleep with a smile on his face – glad that it was Simon's turn today.

Simon muttered something about the lesser of two evils. 'You don't want to go anywhere *yet*, surely,' he said.

'I want to go down the Mile End Road, stake out the flat where the twins live.'

'Alison, no one gets up until midday on Sunday and I'm not taking my beautiful car down the East End.' Simon wasn't sure which protest to make first.

'They might. I can't afford to miss them. We'll stay in it all the time. It won't come to any harm.'

'I'll get dressed. Why don't I have the guts to stand up to you?'

'Because it's easier just to do what I want.'

'Is that what Nicholas says?'

'You can have ten minutes, actually. I'll make some sandwiches and fill a flask.'

Alison put on some of her own clothes – it was such a relief to be free of Mary Lewis's cheap garments for a few hours. She knotted a silk scarf over her head to cover her hair and borrowed Jake's sunglasses to hide her hangover. Willy and Jenny would never recognise her, having no reason to expect to see her lurking outside their flat in a strange car.

Simon appeared, washed, shaved and clad in a pair of jeans which were getting a bit tight for him. Alison handed him a mug of coffee without comment.

'What're you looking for?' he asked after he'd had a few sips.

'They're an odd pair. They're friendly enough but they don't encourage you to get to know them. They're not about to invite me round to dinner like the MacAlistairs. I want to see what they get up to in their spare time, where they live, who with. If they go out, we might get the chance to look round their flat.'

She picked up the flask and the Fortnum's carrier bag, which she had filled with sandwiches and fruit, and sailed out of the flat without waiting for an answer.

'A little light house-breaking,' Simon murmured as he followed her. 'We might get off with a couple of years if we have a good barrister.'

Jake and Simon's flat was on the third floor of a small block just off Neal Street and the car was kept in a garage underground. The lift took them straight down into the garage and Simon used a key to unlock the lift door.

'It's a good job I'm coming with you,' he remarked. 'If only to keep you out of next Sunday's papers. "Top Businesswoman in Cat-Burglary Scandal!"'

'Drive more slowly,' Alison commanded, as they took a left turn off the Mile End Road some twenty minutes later. She took her sunglasses off briefly to peer at the house numbers. 'We want number six. That's forty-two. It's on this side, then, but it must be at the other end of the street.'

Simon stopped outside number twelve and backed neatly into a small space between an orange Volkswagen Beetle and a gleaming white Lotus Elite. He lined the E-Type up exactly six inches from the kerb.

'Nice car,' he commented, nodding at the Lotus. 'Early sixties model, at a guess. Real collector's item.'

'Boys' games,' Alison said, checking the house numbers again. 'Bit further up.'

'I may be new to this espionage business, Alison, but they might think it a bit odd if they look out of the window and see a conspicuous car like this one parked on their doorstep for several hours; with two occupants who don't get out, one of whom looks suspiciously like their colleague, Mary

Lewis — except that she's drawing attention to herself by wearing sunglasses on the most overcast day of the year so far.' Simon paused for breath then concluded in his best summing-up manner: 'But correct me if I'm wrong.'

'Fair enough.' Alison didn't take the sunglasses off though — the day was quite bright enough for her red eyes.

Simon switched on the radio and opened up the *Sunday Times* which he had bought on the way.

'Want a bit?'

'I can't keep watch and read the ... oh, right, I'll have the colour supplement.'

They sat reading and drinking coffee from the flask. No one came either up or down the road for over an hour. Then, shortly after ten, Alison gave a little hiss and pulled the *Sunday Times* Business section up to hide her face.

'The boy twin, I take it,' Simon said as William walked down the front steps of number six in a grey and blue tracksuit and Reebok trainers. 'It's all right, he's going the other way. Want me to shadow him, Q?'

It had not occurred to Alison that the Siamese twins might go out separately. She chewed her lower lip as she weighed up the alternatives. 'He's going jogging, judging by his get-up. The chances are he'll be back soon. We'll stay here.'

In fact William's jogging suit turned out to be merely a sop to fashion. He was back in under ten minutes with a pile of Sunday papers under his arm and what looked like two Mars Bars in his hand.

'Sunday reading matter and breakfast,' Simon murmured. 'They won't be out for ages. If at all. I often don't go out all day on Sunday, you know. That's what Sundays are for — loafing around, reading the papers. Not for getting up at the crack of dawn, missing breakfast and driving demented women around the slums of London, spying on people.'

'I wouldn't call it a slum, actually. These houses are quite smart.'

'I wouldn't say no to a Mars Bar myself.'

'Shut up moaning and have one of these sandwiches.'

'Ah. Cheese doorsteps. My favourite.' Simon bit into one.

'I was in a hurry and your breadknife isn't very sharp.'

'And no pickle.'

'How do professionals stand it?' Alison asked. 'It always sounds so exciting in books − a stake out. They don't mention the hours of boredom, staring at nothing. And they get paid for it. What am I getting out of all this? Other than backache?'

'Shh!' Simon said.

'What?' Alison looked up and down the road in alarm.

'The omnibus edition of *The Archers* is starting.'

They were able to listen to the whole of it without interruption and were well into *Pick of the Week* when the front door of number six opened again and both twins came out, wearing similar blue jeans, black woollen sweaters and leather jackets. Jennifer had what looked like a Gucci bag slung over her shoulder.

They turned right at the foot of the steps and began to walk straight towards Alison and Simon. As they reached the E-Type, they stopped on the pavement.

'Bloody hell!' Alison said. She flung her arms round an astonished Simon's neck and pulled him to her in a simulacrum of a passionate embrace so that his face hid hers. Simon mumbled a stifled protest.

'They're not stopping here!' He managed to free himself at last and wiped his sticky mouth on the back of his hand. 'God! That was unpleasant. I haven't kissed a woman since I was seventeen and I didn't enjoy it then either. Your mouth tastes like the inside of a parrot's cage.'

Behind them the Lotus's engine purred into life. Alison pulled down the sunshield and the vanity mirror gave her a clear view back along the street as Jennifer, in the driving seat of the Lotus, manoeuvred it nimbly out from behind Simon's car and pulled away towards the corner. She turned left and they could hear the powerful engine accelerate easily away.

'Shall I follow them?' Simon asked, starting his own engine. He was beginning to enjoy this.

'How much does a car like that cost?' Alison asked.

'You can pick one up for twenty-five, thirty grand.'

'On a trainee programmer's salary?'

He shrugged. 'So the girl has rich and generous parents. Follow? Or not?'

'Home, James. I've seen all I need to see.'

'What? No house-breaking?'

Alison gave him a withering look. 'Don't be silly, Simon. We're not criminals.'

Simon made a three-point turn in the road and drove back the way they had come.

'There's nothing like getting up early on a Sunday and doing something really *useful*,' he said.

Nick's phone rang at about ten that night. He groped for the extension by the bed.

'Trevellyan,' he mumbed sleepily.

'Hope,' said the voice at the other end.

'Alison?' Nick sat up and switched on the light.

'You sound half asleep,' she said.

'I was fully asleep.'

'It's only ten.'

'I haven't had much sleep these last few nights.'

'Sorry. Shall I ring off?'

'Don't you dare. Oh God!'

'What's the matter?'

'I seem to have fallen asleep in my clothes and I'm in dire need of a bath.' He switched the light off again to shut out the sight of these distressing matters and lay back to listen to her voice in the darkness.

'Ugh,' she was saying, 'I'm glad I'm not there then.'

'*That* is one of the things I want to talk to you about.'

'Yes, I know. I've just had to sit through Simon's lecture. The one that goes I-don't-know-why-poor-Nicholas-puts-up-with-you-when-you-treat-him-so-badly-Alison.'

'I suppose poor Nicholas would rather be treated badly by you than doted on by anyone else. I was so hoping you would come home this weekend, though.'

'I've got to get on with this USM listing business. God knows I've been putting it off long enough.'

'Yeah, I know.'

'It sounds as if you've got your plate full, anyway, if you've been working nights. Or have you already made an arrest?'

'No, and no sign of a quick one either.'

'What is it?'

'Rape. Schoolgirl. Two schoolgirls.'

'Oh, no! How awful. I've got something to ask you and then I'll let you get back to sleep.'

'What?' Nick said warily.

'Can you do a check on someone's movements for me?'

'This isn't a police state, Alison.'

'But people's passports are checked when they enter and leave the country, right?'

'Oh, I see.'

'And you need visas for both America and Australia.'

Nick switched the light back on again and reached for the pad and pen he kept by the bed. 'Fire away. The more help I give you, the sooner you'll be home.' Alison explained about Gerry Walsh and about her idea of checking credit references to see if any of her colleagues had financial problems. 'I'm not making any promises, Alison, but I'll do what I can.'

'Haven't you got a few friends in the right places? People who owe you?'

'I may have.'

'See you soon.'

'I love you, Alison.'

'And I, you,' said Alison who, after more than two years, still found those three little words hard to pronounce. 'Goodnight, darling.'

She hung up.

Chapter Sixteen

'The first aim of self-defence is to give yourself the opportunity to get away.'

Shirley Walpole stood at the front of the church hall on Monday evening feeling, as she always did when she had to speak in public, slightly nervous – although no disinterested observer would ever have guessed it.

Two dozen eager young faces were turned her way, four dozen young ears strained for her every word. She wore a loose black track suit and dusty trainers and she balanced now on the toes of her shoes and took a deep breath.

'Your assailant will grab hold of you,' she explained, gaining momentum. 'He may grab you from behind, round the neck most probably. He might seize you by the hair. Your priority is not to engage in some sort of stand-up fight since he'll almost certainly win it. Your priority is to force him to let go of you, wind him if possible and run like hell to raise the alarm. Any suggestions how you might do that?'

After a brief pause, Sarah Deacon raised her hand.

'Just call out, Sarah,' Shirley told her, 'don't stand on ceremony.'

'You might throw something in his face,' Sarah said confidently, 'sand or earth.'

'Very good. Remember, please, that the law forbids you to carry anything for use solely as a weapon. But there are plenty of things you can legitimately carry in your handbag or pockets. Hairspray, for example. A burst of that in a man's eyes ought to give you just those few

141

seconds you need. Ground pepper is also much recommended. If your neighbourhood beat bobby decides to search you for offensive weapons, tell him you're just off to your cookery class.' The girls laughed dutifully. 'Or, as Sarah says, if all else fails, grab up a handful of earth or sand and fling it straight in his eyes. Any more suggestions?'

'Knee him in the goolies,' called out a tiny girl of about twelve who looked more like a boy with her cropped red hair, grubby jeans and flat-chested sweatshirt. Some of the other girls giggled and she glared at the culprits defiantly.

Shirley smiled. 'Not always as easy as it sounds, I'm afraid. There are more vulnerable spots, surprisingly enough, and I've done a handout which you can collect on the way out but which I'll just run through now. The eyes, nose and Adam's Apple are some of his most vulnerable points and some of the most accessible.

'Try to scratch at his face, if at all possible. Use a comb, a ring or just your nails. He will try very hard to avoid being marked as it will help identify and convict him. If he thinks you're a real threat to his face, he may give up and run off. The solar plexus is the next most vulnerable spot.' Several of the girls looked puzzled and Shirley asked, 'Can anyone tell me, or show me, where that is?'

A small, dark-haired woman raised her hand. She was nondescript in baggy jeans and a man's tee shirt and spoke rather indistinctly through a gold crucifix on a chain which she was nervously holding in her mouth.

'It's about here,' she said, pointing with ragged nails to a spot half way between the chest and stomach. Everyone turned to look at her and she swopped the crucifix for a strand of hair which she chewed hard as she examined the floorboards minutely.

'Excellent,' Shirley said. 'A sharp blow there can drive all the wind out of him — even his dinner, with a bit of luck. Punches must be quick — that's to say you must withdraw your hand at once. Don't give him time to grab your wrist as you strike. The groin comes next after the solar plexus. Then the shins. There's a school of thought which advocates bringing a high heel down smartly on the shin or instep. Personally, I prefer a pair of trainers or flatties I can run in.'

'All this theory is fine – ' the tiny redhead piped up.

'You'll get plenty of chance at rolling around on the floor, I promise you,' Shirley said. 'This is an introductory session. We shall look at various holds he might use on you and how to break them in the coming weeks.'

'But the rapist is active now! Here. In Hopbridge. Perhaps tonight as we walk home.'

There was silence as all the girls remembered what had sparked off their enthusiasm for self-defence as word of the class had shot round the school and the town that afternoon. Many of them were classmates of Elizabeth Parrish or knew her, at least by sight. Many of them had long dark walks home that damp November night.

'Fair point,' Shirley conceded. 'I stand rebuked and we shall get straight down to the basics now. I shall also ensure before we break up tonight that nobody is walking home alone.'

'Now, I'm a judo practitioner but I don't intend to get involved with the theory of judo at the moment. I intend to teach you basic survival techniques. But one of the fundamental tenets of judo is also fundamental to any form of self-defence – that of using your opponent's strength against him.'

'Sounds great in theory,' said the tiny girl.

'I'm talking about balance,' Shirley said patiently. 'Balancing is as basic to us as breathing. We don't think about it until it goes wrong. But just imagine – or remember if it's ever happened to you – when a fever or an ear infection or a blow to the head throws you off balance for a while. You feel helpless. You feel ... subhuman. You almost lose your sense of identity.

'To explain what I mean: imagine someone, someone much bigger than you are, is trying to push open your bedroom door. You're standing on the other side trying to push it shut again. He's much stronger than you are, so however

143

hard you push he's going to win and crush you back against the wall.

'But just suppose, instead, that you resist only for a second and then suddenly stop pushing. What happens? Your assailant comes hurtling into the room and falls flat on his face. He's lost his balance and you've got your chance to run. That's the principal we're going to look at this evening. In Judo we say "Minimum effort, maximum efficiency."'

'The bigger they are, the harder they fall, in other words,' said the red-headed girl.

'Exactly! Pull out the mats and pair off.'

There were an odd number of students and the tiny girl headed for Shirley.

'You look big enough to me,' she said, with satisfaction.

Shirley, who towered a head over her, asked: 'What's your name?'

'Ginny Miller.'

'How old are you, Ginny?'

'Seventeen.'

'Christ!'

'Don't say it. You thought I was about twelve.' She grinned suddenly all over her freckled cheeks. 'That's why I come on a bit aggressive sometimes. Sorry.'

'No apology needed.'

'Only my kid sister, Karen, is in Liz Parrish's class at school. They're friends. I know her well. She's such a quiet, frightened little thing.'

'Unlike you.'

'Let's just say that at the moment I'm an angry little thing.'

'Good. It's time we women got angry. I don't think I need to warn you not to be too gentle with me either, do I?'

Ginny shook her head.

Shirley looked round to check that everyone was ready. She noticed that Sarah Deacon was facing the woman with the crucifix and the ragged nails. They seemed to know each other.

*

Alison was curled up with a bottle of Côtes du Rhône and the *Hacker's Handbook* — finding it short on plot and characterisation — at eight o'clock, when someone knocked on her bedroom door. She had laid early claim to the bathroom that evening and was in her dressing gown. She went to the door and called through it: 'Who's there?'

'Mary?' said Nick's voice. 'It's me, Nick, your country cousin.'

Alison hurried to open the door. He came in. She shut it behind him and locked it.

'Nick! It's so lovely to see you. I thought you'd be far too busy to come, with a rapist on the loose.'

'I was in need of an evening off. I'll get the first train back in the morning.' He put his arms round her and hugged her. Then he stepped back and scrutinised her.

'Stripped for action, I see. You must be clairvoyant.'

'No, I'm not,' Alison said. 'You should have let me know. What if I hadn't been in?'

'I'd have let myself in and waited for you.'

'Let yourself in?'

'Sure. Haven't you seen people open locks with a credit card on the telly?'

'Yes ... but ...'

'Well, it doesn't work. But I do know how to pick a lock, as it happens.'

'Full of surprises, aren't you?'

'I have got a surprise for you, actually.'

'Don't I get a kiss?'

'Several. Mmmm. Alison, I've missed you.'

'Shh,' she hissed, 'don't call me that. I'm Mary.'

'The room isn't bugged, is it?'

'Who knows?'

'Well if it is, they're going to get quite a earful.' He looked round the bed-sitting room, tearing his eyes away from Alison for the first time.

'What a dump! I haven't lived anywhere as grotty as this since Oxford. Where's the bed?'

'That's it. The couch. It folds out.'

Nick looked at it doubtfully. 'It doesn't look very robust for what I have in mind. It'll have to be the floor.' He pulled her down on the rug and began to unfasten her dressing gown.

'Is this the surprise?' she asked. 'Because it's not very surprising.'

'Tell you later,' Nick mumbled, forgetting childhood injunctions not to talk with his mouth full.'

Gerry paused at the door and listened. Philip had a long-standing opera date at Covent Garden that evening and he'd bussed up from the Barbican in the hope that Mary would come out for a quiet drink. He'd decided to come in person since it was too easy for her to say 'No' over the phone. He knew she liked him but she hadn't given him much encouragement so far. That was fine by him — the thrill of the chase was the best bit.

But the sounds he was hearing now were oddly familiar, coming from the room of someone who was Steering Clear of That Sort of Thing.

He heard a voice raised in muffled ecstasy.

'Alison!' it moaned. 'Alison!'

Gerry smiled to himself as he turned and tiptoed back down the stairs.

It wasn't very much later that Nick and Alison were talking again. Nick fell back on the rug and let out a long sigh.

'Oops, sorry. Couldn't hold on any longer.'

'Never mind.' Alison propped herself up on one arm and examined his thin, smooth body. 'I'm quite glad to have evidence that you haven't been getting it elsewhere.'

'Thank you for that vote of confidence.'

'I thought you might be consoling yourself with Shirley Walpole.' Nick didn't reply at once and Alison ran her finger gently down the narrow downy stream which ran from the thicker pond on his chest, flowing finally into the delta of his pubic hair.

'No,' he said at last. 'Not for want of her trying, though.'

Alison had been about to ask what his surprise was when she realised what he had said.

'What did you say!' she yelped.

'She made a pass at me.'

146

'I don't believe you. Just like that?'

'Just like that.'

'Well, I don't think you should boast about it to everyone,' she said cuttingly.

'Not everyone, silly. I haven't told anyone except you and I was in two minds about that. I didn't want to deceive you but I didn't want you to get your knife into her either.'

'Whatever did you say to her?'

'Well I didn't want to hurt her feelings so I said that I was very flattered, and that she was a very attractive woman and that I was completely faithful to you.'

'And what did she say to that?'

'She said it would be just an uncomplicated fuck, I quote, and that she wouldn't tell you if I didn't.'

'That little cow-eyed —'

'I was a bit embarrassed. But she seemed quite unbothered by it.' Nick clicked his tongue, put on a Victorian-spinster expression and said, 'Honestly, women today.'

'My God. I turn my back for five minutes ... Were you tempted?'

'No.'

'Not the slightest little bit?'

'Nope.' Nick yawned and stretched. 'Give me the deep peace of the marital bed any day. Not that it is very peaceful, on reflection, you make more noise than any woman I —'

'Yes, yes. So you keep saying.'

'It's infuriating really,' he said smugly. 'Ten years ago when I was twenty-four, twenty-five, the sexual revolution was still in full swing, I was unattached and as randy as hell and women hardly gave me the time of day. Now I'm living in monogamous bliss and they've invented all sorts of lethal new diseases and beautiful women keep hurling themselves at me shouting, "Take me, take me." It's so unfair. Ow! You're hurting me! Owww!'

'Good! You complacent bastard! You're just telling me all this to make me jealous so I'll come home, aren't you?'

'Partly,' he admitted, 'and partly just being honest with you. Come home, Alison. You're the only woman in the world I want. I wouldn't care if all the women in London were standing in their shifts from here to the eastern world.'

147

'What?'

'Sorry, I keep forgetting you only went to Cambridge.'

'I may not be able to quote English literature like you, Nick Trevellyan ...' She leant over him, kissing him.

'Irish literature actually, or Anglo-Irish if you want to be ... mmmmm, that's nice ... pedantic.'

'Whatever ... but I could buy you up a hundred times over.'

'No, you couldn't,' he said, pulling her down on top of him. 'Firstly, I'm not for sale; secondly, I'm already yours, body and soul.'

After a much longer intermission he said: 'Time for some refreshment, I think.' He got up and fetched Alison's bottle of wine and two chipped cups. 'You really know how to entertain in style,' he said as he poured. He sank down on the floor beside her, handed her her wine and nestled comfortably back against her.

'Now we've got the serious business over, time for my surprise. I have some news for you. You are now lying in the arms of a Detective Chief Inspector.'

'Nick, that's wonderful.'

'Reg called me in and told me this morning, unofficially.'

'Was he pleased?'

'Well, his attitude towards me is always so ambiguous, as you know.' He thought of something. 'Hey, I think I'll buy myself a new jacket to celebrate.'

'It doesn't mean a move, does it?'

'No. It seems there's enough crime in the Hop Valley nowadays to warrant a Chief Inspector.

'I bet Shirley Walpole will fancy you even more now. Does she know?'

'It's not official until tomorrow. Anyway, I wanted you to be the first to know. Pity old Bill's not there to celebrate with.'

'How are you getting on with her, when she's not lusting after your body?'

'I like her. If she thinks I'm talking a load of bollocks she says so, whereas Bill would just sit there with that long-suffering look on his face saying, "Yez, zir".'

'Huh! She can just damn well show a bit more respect

now you're a DCI. Seriously, isn't it going to make things a bit awkward for you?'

'It's not unusual. When men and women work together in the very intense atmosphere that detective work generates, it's natural that equally intense feelings should flare up. If an inspector-sergeant team is really going to get results, they're going to get very close emotionally, almost be able to read each other's thoughts. Remember, they may depend on each other for their lives at times. You hardly ever find partners who tolerate each other — it's either love or loathing. That's one of the reasons I disapprove of romantic entanglements between my subordinates. They never last once the case is over.'

'Let's hope Shirley doesn't start to loathe you, then.'

'I think we have too much liking and respect for each other for that.'

'I suppose a sexual crime arouses even stronger emotions, one way or the other.'

'I think you can be sure of that. By the way, I did those enquiries for you. None of your colleagues would have any trouble getting a credit card and none of their names showed up on the police computer. I know negative information like that is little better than useless.'

Chapter Seventeen

'Well if everybody's suitably bruised and battered,' Shirley said an hour later, 'let's form some groups for walking home. It might be useful if you did something similar at school – it's often dark by the time school ends at this time of year, if it's a bit wet or stormy, or if you have to stay late for anything.'

Sarah Deacon stepped forward: a natural leader.

'I'm walking to Riverside Close, about half a mile away. I'm sure a lot of other people live on the Riverside Estate.' She turned to the girl with the crucifix. 'Tessa?'

'Kevin's meeting me,' the girl said with a slight air of defiance. Two other girls said that their fathers were calling for them in the car. Four girls stepped forward to claim occupancy of the Riverside Estate and set off into the night with Sarah.

'Same time Thursday,' Shirley called after them. They were excited and boisterous and their chatter could be heard for some time as they bounced down the street.

'If anyone's left over, anyone who lives in an out-of-the-way place, I'll run them back by car,' Shirley said. 'My car's parked at my place, just round the corner.' But there were no takers. Suddenly it seemed that everyone had forgotten Shirley.

'Goodnight, girls ... ladies.' Shirley hesitated.

'Sisters?' Ginny suggested cheerfully. 'Goodnight, Shirley.'

Shirley set off to walk back to the quiet room she had rented in a family house until a suitable flatshare or bedsit should turn up.

Always assuming she was going to be here any length of time, she thought — rubbing a sore elbow, courtesy of Ginny who had taken the injunction not to be gentle with her litcrally. She had jumped at the chance of coming here as a temporary replacement for Bill Deacon, obscure, out of the way bit of the county though it was. You didn't get noticed or gain commendations by being a minnow in the huge pond of Headquarters.

And Nick Trevellyan had a reputation for solving crimes and not taking all the credit for himself either — not like Ted Seymour. She had hoped to come away with a good report from him and her feet firmly on the next rung of the promotion ladder — Detective Inspector Walpole. She had been told he was a nice man as well as a good copper but had not expected to find herself caught so physically and emotionally off balance.

No, she had made a complete fool of herself where he was concerned and she couldn't really expect him to forget it. Admittedly his manner to her had not changed since that night but surely embarrassment would make him want to get rid of her as fast as he could.

And where was Nick, anyway? They had reached that stage of an investigation where all the routine procedures were under way — forensic tests, house to house — and they were waiting, more than anything, for a lucky break. He had said they both needed a rest and had disappeared at about four o'clock. There had been no answer at his flat when she'd tried to contact him to tell him her wonderful idea — the self-defence class. She had had to okay it with the superintendent.

She felt very cold and lonely tonight, just as she had on the night she had made such an idiot of herself. Drizzle was running down the back of her neck. Her trainers were letting in water. She turned up the collar of her jacket.

How she wished at that moment she had a man coming to meet her like that odd, shy girl Sarah had called Tessa. She didn't look the type to have

151

a boyfriend, or was it her husband even — she was one of these women whose ages were hard to gauge? It was always the dim, plain little things who were happily married too — was it that their expectations weren't unreasonably high? Shirley would have settled for anyone warm tonight: anyone prepared to give her a hug and see her safely home; mix her a gin and tonic and ask after her day.

But the police force was still in the dark ages when it came to women combining family and career — especially in CID. The hours were long and uncertain, you were always breaking dates, leaving them standing impatiently outside the cinema until they'd missed the start of the film, coming home too exhausted to offer them a civil word.

The most senior police women in the country tended to be single and even then there wasn't one Chief Constable or even Deputy among them.

Shirley Walpole — young, attractive, personable, as she was — was beginning to lose confidence in herself.

She suddenly laughed out loud, then glanced round to see, to her relief, that the street was deserted. Other people had more sense than to be out on a night like this. So much self pity, she mocked. Poor, Pathetic, Little Shirley Walpole. Shirley's great gift, had she but known it, was the ability to step outside herself from time to time and laugh at her own foolishness. It kept her sane.

The little nineteen-thirties semi — her temporary home — was in darkness and she remembered that the Harkers, her landlords, had said they were going to stay with their married daughter in Stroud for a few days. She took her front door keys out of her pocket and made them into an armed fist with her right hand before walking up the short unlit driveway, past her modest white Austin Metro. She let herself in at the front door.

It didn't occur to Shirley that she had been the only one left to walk home alone that night.

*

Rain was pouring down relentlessly over a grey London dawn and Alison, having been up since six to accompany Nick to Paddington Station, was feeling more than usually sorry for herself. Spending an evening with Nick, lying the night in his arms on the lumpy sofa bed, had reminded her that she wanted to go home; and saying goodbye to him that morning had been painful. As the first train to Taunton had pulled out of the station she had been tempted to drag open a door and jump on it with him.

But she had her pride.

She comforted herself with a full English breakfast at the buffet at Paddington then caught a bus as far as Bank. She walked the rest of the way to the office, dodging puddles and narrowly avoiding being blinded by short and careless umbrella owners.

The buildings of the City of London seemed more than usually dirty this morning – uniform in their dreariness. At home, heather coloured the moors all year round and the sea was clear steel with white foaming tips. The deer were red and the stone houses pink – even in November.

Alison was homesick.

She let herself in at the front door of Orion with her cardkey. Although it was still barely eight o'clock she knew that she wouldn't be the first in. Sure enough, she could make out the figure of Zac through the tinted glass of the computer room door.

He had the top of the printer open and was tinkering with it. As Alison stood impatiently pressing the button for the lift, she saw him close the lid and give the printer a sharp kick. She tapped on the glass and had the pleasure of seeing Zac start guiltily. He crossed the room and wrenched open the door.

'The lift's not working,' he told her with evident enjoyment.

'Like the printer?' she suggested.

Zac held the door wide, cupped his hand to his ear and listened with exaggerated attention. Alison realised that the printer was once more clattering out its listings. She nodded with respect.

'I suppose the trick is knowing where to kick.'

'The lift won't be fixed before tomorrow,' was all Zac said in reply. 'The exercise will do you good, woman.' He went back inside and the door swung shut on its heavy spring with a click.

Alison went into the kitchen and poured herself some coffee before trudging up the stairs. She returned Gerry's cheerful 'Good morning, Mary', took off her coat, unwound her scarf and stood steaming slightly in front of the radiator. There was a small puddle of rain on the windowsill so she hung her bag over the back of her chair and sat down to sip her cooling coffee. Gerry was pounding away at his keyboard as if making an attempt on the Clive Zacharzewski speed record.

'Someone's switched my terminal off,' Alison remarked. She reached a hand behind it to feel for the On/Off switch and started back in shock as Gerry yelled:

'Don't touch that!'

What seemed like less than a second later he was round her side of the desk and was unplugging her terminal from the wall socket.

'What's got into you?' Alison demanded. 'You frightened the life out of me.'

Gerry turned the terminal round and pointed silently at two bare wires sticking out from where the On/Off switch ought to have been. Alison gasped.

'I don't know about *frightening* the life out of you,' he said. 'Look at you. Your hair and clothes are damp, your shoes are soaking, and on top of all that you're nicely earthed in that rain puddle on the windowsill. Another second and there wouldn't have been any life left in you to frighten.'

Alison pushed her chair on its castors as far away from the terminal as she could get. Gerry's hand rested comfortingly on her shoulder.

'It's okay, sweetheart. I've disconnected it. There's no danger now.'

'I . . .'

'Here, have a sip of your coffee.' He raised her hand, which was still automatically clutching the mug, to her lips. 'Then take a few deep breaths.'

'What the hell's going on?' Jilly, who had just come

154

panting in at the door with Zac, was staring wide-eyed at Alison's pale face and jerking body. 'What's all the shouting about.'

'Is she having some sort of fit?' Zac asked with interest.

'Just a nasty accident, narrowly averted,' Gerry said.

'Accident!' Alison echoed.

'Well, what else could it have been?' Gerry asked reasonably. 'A potentially lethal combination of a loose wire, a wet day and a leaking window, that's all.'

Zac, who seemed to have grasped the situation without delay, was examining the bare wires. He also looked at the On/Off switch which lay harmlessly on the desk where it had fallen. Finally he shrugged.

'One of the cleaners, maybe. They're a bit inclined to wrench the equipment about. I've often had to speak to that little Malaysian one about pulling the terminal plugs out by their wires to plug her wretched hoover in. She probably knocked the switch off somehow and didn't bother to report it.'

'Come off it,' Alison muttered faintly.

'It is a rather bizarre sort of thing to happen by accident,' Gerry agreed. 'But look at it another way. Who would want to electrocute Mary?'

'Sorry. I'm being silly.' Alison had recovered some of her colour now and some of her wits. 'Of course it was an accident. As Gerry says, what other explanation is possible?'

It was not the time for her colleagues to start asking questions about why anyone should want to harm her.

But was her cover blown? Had John Hacker recognised her, remembered her photo from somewhere? Noticed her presence in the computer at night looking for him? She had been one of the first out of the office yesterday evening — anyone might have found the few seconds necessary to tear off that switch after she'd gone. Or either Zac or Jilly could have done it this morning. Jilly was dry and wearing indoor clothes: she'd obviously been in the office for some time.

Probably ruthless, Nick had said. Somehow those had just been words until this moment. She would be watching her back from now on.

'I think we should get it looked at,' Jilly was saying. Alison shook her head.

'Let's not make a stupid fuss. There's no harm done.'

'But I'm responsible for health and safety,' Jilly protested.

'I'm going to check the rest of the terminals,' Zac said. 'We don't want any fatalities. Knowing Philip, he's probably skimped on the insurance.' With this callous parting shot he started making his way round the office.

'I think you'd better go and lie down, Mary,' Jilly said. 'Or maybe you should take the rest of the day off.'

Alison felt very tempted to agree but it was a well-known fact that a freelance contractor had to be dying of bubonic plague before he lost a day's pay.

'Just give me a minute,' she said.

'All clear,' Zac called out. He rejoined them. 'Just a one-off – not a concerted campaign of terror. We'd only have lost one, hardly put the deadline back at all.'

'My God!' Gerry said. 'Can't you see how shaken Mary is? Can't you save your cheap remarks for another time?'

'Just trying to cheer the girl up.'

'I suppose it was just one of those things,' Jilly said uncertainly. 'We'd just all better be a bit more careful in future.'

'Well, it could have been worse,' Zac said.

'I don't really see how.'

'It could have happened to me, woman.'

Gerry turned away in disgust and went back to his own seat. He resumed his work and ignored Zac pointedly for the rest of the morning.

Zac fetched a small screwdriver from the top drawer of his desk and reconnected the On/Off switch to the wires. He switched it on to test it and pronounced it in full working order. Then, with unexpected sensitivity, he swopped Alison's terminal for his own.

'You know,' he said as he resumed his work, 'I find this all very puzzling.'

*

156

'I'd just rather you'd spoken to me first,' Nick said. 'It looks a lot like you were going over my head, going straight to the superintendent.'

'I don't see that it matters, sir.' Shirley studied the map of the Hop Valley on the wall above his head and would not meet his eye. 'The important thing is that the women in this town learn to protect themselves.'

'Develop false illusions about their ability to do so, in other words, rather than stopping taking risks.'

'Those are certainly other words.' Shirley's voice was now quite loud. 'So you want women kept in purdah while men like the rapist walk the streets.'

Nick's voice rose equally loud and said: 'For God's sake sit down, Sergeant, and don't stand there at attention looking as if you were being court-martialled.'

Shirley didn't smile. She sat. And waited.

'I understand what you're saying, Shirley. I agree that, normally speaking, women shouldn't be frightened off the streets after dark — '

'Which is fifteen hours a day at this time of year.'

' — as you say. But these are exceptional circumstances and we haven't the manpower to protect them from this maniac.'

'Which is why I want to teach them to protect themselves!'

'I know you're very keen on this judo, Shirley. I know you've been doing it for years. But is it really any good in a life or death situation?'

'Yes, it damn well is! Women are not that much weaker physically than men, sir. It's largely a cultural thing. It's just that they're brought up to think of themselves as helpless. They wear high heels so they can't run to safety, tight skirts so they can't climb or kick. They're brought up to be nice to men, to smile and flirt and simper, to make men like them at any price.'

'Exactly my point,' Nick broke in. 'So when a man attacks them, they don't gouge his eyes out because they're afraid they might *hurt* him.'

'I've never had that problem myself,' Shirley said gruffly. 'However, I take your point and that's one of the things I'm

157

trying to knock out of them. I'm doing it in my own time,' she concluded.

'All right, Walpole. You win. Not that you'll be getting much own time until we've caught him. I just wish you hadn't gone straight to Reg about it, though.'

'You were nowhere to be found,' Shirley pointed out. 'I wanted to get started. Monday night's a good night for classes – there's not much else on. I called round at your flat, you weren't in. I rang that Little Hopford number you gave me and just got an answering machine.'

'All right, I apologise. I'm being unreasonable, perhaps, but I'd still rather the women of Hopbridge kept out of Riverside Park at night until I've got him behind bars.'

'I got a bloody good turnout considering the short notice. Word went round like wildfire.'

'How many?'

'About two dozen. Sarah Deacon was there.'

'Oh, yes?'

'She's a really nice kid ... young woman. Quite a few other girls from the comprehensive were there too and some of the nurses from the hospital. The nurses' home is pretty isolated and badly lit although they're stepping up security for the time being.'

'When are you meeting next?'

'Thursday night. I want to see them twice a week until they've grasped the basics. It's two hours. I'll make them up later.'

'Let's hope these classes won't be needed for long. Let's hope we can get him soon.'

Shirley shrugged. 'He's just one. Even if he walked in and gave himself up this very minute, they'd still be needed.'

'Is there anything I can do to help?' Nick asked with an attempt at conciliation. 'Volunteer to be hurled round the room and have my eyes gouged out?'

'It's women only,' Shirley said coldly.

At that moment the door opened and Carol Halsgrove reported in again from another overnight stint at Liz Parrish's bedside.

'The hospital are saying she could go home now, sir,' she told Nick. 'They say that there's nothing physically wrong with her that won't heal just as well at home and that staying in hospital may be delaying the healing process psychologically.'

The phone rang before Nick could reply. He listened for a moment then said: 'It's not exactly the most convenient moment. Yes, I know. I can hear you are. All right. There's no point in your spreading it round the office. Stay in bed and get back to work as soon as you can.'

He hung up. Carol raised an eyebrow.

'Paul,' Nick said. 'He's got a filthy cold – you can hear it over the 'phone. I trust you're not going to go down with it too.'

'If you mean that I might catch it from him, I should say that's very unlikely,' Carol said coldly. 'I haven't so much as seen him since this business flared up.'

Nick opened his mouth to say something but thought better of it.

'Let her go home,' he said instead. 'Mrs Parrish must be exhausted, spending every spare moment at the hospital. We'll send a doctor round to her once she's well enough to be examined. We'll send Mike Brewster. He's surprisingly good with children.'

'*If* she's ever well enough to be examined,' Shirley said.

'Thank God Pauline Taylor was able to give us a description,' Nick said. 'It's all we have to go on. What's happening about her, Shirley?'

'The threat that I'd have her taken into care if Taylor laid a finger on her seems to have concentrated his mind wonderfully. She's bearing up and Mrs Taylor seems to be siding with her for once. Pauline – '

'Has this Taylor got any sort of record?' Nick interrupted.

'Lord no! He's the epitome of respectability and a pillar of the church.'

'Only he's obviously a man of violence.'

'Only at home, though. A fireside tyrant – except that he's too mean even to light a fire in his grate. We know how interested the courts are in that. Anyway, as I was saying, Pauline's decided to have an abortion, naturally enough, and it's fixed up for next week some time.'

159

'Can we do genetic fingerprinting on the foetus?' Carol asked, wrinkling her nose in distaste.

'In theory, most certainly,' Nick said. 'And we shall.'

Chapter Eighteen

'I think I've just about had enough.' Gerry got up at six-thirty that Tuesday evening, stretched his stiffening muscles and put his coat on. 'Coming, Mary? We could grab a pizza or something.'

'I'll just hang on for a bit,' Alison said. She had had enough too – enough of this job, that bedsit, this drab brown hair. Tonight was going to be the night.

'I think you ought to call it a day,' Gerry said, 'especially after this morning's little incident.'

'I'm fine. I'd almost forgotten about it.' Like hell she had. Tonight was going to be the night, especially after this morning's 'little incident'. She was going to get him before he got another chance to get her.

'See you tomorrow then.' Gerry went whistling on his way. Alison stepped out on to the landing and listened. She heard the front door slam behind him. She went into Philip's office and looked out on to the street. Gerry, with his long, carefree stride, was already turning into Moorgate.

She surveyed the building mentally. She knew that Zac was still downstairs in the computer room. Otherwise the place was deserted. Jilly had her orchestra on Tuesdays and always left by six that day. Ruth and Philip had been out with a client all day and would go straight home from there. Willy and Jenny were away on their course. It was the ideal opportunity.

She would have to wait until Zac had gone. Meanwhile she might as well make herself some coffee. There wasn't much point in doing any more work since she would

161

be leaving soon, going home – tomorrow with a bit of luck.

Fingers crossed.

The main lights were off but a sort of nightlight shone on each landing – all the other offices were locked and empty. She could see Zac sitting at the operator's terminal, oblivious as always. There was no knowing how long he would stay.

The coffee pots were empty and she filled a fresh filter and stood waiting for it to percolate. Then she went back upstairs. It occurred to her that if she sat in Philip's office, she would see when the lights went out in the computer room on the ground floor. Then she would know Zac was on his way out.

She settled in the dark office to wait. Philip's swivel chair was high-backed and comfortable. She reclined it and closed her eyes. She hadn't had much sleep lately, what with boozy nights with Jake and Simon and the MacAlistairs. Then she had been up early that morning to see Nick off. Then someone had tried to kill her. These little things took it out of you.

As Zac sat pounding away at the operator's console, there was a soft tap on the window. He glanced at his digital watch – nine-nineteen. It was dark outside and the computer room was lit by fluorescent lights and Zac could see nothing. He got up, switched off all but one of the lights and squinted through the tinted plate glass. He could just about make out the figure outside.

'What the hell do you want?' he shouted.

'Let me in, can't you?' the figure mouthed through the glass, pointing at the front door.

Zac let out an impatient exclamation. Why would nobody let him get on in peace? If it wasn't the Lewis woman peering at him through the door it was that apology for a nightwatchman, Cleary. He stormed out of the room and dragged open the street door.

'Thanks. It's turned bloody cold out there.' His visitor shivered in demonstration despite being well wrapped against the cold in a black leather blouson, the street credibility of which was ruined by a blue woollen hat, muffler and gloves.

'Can't you see I'm busy?' Zac thrust his cardkey, which hung from his belt by a chain, into the door and punched 1234 onto the bank of numbers. The door clicked and he pushed it open. His visitor followed.

'I just wanted a quiet word.'

'Funnily enough, I've been wanting a quiet word with you.' Zac sat down at the console again. 'But after you.'

Alison awoke feeling disorientated as she always did after sleeping during the day. She blinked around. It felt as if it ought to be morning but she knew that it wasn't. Her mouth felt bad from sleeping without cleaning her teeth. Half a cup of very cold coffee sat on the desk. She punched a key on the terminal in front of her on Philip's desk and it told her the time was 21:27. The heating had gone off a while ago and she shivered.

She crossed to the window and peered out.

Down on the ground floor, the printer stopped work and demanded more paper. Its plea went unanswered as the last light in the room was snapped off.

Surely Zac must have gone home by now. Yes. The computer room was in darkness.

Outside in the street, but too close to the building to be in Alison's line of vision, a shiny new knife, and the blue woollen muffler which enveloped it, slid silently down the nearest drain.

'You little bitch.'

Alex thought for one horrible moment that he was going to cry. He concentrated on his anger instead. The rhythmic thump of the dance music exacerbated the rage in his head.

'Sodding, *frigid* little bitch.'

'Let's not go through all that again,' Sarah Deacon said with a sigh. 'I've told you, I'm not ready for that. And the fact that "everyone else does it" cuts no ice with me.'

'You needn't think I'm going to wait around 'til you've finished your bloody "A" levels, let alone your bloody university course. Who do you think you are, anyway?'

'I don't expect you to wait for me. That's why I'm telling you it's over. It's been fun, Alex, and I'm very fond of you

163

but I'm too young to get serious about anyone. I think it's best if we stop seeing each other.'

'Fine.' Alex wound his motorcycle scarf around his head as he began to get up – that way no one could see his lip trembling. 'You can bloody well walk home then, you little . . . and I hope the rapist is out tonight.'

'Alex! What a terrible thing to say!' But he had already walked out of the disco. Sarah looked around helplessly. All the people who had been following the quarrel with interest glanced quickly away and resumed their own conversations.

'Cheer up, Sarah.' A boy she knew slightly from school came over and put a friendly hand on her shoulder. 'Look, would you like to dance?'

'No thanks, Tom.'

'Want a coke?'

'Thanks. I really appreciate it.' Sarah collected up her things. 'But it's late. I think I'll be getting home.'

'Sure you'll be all right like?'

'Quite sure.'

She'd missed the last bus. She hadn't intended to lose her lift home on the back of Alex's motorbike. She'd hoped the split would be civilised. It hadn't occurred to her that he cared that much.

She could ring home and ask her mother to come and fetch her in the car. But her mother was a little distant at the moment, brooding about her father's health and low spirits, facing up to the fact that he was now well past the half-way mark – that they both were. Besides, she was a big girl now – sixteen – time she could cope on her own. She would walk it.

There was a short cut through the park, of course, that cut off nearly a quarter of a mile. Only Sarah wasn't stupid enough to try it. It would have to be the long way round.

She thought over what Shirley Walpole had taught her as she trudged along the road, keeping well to the outside of the pavement, near the kerb. Don't keep both hands in your pockets: Sarah guiltily removed her hands from her pockets where she had thrust them deeply and despondently. But she had forgotten her gloves and her hands soon felt cold and she put them back.

Hopbridge was well lit until midnight, that was a mercy. Frost was beginning to form, sparkling in the brief circles of light under the lamp posts. She remembered that black ice was forecast tonight. It was just as well she hadn't gone home on Alex's bike, just as well she hadn't called Mum out in the car. Mum didn't like driving at night when there was ice.

She began to walk more quickly to stave off the cold and to get home to her safe bed the sooner. It was not quite midnight but few cars passed her. One slowed down behind her but thought better of it and accelerated away. Who was that? A kerb crawler who had slowed down enough to ascertain that she wasn't a pro, a neighbour whose kindly impulse had died down at the last moment, a Good Samaritan who had belatedly realised that the last thing a young girl walking home in the present climate of fear needed was the offer a lift from a stranger?

She crossed the road to face oncoming traffic and gathered a handful of coins into her fist. As she turned into Riverside Gardens, the street lights went out. Midnight. She had promised, like Cinderella, to be home by midnight. She was almost there.

She was relieved to see lights still blazing in the kitchen and hall of number five Riverside Close. As she let herself in with her latch key and called out, 'Only me,' her mother emerged from the kitchen and said: 'Hello, darling. How was the disco? I didn't hear Alex's bike – he must be getting more considerate of the neighbours. Would you like some cocoa?'

Susie staggered back in astonishment as her tall, sturdy daughter flung herself into her arms sobbing.

'Oh, Mum. Mum.'

Ted Cleary was a retired policeman. He had never risen above the rank of constable, being lazy by inclination. A time-server, he had served his time, retired on full pension and taken on this nice cushy number looking after this office block in the City at night. A brawny, red-faced man, his looks yelled 'Irish' at anyone within eyeshot.

He had a little office with a gas heater and a kettle in the basement and made a tour of the building punctiliously

165

every hour. There was no need for dogs or anything heavy like that, no danger in a job like this. Since he had the gift of cat-napping he was able to put in a few hours' sleep each night, freeing him to tend his garden in the ungentrified part of Camden Town during the day.

He did his nine o'clock tour, glancing at each floor to see if it was occupied. It looked as if the tall, buxom, brown-haired girl on the top floor had gone. He hadn't heard her leave but there were no lights on up there. The bad-tempered Pole, who never had a civil word for anyone, was still at his post in that bare room on the ground floor.

He made his way back to his cubby hole, put the kettle on for a nice cup of tea — he couldn't be doing with that bitter coffee they made in the kitchen — and put his feet up.

It must have been twenty minutes later, just when he was settling down for his next cat-nap, that he heard the screaming.

As Ted told his proud wife and admiring neighbours the next morning, at least he knew what to do, being a retired policeman. He had checked that The Pole was dead — not that there was much doubt about that, with a gash across his throat like the Grand Canyon. He had dialled 999 and asked for the police, giving just the right amount of detail with succinct efficiency. He had taken a cursory look round for the weapon without success. He had told the brown-haired girl sharply not to touch anything further, had washed the blood off her shaking hands at the kitchen sink and made her drink a nice cup of hot sweet tea while they waited for the sirens and while he phoned his cousin at the nightdesk at the *Daily Mirror*.

It was shortly after midnight and the desk sergeant at Hopbridge police station had just sent a constable down to the canteen for some more coffee. You didn't expect much action in Hopbridge on the nightshift on a weekday.

The door to the waiting room was controlled by a buzzer. People who wanted an audience with the sergeant after dark had to ring a bell and he would buzz them in. There was no one in the waiting room and hadn't been for the past two hours.

166

As he stood there, wondering whether he should have added a bacon sandwich to his canteen order, he heard the outer door swing open with considerable force and there was a frantic pounding on the inner door as whoever it was ignored or didn't see the bell. Sergeant Nicholson peered cautiously out. The face pressed desperately up against the door was that of a girl of about twelve and was streaked with earth and tears. He buzzed her in without further delay.

'It was him!' she yelled. She banged on the desk and he realised that it was anger and excitement which was driving her rather than terror.

'Calm down, love.'

'Can't you hear me, you wally' She wiped her coat sleeve across her mucky face. 'It was the Riverside Rapist. I fought him off. And don't call me "love".'

Nicholson was in action at once. This was his big moment.

'Where?'

'In the park. By the north-east exit. Ten minutes ago. I ran all the way here.'

'Did you get a good look at him?'

'He wore a woolly hat, a balaclava, to hide his face. He was medium height, quite heavy build. Dressed all in dark clothes –'

Nicholson was already on the radio although he knew that ten minutes was too long and the rapist would be gone. He called for all patrol cars and all beat constables to look out for a frightened man matching the description.

'Sit down, love ... miss. I'll get the Inspector in charge of the case out of bed. He'll want to talk to you. You're sure you're not ... hurt?'

'He didn't rape me if that's what you mean. I put up such a fight he took fright and ran off. I'm a bit bruised but that's all.'

'I'll get the doctor to give you the once over all the same. Just as soon as Mr Trevellyan's talked to you.' Nicholson picked up the telephone to call Nick. 'What's your name?' he asked.

'Ginny Miller,' Ginny said.

'Give me your address and telephone number. Your parents must be worried sick.'

Nicholson got through to Nick at his flat without difficulty. Nick said he would be there in ten minutes. Then he efficiently rang the Millers, found the collapsing Ginny a comfortable seat and a kindly WPC and ordered her the inevitable cup of hot, sweet tea.

'Can I clean myself up a bit?' Ginny asked miserably. Her first excitement had faded and she realised that she was cold and filthy and starting to shiver.

'Not just yet,' WPC Myra Greenslade explained. 'He might have left something on you – some of his blood, even, if you managed to scratch him. I can't tell you how valuable that would be to us.'

'But what the hell were you doing in the park at night?' Shirley said in fury. 'I could shake you, Ginny. How could you take such a risk?'

Ginny had had her nails cleaned by a professional. Then she'd been allowed to scrub up in the women's changing rooms and found some clean clothes to borrow while hers were bundled into a plastic bag and joined the nail scrapings in the evidence pile.

Now she was in Nick's office. Since she wasn't under seventeen, despite appearances to the contrary, Nick had asked her parents politely to wait outside. He didn't need their panicky recriminations to impede his investigations. He didn't need Shirley's either. This latest attack, given that the plucky girl wasn't hurt, might be the best piece of news he'd had in a week.

The patrol cars had not been able to find anyone answering the rapist's description and it was assumed that the ten minute delay had given him enough time to get home.

'What were you thinking of?' Shirley asked again.

'I was late.' Ginny looked briefly sulky. 'I promised to be in by midnight. I got held up and I didn't want Mum to be worried since she always waits up for me. It's a short cut. I thought I would be okay. I thought I knew how to take care of myself after your class last night.'

Nick looked at Shirley. He would have looked superior if

168

he'd known how. Instead he looked sympathetic which only made her feel more guilty than she did already. She sat down on his desk with a sigh. He laid a hand on her shoulder and squeezed.

'And I was right!' Ginny concluded triumphantly. 'I did just what you said, Shirley. He grabbed me from behind with his hand across my mouth to stop me screaming. I brought my heel down really hard on his instep which made him let go. Then I turned round and got him straight in the eyes with some black pepper I've been carrying around in my pocket all day, and than I ran like hell. And I didn't stop running until I got to the police station.'

'You were *lucky*,' Nick told her, 'rather than right. Did he say anything at any time during the attack.'

'When I hurt his foot he said something like "Shit!" or "Bitch!" — just what you'd expect. Then again when he got the pepper in his eyes.'

'Not enough to identify an accent, I suppose?'

Ginny looked doubtful. 'Not that I heard.'

'Any idea where he came from?'

'It must have been a clump of bushes I'd just passed. I was keeping a good lookout, since I was a bit nervous. I didn't hear a sound. He came up behind me without a sound.'

'You must be exhausted,' Nick said. 'Have a quick word with the doctor and then I'll let your mum and dad take you home and put you to bed. Tomorrow morning you can come out to the park with me and show me the exact place.' He offered her his hand and after a moment's hesitation she realised what he meant, took his hand and shook it vigorously up and down.

'You're a very brave and a very stupid young woman,' he told her.

Ginny smiled weakly and then burst into tears.

Chapter Nineteen

When Bernie Ackroyd told people he was a policeman they assumed he meant constable or, at best, sergeant. They also took it for granted that he was, if not exactly bent, one of those coppers who had spent so much time in the company of criminals that he was no longer quite sure where the border lay. All of which said a good deal more about them than it did about Detective Superintendent Ackroyd.

Admittedly Ackroyd was a rough-looking man with an unreconstructed East End accent and a face which said that he'd seen it all; heard it all. Jewish by birth, though not by inclination, he had, at forty-one, lost belief in anything but the roughest sort of justice.

He had joined the Metropolitan Police at twenty and had risen through the ranks just about as rapidly as was possible for someone not in the fast stream. He suspected that his accent, his lack of social graces and his inability to play golf or roll up his trouser leg would prevent further promotion; but since higher rank meant more desk work, since his Superintendent's salary had allowed him to move Linda and the kids out of Bermondsey and into a nice little estate in Finchley, since his pension would keep him warm in his old age, he was not complaining. His work was his main hobby although he also played a mean game of poker.

He had commandeered Philip's office on his arrival at Orion and was now looking across the desk at his sergeant, savouring the feeling that the thrill of the chase was about to begin.

Detective Sergeant Steve 'Morrie' Morrison was about the

170

same age as his boss and came from a similar background but lacked the drive. People were inclined to describe him, to his irritation, as 'nice'. No one ever described Bernie Ackroyd as 'nice'.

But there were moments when Morrie, too, felt as if he had tasted blood.

'So,' Ackroyd began, 'it's down to one of our little band of staff, as far as I can see. That should make life easy.'

'A closed circle of suspects,' his sergeant agreed eagerly, 'just like one of those old-time detective novels.'

Ackroyd didn't reply. He didn't need to. The contemptuous twist of his mouth was enough. 'You need one of those magnetic cards to get into the – what do they call it? – the computer room,' he continued. 'In fact, you need one to get into the whole bloody building.'

'Someone could have lost one or had one stolen,' Morrison interrupted.

'And,' Ackroyd went on more loudly, 'a code number.'

'Which was 1234,' Morrison pointed out. 'It wouldn't take a genius to work that out.'

'Good point.' Ackroyd was a fair man. He grinned suddenly. 'You're not quite brain-dead yet, Morrie.'

'So – '

'However, let's think this through. If someone from outside found a card lying in the gutter, sneaked in and killed Zaca ... Zacaz ... Bugger it! It's always helpful when you can pronounce the victim's name.'

'They called him Zac.'

'Fine by me. Killed Zac – then we're looking for a homicidal maniac and I don't give much for our chances. So let's forget that scenario. Say someone steals one, right, never mind how for the moment. The front door's locked at six o'clock, magnetic card or no magnetic card. So, he has to let himself in during the day and hide out until later that night. Right? Where? The night watchman was doing his rounds.'

'So he says.'

'You checked him out?'

'West End Central say he's a lazy bugger but as straight as they come.'

'Good. That's that out of the way. Although I have my own suspicions as to who it was tipped off the press so fast.'

Ackroyd didn't like the fourth estate, nor they him. They liked to portray him as the unacceptable face of modern policing: a slow-witted philistine who'd just as soon beat a confession out of the obvious suspect as put himself out finding the real criminal. None of these things was true of Ackroyd but he wasn't photogenic and he was aware that the camera made him look like a thug. The press were surrounding the building this morning and he knew they'd taken several unflattering shots which he would be forced to wince over in tomorrow's papers.

He shrugged the press off his broad shoulders and went on. 'So, we assume for the moment that Cleary did his round on the hour from the time he locked the front door at six o'clock, the way he says. There were these people working on the fourth floor and coming down to the ground floor to make themselves coffee every five minutes if I know office workers.'

'He hid in one of the toilets,' Morrison suggested.

'And going to the bog every five minutes as a consequence of all the coffee. They had to come up and down the stairs since the lift was out of order so they passed every landing, every office, and every bog in the building.'

'As I said,' Morrison pointed out, 'a closed circle.'

'You may be right, Morrie. You and your wretched "locked-room" stories. Cleaners?'

'They don't have cardkeys. The night watchman lets them in early in the morning and counts them all out later. They don't go into the computer room in case they damage something.'

'The modern legend of the cleaner who almost starts World War Three by plugging her hoover in?'

Morrison looked blank. 'Whatever. I don't know anything about these wretched machines.'

'Let's start fetching them in,' Ackroyd said. 'Who's this bint who found the body?'

'Girl called Mary Lewis. Address in Ronalds Road off the Holloway Road. Bedsits.'

'Bedsit? I thought they all earned a fortune, these computer wizards.'

'She's freelance. A bird of passage, I'd say. No husband, no boyfriend – alone in the world.'

'Is that so? How did she seem?'

'Shocked, but keeping a stiff upper lip.'

'Let's see if we can get that lip trembing a bit, then, shall we?'

Alison was more inclined to bite her lower lip as Sergeant Morrison led her into the office. She always did that when she was thinking. Should she admit that she wasn't Mary Lewis? She knew what Nick would say: Tell them the truth, the whole truth and nothing but the truth, and tell it to them *now*.

In English law you could call yourself whatever you wanted: you could be Alice Adams on Monday, Barbara Brown on Tuesday, Cathy Clark on Wednesday ... Denise Duffy on Thursday.

For Christ's sake, Alison, pull yourself together.

Except that the police looked with the utmost suspicion at anyone whose name differed – in the slightest phoneme – from their birth certificate, without a bloody good reason. After all, why should any law-abiding citizen want to masquerade under an alias?

At her first sight of Bernie Ackroyd, Alison relaxed. He looked like a used car salesman. In his grating East End accent he introduced himself and his sergeant and invited her to take a seat. She answered him graciously and did so.

Posh voice, Ackroyd thought. Didn't really go with the rest of her. He could tell that she wasn't planning to invite him to any Hunt Balls. People were inclined to underestimate Ackroyd. It was his principal strength.

Alison sat and looked at him with less certainty. He was a Detective Superintendent, after all, and you didn't get to that rank by being thick. But then so was the notorious Ted Seymour, whom Nick had once described as the sort of General who gets shot by his own side. Alison had never met Seymour who was, like Bertie Wooster's Aunt Agatha, an invisible menace, but even Nick, she remembered, had never accused him of being thick.

It would be so much easier to remain Mary Lewis for the time being.

'So, you're the one who found the body,' Ackroyd stated. 'Mary Lewis.'

Alison's instinct told her to trust him completely.

'Can we talk about that?' she said.

The Chief Inspector's mind wasn't on the matter in hand this morning, Shirley thought with irritation. He'd been perfectly normal when she'd picked him up at his flat in her car at eight, accepting with modest pleasure her congratulations on his now public elevation and promising a celebratory drink as soon as the rapist was behind bars.

Then he'd asked her to stop at the bus station on their way to Ginny's house so he could pick up a morning paper. He had come back looking anxious and pale and since then she had addressed several remarks to him without any sign that he'd heard a word she was saying.

Ginny had recovered her spirits after a good night's sleep − Dr Brewster had given her a mild sedative. She was enjoying the day off school, the momentary fame, and was looking forward to dining out for the next few months on the full inside story of how she'd fought the Riverside Rapist and won.

They parked by the north-east gate to the park and Ginny led them easily to the spot where the attack had taken place.

'I ran off to the exit, and I'm certain he ran off in that direction.' She pointed towards the water meadows. The Scene of Crime team had already marked off a wide area with white tape and Shirley directed them to the clump of bushes which seemed the rapist's most likely hiding place. He was a little nearer the exit than last time.

Nick stood staring across the meadows, his newspaper folded under his arm. Strangely, he had bought a tabloid this morning as well as his usual *Times* and Shirley could make out the bizarre headline: 'Cutthroat Dealings in the City of London!' She hadn't been aware that Nick was interested in high finance.

'Sir?' Nick didn't hear. 'Sir!'

'What?' He forced his mind back with an effort of will from the City of London to Riverside Park. 'Found anything?'

'The mixture as before,' Shirley reported with a shrug. 'Footprints, size nine. Torn blades of grass. These bushes aren't as prickly as the other lot. He may not have left any fibres this time.'

'Let's leave them to it,' Nick said. 'See what they come up with. Ginny, you've done a great job. Someone will run you round to school now.' Her face fell. 'There won't be anything interesting happening here, I promise you.' He told a young constable to drive her and Ginny went obediently off.

'What now?' Shirley asked.

'We're going to talk to a few of my favourite suspects,' Nick said, 'and see where they claim to have been at midnight last night. But first I have to make a telephone call.'

He got Shirley to stop the car at the nearest call box and rang the office number Alison had given him. He was answered by an assured constabulary voice which said the office was closed owing to unforeseen circumstances and asked insistently for his name and business. Nick hung up without disclosing either, feeling strangely guilty.

He then rang Alison's home number which he knew to be a pay-phone on the landing outside her room.

She was just unlocking her door when the phone rang. Ackroyd had finished with her for the time being, had taken her statement and fingerprints and told her brusquely to go home and stay there. Philip had protested loudly at having his fingerprints taken but it was not the first time Alison had suffered this messy indignity and she had made no fuss.

She picked the telephone up and said 'Hello' with as little expression in her voice as possible. She was not surprised to find that it was Nick, recognising him from his first hesitation as if his very breathing were known to her. She had noticed the glaring headlines on her way home and had been expecting some reaction.

'May I speak to Mary Lewis, please?'

Alison replied in a passable London accent: 'I'll just see if she's in.' She made some convincing off-stage sound effects of knocking on a door and waiting before picking up the

175

receiver again. 'I'm afraid she doesn't seem to be here right now. Can I take a message?'

'Yes, please. Tell her Nick rang. Tell her to be careful. Tell her I love her.'

'Will do.' Alison hung up without further comment. She knew he knew. He knew she knew he knew.

He'd done his best. He got back in the car and Shirley drove them round to the O'Sheas' house in complete silence.

Tessa O'Shea had worked the nightshift at the hospital again and was just getting ready for bed when Nick and Shirley knocked on her door that morning. It was Kevin who answered the door and he led them into the kitchen without a word. Tessa was sitting at the formica-topped table drinking a cup of what looked like cocoa. Neither detective, having done their share of nightshifts in their uniformed days, found this in the least incongruous.

'Not at work, Mr O'Shea?' Nick asked pleasantly. 'What is your job, by the way?' O'Shea mumbled something inaudible. 'I'm sorry. I didn't catch that.'

'Nothing. I said I don't do nothing.'

'He's on the dole,' Tessa elaborated. 'Social security.'

'Have you no trade?' Nick asked. O'Shea shook his head. 'I'd like to know where you were at around midnight last night, Kevin.'

'Why?' Tessa looked up from her mug. 'There hasn't been another ... No, I would have heard about it. They'd have brought her to the hospital.

'Attempted rape,' Shirley said. 'The intended victim was too much for him. She got away.'

Tessa sighed. 'Thank God.'

'She may have hurt his foot,' Nick said. 'He may be walking with a slight limp this morning.' Everybody glanced at O'Shea who seemed to have no difficulty in walking. 'He would have come home muddy and dishevelled and probably in a bit of a panic.' His voice rose and took on an unaccustomed bullying tone. 'You haven't answered my question, Kevin.'

'I was here. In bed,' O'Shea said finally. 'I went to bed at about eleven.'

'Do you own a balaclava?' Kevin stared before shaking his head. 'What size shoes do you take?'

'Nine.'

'I'd like to see your shoes and boots, please.'

He pointed towards the kitchen. 'Out the back.' Nick nodded to Shirley. She pulled the sketch of the boot soles from her pocket and went out through the tiny kitchen into a rear lobby where coats hung and shoes sprawled higgledy-piggledy on the floor.

'We got some skin scrapings from under the girl's nails,' Nick lied. 'You probably know that it's now possible to do what we call genetic fingerprinting. We'll be taking blood samples from all the young men in the valley and matching them to the skin. It's accurate to one in several million.'

O'Shea looked back at him blankly. Either he was innocent or he knew that his skin had not been scratched. He had not glanced down at his hands as Nick spoke of scratches either, as a guilty man might be expected to do. What had he wanted? A sudden grovelling confession? He knew that it didn't usually happen that way.

But there was something so bovine and slow about O'Shea that he might not really have taken in Nick's words. But then he still had that alibi for the Liz Parrish attack. Also he didn't quite fit that damned profile. Nor did he fit Pauline Taylor's description. But, and this was a very interesting but, he did fit Ginny's. So many contradictory buts.

They had interviewed Pauline and Ginny again after going over both statements. Each girl stuck unshakably to her description. The Riverside Rapist was a tall-short, slim-stocky man. All they agreed on was that he was young and silent and wore a balaclava. The prospect of two rapists on the loose was almost more than he could bear. And in the Hop Valley, where no rape had been reported in three years, it was a coincidence he was not prepared to accept.

Shirley came back into the room and shook her head.

'You want a blood sample from Kevin?' Tessa asked Nick.

'Among others.'

Kevin shrugged indifferently.

'How long do the tests take?' Tessa asked. 'To check, I mean.'

Nick hesitated before reluctantly admitting: 'About three weeks.' There was still a chance that the SOCOs might come up with a hair from the park. They'd be able to fingerprint on that. Failing that it would have to be Pauline Taylor's growing baby.

Chapter Twenty

'I don't believe it,' Bernie Ackroyd said.

It was past two, he was hungry and more than a little irritated by the well-dressed man in front of him who looked like someone who'd had a decent lunch. 'You're telling me that you put both these people, this Alison Hope and ... what's his name? ... Gerry Walsh, in here together to look for this fraudster of yours and neither of them knew that the other was doing the same job?'

Philip nodded miserably. Bernie blew a loud exasperated noise out of the side of his mouth.

'Explain.'

'I'd asked Alison to help,' Philip said uncomfortably. 'I really couldn't think of anyone else at the time. Then, just as she was all set to start work, Gerry turned up out of the blue from the States. He's an old ... mate ... and as clever as they make them so I roped him in to help. But I couldn't just put Alison off after all the trouble I'd gone to to get her. And I couldn't tell either of them the truth in case they thought I was an awful fool.' He hesitated then added, 'I feel like an awful fool.'

'Yes, Mr Hunter.' Bernie wasn't about to disagree with this self-assessment. 'Major fraud is usually considered a job for the police, you know.'

'I know.'

'Am I to take it that neither of these friends of yours is the fraudster, then? The person you call "The Hacker"?'

'Absolutely not.' Philip looked shocked.

'I was a bit short of motive until I talked to your Alison

179

Hope this morning. I'm now working on the hypothesis that Zac had rumbled your hacker.' He stopped short as a horrible thought hit him. 'You're not about to tell me that he was looking for the hacker on your behalf too, I hope.'

Philip shook his head. 'Hardly. I think I'd have called him my prime suspect.'

'So we assume that he rumbled the hacker by accident, perhaps caught him red-handed in the computer room last night.'

Philip shrugged. 'The hacking has all been done from remote terminals. It'd be a pretty foolhardy hacker who'd try anything from our own operator's console. Why take the risk?'

'And you back up Alison Hope's story that she went into the computer room just before half-past nine to try to locate the hacker, using this operator's console?'

'Not specifically. I mean, if that's what she says, it's perfectly likely.' He shrugged. 'We haven't been in touch since she first arrived in London, we thought it would be too risky. I didn't know what her next move was likely to be.'

'But Zac might also have stumbled on the hacker when he was sitting there using the console?'

'He might easily. And not much gets ... got past him. Look, Superintendent, is anything about this fraud going to have to become public?'

'Depends if it has a bearing on the murder,' Bernie replied. 'If it has, then it will come out at the trial.'

'I've worked so hard to keep it quiet,' Philip said in dismay.

'Well, look on the bright side.' Bernie spoke coldly. 'Perhaps your hacker will panic and give up now he's blundered into murder.'

'That's true.' The idea was new to Philip – and welcome – and he smiled.

'Where were you between nine-fifteen and nine-thirty last night?' Bernie asked.

'Me!' The smile disappeared in an instant.

'Purposes of elimination,' Bernie said blandly.

'I was at home all yesterday evening.'

Bernie examined the pad in front of him where he had

180

been doodling some round shapes which might have been breasts. 'You live in the Barbican?'

'That's right.'

'Just five minutes' walk from here.'

'What am I supposed to be doing?' Philip asked angrily. 'Hacking my own system, robbing my own clients blind and destroying my own livelihood? Then murdering anyone who gets in my way?'

'Was anyone with you?' Bernie continued, as if Philip hadn't spoken.

'Yes, as a matter of fact. I have a friend staying at the moment. Gerry Walsh, as it happens.'

'You didn't think it too risky to be in touch with Mr Walsh then,' Bernie queried sharply. Philip shrugged again. His shrugs were beginning to get on Ackroyd's nerves. He gritted his teeth and made a conscious effort not to dislike the man too much. But he was picking up the clear message that Hunter was much more worried about news of the fraud leaking out than about the death of a colleague.

'What time did Mr Walsh get in?' he asked.

'Not long after six-thirty. We had a drink and some supper, watched a video. We were just about to go to bed when your people rang me at about eleven.'

'Neither of you went out, even for a few minutes.'

'Absolutely not.'

'It seems you and Mr Walsh alibi each other nicely then.'

Bernie looked across the desk at a young woman of about twenty-two who would have been attractive if it hadn't been for those hyperthyroid eyes and bad skin. She sat composedly, her hands still in her lap, waiting for him to speak.

'You are Jennifer Tatton?' He checked her address. He had sent Morrie off to interview all the other lessees of the building although they were mostly nine-to-five people and Bernie did not expect any real help from them. In Morrie's place he had DC Terry Rawlinson to take notes. He didn't care much for Rawlinson who had a reputation for being a cheeky young sod. But he was frightened of Bernie Ackroyd

181

and uncharacteristically restrained in his presence. Also he could take shorthand.

'I understand from Mr Hunter that you're on some sort of course this week,' Bernie said. 'So you're not actually in the office.'

'I'm doing the SSADM course,' Jennifer replied. 'Along with my colleague, William Marks. It's a two-week course. We're missing some of it now.'

Rawlinson had written down 'Sadism Course'. He examined his own shorthand and looked up, puzzled.

'SSADM?' Bernie queried.

'It's a systems design methodology,' Jennifer explained leaving him not much the wiser.

'Interesting?'

'Only if we have very different definitions of the word, Superintendent.'

She was remarkably self-assured for her age, Bernie thought. One of her colleagues had been murdered in a particularly brutal manner and she sat here making put-down remarks to poor old Plod. Obviously his attempts to put her at her ease with a little small talk were superfluous.

'So where is this course being held?' he asked.

'Over Holborn way.'

'Within easy reach of here, then.'

'Certainly.'

'When were you last in the office, Miss Tatton?'

'On Friday. We left about six that evening.'

'We?'

'William and I. We share a flat so we come in and go home together.'

'Did you come to the office last night for any reason?'

'No.'

'What were you doing last night?'

'The course is quite intensive and we have a lot of homework to do. We didn't get away until after seven. We had a quick meal in a burger bar and then went straight home to do our homework. Then we went to bed.'

'Did either of you go out again?'

'No.'

'Does anyone else share the flat?'

'No. Just the two of us.'

'Can you think of any reason why anyone should want to murder Mr ... Zac?'

'He was an unpleasant man.'

'If all the unpleasant men in the world got murdered, I'd need a rather bigger police force at my disposal, Miss Tatton.'

She smiled for the first time. 'Point taken, Superintendent. I can't think of any specific reason but he was a bit of a snooper. I'm fairly sure that he used to go through people's desks when he was alone in the office, although I can't prove it. I realised early on that he was listening carefully to any personal telephone calls I made or took, eavesdropping on my conversations.'

'Now that is interesting.'

'He liked to think that he knew people's secrets because that would put them in his power. He had no friends and that was his method of relating to people, d'you see?'

'Very clearly. And I also see that you're suggesting he might have been blackmailing someone?'

'It wouldn't surprise me. But who, and about what, I have no idea.'

'Perhaps it *would* surprise you to know that somebody was "hacking" into the FIX system and stealing from clients, Miss Tatton.' He watched her reaction closely. Once he had his guilty hacker, the case was over, bar the paperwork.

'Surprise' was inadequate to express Jennifer's reaction. She was speechless for a moment then she said: 'But how?'

'I'm not a computer buff but, as I understand it, they're creating fraudulent accounts, pretending to have sold shares so the brokers then pay them out money at the end of the fortnightly account. Does that make sense?'

She nodded and said, 'It does surprise me. It surprises me very much.'

'I'd like you to keep that to yourself for the moment. Mr Hunter has been to great lengths ...' Bernie rolled his eyes briefly to the heavens. 'And I mean *great* lengths, to keep it quiet.'

'Very well.'

'Well, thank you, Miss Tatton. So, to sum up, between

183

nine-fifteen and nine-thirty you and Mr Marks were alone together in the flat you share?'

'That's correct.'

'And you're willing to sign a statement to that effect?'

'Certainly.'

He dismissed her. When she had gone he said:

'So if Zac stumbled on the hacker during his snooping, it's likely that he would have attempted to blackmail him or ask for a share of the proceeds rather than simply take what he knew to Hunter or to the police as any normal, law-abiding citizen would do. But he underestimated the hacker and the hacker quickly dealt with him.'

'With extreme prejudice!' Rawlinson was flattered at the Superintendent's sharing his thoughts with him and wanted to throw in his two-pennyworth.

Bernie, remembering that it was Rawlinson sitting beside him and not Morrie, sighed and stopped talking.

'Didn't take to her, sir,' Rawlinson ventured, emboldened by his boss's confidences. 'Cold, calculating sort.'

Bernie merely grunted. If there was one sort of witness he hated more than the ones who got his rank wrong and kept calling him 'Sergeant' or 'Inspector', more than the ones who called him 'Officer', it was the ones who addressed him continually as 'Superintendent'.

Morrie knew that.

'Do you really think Hunter might be behind the fraud?' Morrie asked his boss. It was later that afternoon and he had finished his own interviews.

Bernie sucked his teeth — a mannerism which drove his sergeant crazy. 'It's been known. Maybe the business isn't as flourishing as he makes out and he decided to take some cash and run.'

'Why would he put someone — two people actually — in to investigate, in that case?'

'To molify the defrauded clients? Stop them calling the police themselves? To be seen to be doing something if he was challenged? Get someone to ask around, find out just how sound Orion's financial footing is. After all, office space in this part of London doesn't come cheap. Nor do penthouses in the Barbican.'

'Shall I try the estate agents?' Morrie suggested. 'Make sure he's not got that flat on the market for a quick getaway.'

'Nice thinking, Morrie. I like it. Get Rawlinson on to both those jobs. Even he can't mess those up.'

Morrie made a quick telephone call then Bernie said, 'Remember that Hunter has a key to the front door. It's the only one apart from Cleary's. The only one owned by anyone connected with Orion, that is.'

'You're certain it's an inside job.'

'Certain sure.'

'Remember that Hunter has an alibi as well as a key.'

'We'll talk to Walsh about that. After I've talked to the women.'

Morrie said, 'What do you make of the Hope woman?'

'Instinct says she's straight.'

'She found the body,' Morrie pointed out. 'She was found beside it with blood on her hands. She was in the building and had access to the computer room.'

'All duly noted. Motive?'

'Erm ...'

'Perhaps it was a crime of passion,' Bernie answered himself with a laugh. 'She had the hots for Zac, sneaked into the computer room last night to throw herself at his head, got rejected and pulled a knife on him.'

'It has been known,' Morrie objected, echoing his boss's earlier comment.

'Fine. And what exactly did she do with the weapon in between stabbing him and being found with blood all over her hands. We've found no blood on the door handles or anywhere except in the computer room.'

'Oh, shit.'

'Is there any sign of the weapon yet?'

'Bottom of the Thames,' Morrie forecast gloomily. 'One thing for sure, it's not in the building.'

'Long walk to the river from here on a cold night. Get the sewers searched.

'Coo, you're going to be popular,' Morrie remarked. 'And what will it tell us when we've got it? Whoever did this murder is pretty cool. You don't seriously imagine he'll have left his prints on it.'

'All in a day's work,' Bernie said, 'and you never know. People panic.'

He stood looking out of the window onto the street, his hands thrust moodily in his pockets. It was four o'clock and already dusk and the rush hour had started early − the street below bristled with damp people and umbrellas.

'A stroke of luck,' he murmured with a wry smile.

'What?' Morrie asked.

'The boundary with the City runs down the middle of this street. If this office block had been on the South side of the street, it would have been the City of London Police's baby. Rotten luck, eh?'

'You could have been out on the golf course with the Deputy Commissioner all day instead,' Morrie said sarcastically. 'Sir.'

Bernie laughed and put his arm round his sergeant's shoulders. 'You're right, Morrie. It's not rotten luck at all. And we're neither of us quite brain-dead yet. Bring the next female in.'

Morrie went out and returned with Ruth Harper. She took a seat and Bernie asked her for her movements the previous evening.

'I went straight home from seeing a client. 'She crossed her legs and Bernie looked at them with a connoisseur's appreciation. Here was a really attractive woman: petite, blonde, well-dressed, low-pitched voice. She was sexy without being obvious about it − just the way he liked them.

Morrie checked her address. 'You share a house with a Carl Forster, I believe?' She nodded. It was her house and Carl lived there rent free but she didn't feel inclined to spell that out to these two policeman. She could see that the senior one fancied her. She hitched her skirt up a little higher − you used what weapons you had to smooth the path of life and making men want you was one of the best weapons Ruth knew.

'I got home at about six-thirty,' she said. 'I nipped round to Marks and Spencer in Camden Town to get something for my supper since Carl was out that evening and I knew

186

he wouldn't be eating in. I got home again at about quarter past seven, stuck the food in the microwave and ate it. Then I had a bath, listened to a bit of music and read a book. Then Carl got in, rather earlier than I'd expected, at about ten-fifteen.'

And in a filthy temper.

'Did you go out again?' Bernie asked.

'I didn't even bother to get dressed after my bath. I sat around in my dressing gown.' She looked Bernie straight in the eye and tried to telepath to him an image of her in her flimsy silk dressing gown. Bernie's imagination was more than equal to the task and he smiled.

'Did anyone call at the house or telephone?' he asked, when he'd finished his little fantasy.

'I'm afraid I was rather naughty, Superintendent.' Ruth giggled. 'I unplugged the phone and put the answering machine on. I often do if I'm alone at night. Most of the calls are for Carl – he's a journalist, you see.' And she was sick of telling other women that he wasn't there. 'I heard the machine go on a couple of times but they both turned out to be hang-ups. I find that so infuriating, don't you?'

'I usually manage to answer the phone, if I'm in,' Bernie replied tersely. It wasn't that her story was implausible – just that it was inconvenient. And he hated grown, sober, women who giggled. 'Where was Mr Forster, by the way?'

'He said he had a union meeting at the office at six-thirty and that he'd go for a pizza with some of the other reporters afterwards.' And when she'd rung the offices of *Computing Tomorrow* on first arriving home at half-past six, there'd been no reply.

'So,' she opened her eyes wide, 'I have no alibi, Superintendent.'

'No, miss,' Bernie agreed, disliking her more with each moment that passed. What was she? Late-thirties? Someone ought to tell her that the little girl act didn't suit her anymore. 'Did you like Zac?'

'Not much. No one did. Although Carl didn't seem to mind him, said he was "good value". He used to enjoy winding him up.'

'So they were acquainted?'

187

'Oh, yes. I've been working here for ages even though I'm freelance. Philip says I've got a job at Orion for as long as I want it.'

'That's nice. Were you aware that Mr Hunter was concerned about some hacking that was going on?'

'On FIX?' Ruth stared at him. Then she smiled. This sounded like a scoop. Tonight she could be sure of Carl's full attention. She wanted to get as much detail as she could.

'He said nothing to me. What sort of hacking?'

'Theft. Creating false accounts on stockbroker's files.'

'Ingenious,' Ruth breathed. 'I had no idea.'

Chapter Twenty-One

Jilly MacAlistair was the first person Bernie had talked to who seemed genuinely upset by Zac's death. She had arrived for work as usual at about eight that morning, not having read a morning paper or heard the radio news, to be taken, apparently, unawares by the scene of chaos which greeted her.

She was sitting in front of him now, quietly despondent. A few tears dribbled from her eyes and she did not bother to wipe them away. She wore no make-up to be damaged by the tears. She was not an attractive woman but somehow he warmed to her more than to the Harpie — Bernie smiled at his own little pun — who had a quality of desperation about her which repelled.

'You seem to have known Zac better than anyone,' he said.

'I suppose Duncan and I were his best friends,' Jilly agreed. 'Perhaps his only friends.'

'Everyone says he was a . . . ' Bernie hestitated, not wanting to hurt her feelings ' . . . temperamental sort of bloke. Not easy to know.'

'You mean he was a bad-tempered, cantankerous old sod?' Jilly gave him a little smile.

'Well, yes.'

'I can imagine they've all been telling you that and it was true, I suppose. But he wasn't always like that. Fifteen, sixteen years ago, at university, he was a happy young man with all his life ahead of him. Now's he's dead.' She paused. 'I can't quite take it in.'

'It's always like that in a case of sudden death,' Bernie told her kindly.

'It never happened to me before, you see, no one close to me ever died before. I keep expecting him to walk through that door and ask why no one's getting any bloody work done today.'

Bernie wished he would, then he could tell them who'd done it.

'Can you tell me what happened to change Zac from that happy young man to the curmudgeon I've been hearing about?'

'A series of disappointments. The sort of things that happen to a lot of people only they manage to cope. Zac didn't. He became bitter.'

Bernie leant back in his chair. 'Tell me about it.'

'He was a bit older than me and Duncan, had been out in the world working for a couple of years before coming to university. We were both straight out of school and as naive as could be so we rather looked up to him. He enjoyed that, being seen as a sort of mentor. And he was academically brilliant. Duncan was bright too, of course, but he had to work quite hard at it. I was just there to enjoy myself and get a good enough degree to make a decent career for myself. Zac came effortlessly top in every exam.'

'So what happened?'

'He fell in love. In fact they were engaged. This was at the start of our final year. I could never see it working, myself. He was working-class and had a bit of a chip on his shoulder. She, Amanda, was home countries, private school. I suppose she fancied a bit of rough for a while. This was the early seventies, before anyone had even heard of Maggie Thatcher, and all the old sixties stuff about working-class credibility and middle-class guilt was still fashionable.'

'Only in middle-class universities,' Bernie observed.

'Anyway, she broke off the engagement halfway through the final year and Zac just went to pieces. He had a sort of breakdown and almost failed his finals. In fact he got a third on the strength of some continuous assessment work he'd done earlier in the year. But all his dreams were gone: marriage to Amanda, first class honours, a

190

few years of research and a comfortable niche as a lecturer.'

'It was bad luck,' Bernie said. 'But, as you pointed out earlier, similar things happen to a lot of people and they don't let it ruin their lives.'

'Well Zac did. Oh, there were times when he could be quite manic, almost like the old Zac. I remember at our wedding, he was Duncan's best man, he made a very funny and rude speech, drank lots of champagne, danced and flirted with the bridesmaids. When we got back from our honeymoon he was back on the bottom again.'

'And you and your husband have kept in touch with him all these years?'

'On and off. Since he came to work at Orion, naturally, we've seen more of him.'

'Would you say he had any enemies?'

Jilly thought about it. 'Hardly anybody liked him but he didn't let anyone get close enough to become an enemy.'

'Were there any women in his life, to your knowledge?'

'Not for years.'

'You've worked on FIX for a long time,' Bernie said, changing tack.

'Since the start.'

'Would it surprise you if I told you that FIX was being hacked into, that clients were being robbed.'

'Not really.' Morrie looked up from his notes and both policemen waited for her to continue.'

'You knew about it?' Bernie said. She was the first person he'd interviewed who was willing to admit to it.

'Not to say *know*. I could see that Philip was very worried about something. I knew that he'd asked the clients to change all their passwords and to be very careful who they told them to. I know that he got the dial-up numbers changed. I'm not a complete fool − I can add two and two.'

'Did you speak to Mr Hunter about it?'

'I thought if he wanted to confide in me, he would.'

'And did you know that Mr Hunter thought it was an inside job?'

'It was a fair bet. It usually is.'

'Had you any idea who the culprit might be?'

'If I'd had to lay a bet on it yesterday, I'd have said Zac. Now, I'm rather baffled. All I know is that it isn't me, since that's presumably what you're getting at.'

'Can I ask you where you were last night, Mrs MacAlistair?'

'Certainly. I play in an orchestra on Tuesday nights, in Ealing. I took the Central Line straight there, arriving at about a quarter to seven, as usual. I left at a quarter to nine and went straight home, getting in shortly after nine. Duncan was in, up in his study working on his Apple. Neither of us went out again.'

'That's very clear, Mrs MacAlistair. Thank you. One last thing. Of all the people involved in this project, or connected with it, who would Zac have let into the computer room, turned his back on, not been afraid of?' The most obvious answer to this, he realised, was either of the MacAlistairs.

'All of us,' Jilly said. 'He would not have cared to let anyone see that he was afraid to turn his back on them. Besides, he believed he was cleverer than everyone else, that he could outwit anyone in the world.'

Bernie liked the look of Gerry Walsh, there was something there that he recognised − Walsh was his own man. He came into Philip's office, sat straight down, crossed one long, booted leg over the other knee, folded his arms and waited to find out what Bernie Ackroyd wanted of him.

'Mr Hunter's been telling me about this hacker,' Bernie said, 'the one you were put in here to find.'

'Uh huh.'

'Were you making any progress? Did you have any idea who the hacker was?'

'Nothing but a string of hunches.'

'Hunches?' Morrie repeated.

'I've been around,' Gerry told him. 'Worked and travelled all over. Europe, Australia, America. I size people up quickly. Most people you can read like a book.'

'Got my measure?' Ackroyd asked him.

'Yeah, I think so. You look like a gangster but your mind

twists and turns as quickly as a ballet dancer – and as gracefully.'

'So tell me who you suspected,' Bernie said, amused at the compliment.

Gerry shook his head. 'It wouldn't be fair. Yes, I've got your measure: you've knocked around too, seen it all. You'll form your own judgements. Anything I could say would just muddy the waters. I hadn't a scrap of proof for my suspicions – just a working knowledge of human nature.'

'Okay. Tell me: what did that working knowledge tell you about Zac?'

'That he was an unhappy man.'

Bernie was surprised. 'That differs a bit from the usual view.'

'An unhappy, disappointed man,' Gerry enlarged. 'And a snooper – an embryo, if not an actual, blackmailer. Obviously Zac had found out who the hacker was and the hacker killed him rather than pay up.'

'Apparently. Did you know that the woman you knew as Mary Lewis had been put into Orion by Mr Hunter to do the same job you're doing?'

'Philip just told me that she's really Alison Hope, of Hope Software. But I already knew that she wasn't who she claimed to be; or that she wasn't *what* she claimed to be, shall we say.'

'Which was?'

'A dim little spinster who'd just come back from five years in Papua New Guinea.' He shook his head admiringly. 'Alison Hope: now that makes more sense.'

'What made you so sure she wasn't Mary Lewis?'

'She smelt wrong.' Gerry didn't enlarge on this cryptic comment and Ackroyd didn't need him to. He wasn't interested in Mary-Alison, anyway. He knew she hadn't killed Zac. She smelt wrong.

'Mr Hunter says you were at home with him all last night,' Ackroyd said. 'Is that right?'

'Absolutely right. I got to his place at about six-thirty and we didn't go out again.'

'I don't call him very helpful,' Morrison said when Gerry had gone. He resented Gerry's relaxed attitude – most people

193

had the decency to get agitated when questioned by the police. 'He could have told us who he suspected.'

'He's right. They're nothing but suspicions and would just have muddied the waters. He confirmed Hunter's alibi — that's the main thing.'

'We're not doing anything illegal, for heaven's sake!' Jennifer turned her protruding eyes on her anxious friend. She seldom blinked and her stare had the power to disconcert even those closest to her.

'Are you sure?' William bravely stood his ground, nibbling absently at a fingernail. 'Only, well, what with Zac being killed like that ...' He shuddered. He was a squeamish youth and slashed throats upset him.

'Who cares?'

Jennifer was not particularly squeamish but even she didn't want to visualise Zac's messy death so soon after lunch.

'That's a bit thick, Jennifer!'

'Honestly, William. Don't be such a hypocrite. We both of us hated Zac. And I mean "who cares?" literally too. He had no one, nobody liked him. Whoever ... disposed of him, did the world a favour, if you ask me.'

'How do we know what friends he might have had outside the office?'

'He hardly ever *was* outside the office. It was his life.' Jennifer resumed her typing. 'I'm not stopping now that I've got into Davenports at last. This is the big one. I have a hunch that the market's about to take a major swing. I can't be distracted by Zac, or by that comic-book policeman.'

'I don't think I'd call Ackroyd that,' William protested. 'He looked at me so hard, it was all I could do not to break down and confess everything.'

'There *isn't* anything to confess, William. What *did* you tell him anyway?'

'That we were both here together last night, of course.'

'It's useful that he's given us this half day's paid holiday anyway. I bet that's breaking Philip's heart.'

'Look, Jennifer, are you sure this isn't insider dealing, or something?'

'How can it be? By the time I see the transactions, they've

already been made, they're in the public domain. It just so happens that nobody else knows about them yet except the brokers. If I happen to see what the big institutions are buying and selling this afternoon, which way they think the market is going to swing, and act on that information in my own share-dealing in a way that other private investors can't, how can that possibly be illegal? Immoral, possibly. Illegal, no.'

'I suppose not.'

'These people, the insurance companies and pension funds, they're the people who make the markets — who cause them to shoot up or to go into free fall. They're the key to everything.'

'Which is probably immoral in itself,' William said, easing his conscience.

'The most we could be charged with is stealing electricity from Orion!'

'So which way is the market moving now?' William forgot his concern for Zac in his eagerness for new profit.

'We're heading for a crash, I'd say. Insular Insurance are selling heavily again this afternoon. My analysis shows that they've sold twenty percent of their assets and put the money on deposit, this week alone. And they're not untypical.'

'It makes sense, I suppose,' William admitted. 'My dad says the market went crazy after Big Bang, shooting up until the P/E ratings don't make sense any more. We're probably just about due for a major correction.'

'And the Stock Market started a new account on Monday. That's a bit of luck.'

'You're going to sell stock we haven't got, within the account?'

'That's right. Then we'll buy it at a much lower price next week.'

'Got a list of stock to sell?'

'Here.' She handed him a printout with about twenty company names on it and a column of figures set against each name. 'Sell the number of each share in column two. They each amount to about twenty thousand pounds worth so a ten percent downward correction will bring in about forty thousand pounds. Do it now.'

William picked up the telephone obediently.

'But why would anyone want to kill Zac?' he asked as he dialled their broker's number.

'I expect he was rude to them,' Jennifer said indifferently. 'Or perhaps he found out something he wasn't meant to know. He was a little weasel of a man. He often used to look at me with that smug expression which said he knew I'd been up to something and was gloating about knowing it, thinking that he could shop me at any time. It got right up my nose.'

'How d'you mean, "shop" you?' William replaced the telephone receiver. 'You just said we weren't doing anything illegal.'

'Nothing they can prosecute us for, silly, but Philip would certainly sack us if he found out and make sure we didn't get access to FIX again and that would be very inconvenient. We haven't made enough to retire on yet!'

'That's what I told Ruth, certainly.' Carl Forster pushed back his chair and stood up. 'Can we go somewhere a bit quieter, do you think?' He led the two policemen into an empty office across the corridor, took the telephone off the hook and sat down on the desk. Ackroyd and Morrison remained standing since any of the chairs the room offered would have put them lower than Forster and therefore at a disadvantage.

'Actually I had a date.' Forster shrugged. Bernie half-expected him to wink and say that they were all men of the world, weren't they, officer? He looked the type.

'So you weren't here at all that evening?' he said.

'Tuesdays are pretty quiet as it's the night we go to press, so all the work for that week's edition has been done and we're not getting panicky about the next one. We usually push off early that night. I left at six, met ... my friend ... for a quick drink in the Groucho, then took her for dinner at *L'Escargot* shortly after seven.'

'I hope you got your money's worth, sir,' Bernie said equably. he wasn't averse to a bit on the side himself but at least he had the decency to be furtive about it and to feel guilty afterwards.

Forster frowned. 'I wouldn't say that.'

'I'll have to know your friend's name, sir, since she's your alibi.'

'Alibi? For me? I thought you were just checking up on Ruth.'

'You're connected with Orion, obliquely, sir. You knew Zac.'

'All right. I'm sure I can rely on your discretion, since it can have no bearing on the case. Her name's Debbie Richards. She's a secretary at *Design Monthly*.' The policemen exchanged blank looks. 'It's a fashion magazine,' he explained.

'Address?'

'I'm afraid I don't know it. It turns out, you see, that she lives with her mum and dad. I wish she'd told me that before I shelled out for an expensive dinner. You can get hold of her at *Design*, though, in Old Compton Street.'

'And she was with you until what time?'

'About a quarter to nine. Then I suggested that we go back to her place and she dropped her little bombshell about living at home in Stanmore with Mummy and Daddy. Then we had a few words, and she stormed off moaning about that being all men were interested in.'

She'd known he lived with another woman – why the hell did she think he'd asked her out to dinner? To swop Grub Street gossip?

'And what did you do?'

'Ordered a cognac. Sulked a bit. Went home.'

'Leaving the restaurant at what time?'

'Nine?' Forster guessed. 'What time was the dastardly deed done?'

'Shortly before nine-thirty.'

'Meaning that I had time to get to Orion?'

'Miss Harper says that you didn't get home until after ten.'

'There was a hold-up on the Northern Line. An "incident" at Kennington. Why people can't commit suicide in a more considerate manner is beyond me.' He stood up. 'Want Debbie's phone number?'

'That won't really be necessary, sir,' Bernie said. 'Since

197

she isn't alibi-ing you for the relevant time. Did you kill Zac, Mr Forster?'

'No, I did not.'

'Any idea who might have done so, or why?'

'None at all.'

'Thank you. We'll be in touch if there's anything else.'

Chapter Twenty-Two

Nick was waiting for Alex Porter when he got home from his job at the garage at about six. Alex heard him out calmly then said:

'I was at a disco with my girlfriend until about eleven-thirty. Then we had a bit of a row and I left her there. God!' He remembered suddenly. 'I'm such a shit.'

'Why?' Nick asked.

'I left her to walk home alone. It might have been her. I said ... I said ...'

'What did you say?' Nick asked kindly. 'That you hoped the Riverside Rapist would get her?'

Alex stared at him as if he suspected him of witchcraft. 'How did you know?'

'Because people say things they don't mean in the heat of the moment. We wouldn't be human otherwise. It wasn't Sarah. You have nothing to reproach yourself with.'

'Thanks. I feel very ashamed though.'

'But you'll survive and live to apologise and make the quarrel up.' Alex shook his head doubtfully. 'So, where did you go next?'

'I rode my bike around for about three-quarters of an hour –'

'Where?'

'Up the valley, as far as Hopwood. Then along the top of the moors for a bit. Then back. I needed to cool off. I was hopping mad. Then I came home.'

'And what time was that.'

'About twelve-fifteen.'

Nick looked at Mrs Porter who said, 'I was in bed but I heard the front door go. It must have been about that time.'

'No earlier?' Nick made the treacherous offer. How sound was the alibi Mrs Porter had given Alex the first time round?

'No.' She smiled at him. 'I could easily say that it was a bit earlier if that was when the attack took place, but I don't need to. I have complete faith in my son's innocence, you see, Chief Inspector.' She put her arm round Alex who returned her embrace with warmth. 'Also I didn't bother to get up when he came in so I can't even tell you he wasn't muddy or dishevelled.'

'So I've no alibi,' Alex said, underlining the point. 'But then I didn't know I was going to need one.'

'Did anyone see you on your bike ride?'

Alex shook his head. 'Nasty cold night. I didn't see a soul. A couple of cars might have passed me along the valley road. Not even that on the moors. And they won't remember, will they? At best they'd be able to tell you they saw a motorbike. They won't be able to confirm it was mine.'

'Do you mind if my people take a look at the bike?'

Alex looked interested. 'You mean you might be able to tell from the mud on it where it went last night – confirm my story?'

'Something like that.' Nick smiled, liking the boy. 'You seem to have police work well taped.'

'Sarah used to tell us a bit about it, her dad being a policeman,' Mrs Porter said. 'She finds the scientific part very interesting. We always found her stories fascinating, didn't we, Alex?' He grunted sadly.

'Do you own a balaclava?' Nick asked.

'What? And look like a complete wally?'

'It can get pretty cold on a motorbike.'

'Even so.'

'Was that a "no", then?' Nick asked.

'No,' Mrs Porter said. 'He's never owned a balaclava.'

Alex also wore size nine shoes but, again, none of them matched the sketch the SOCOs had done. Nick was not surprised – the rapist must realise he'd left footprints. The boots he used for his nocturnal excursions would be well hidden − probably not even in the house.

He gave Alex the now familiar explanation about the skin samples. Alex glanced at his hands and held them out for inspection.

'I get scratched all the time at the garage. Then I get oil well rubbed into the scratches. It's a miracle I haven't got gangrene.'

'Are you willing to give me a blood sample?' Nick asked. Alex didn't fit his profile either − the boy was a skilled communicator, charming, able to attract a sensible, pretty girl like Sarah Deacon. But he fitted Pauline's description.

'Now?' Alex asked.

'Preferably.'

'Give me a minute to get changed.'

'I got on to London Transport at St James's, like you said,' Morrie told Bernie. 'There really was a suicide at Kennington last night, just before nine and it did cause a lot of problems on the Northern Line.'

'Okay,' Bernie said. 'But it doesn't prove anything. Say Forster sprints up to Tottenham Court Road tube station after he leaves the restaurant and gets the Central Line through to Bank. He could have been at Orion just before nine-thirty. He kills Zac, then goes to Moorgate to get the Northern Line home to Kentish Town. The Northern Line information service tells him there are delays owing to an earlier incident at Kennington. But he gets a train after a few minutes and arrives home at ten-fifteen. No problem.'

'It would have been a bit of a rush, getting there,' Morrie pointed out. 'It's a ten-minute walk from Bank station to Orion. And he had to be there a good bit before nine-thirty to get Zac to let him in, kill him, dispose of the weapon and be out of the building by the time Alison Hope came down.'

'He might have got a taxi. Put the word out. See if any of the cabbies picked up a fare last night from Soho to the City shortly after nine.'

'It's already in hand.' Morrie smiled with quiet satisfaction. 'Rawlinson's down there now. And the restaurant recognised him from my description and because they remember the girl he was with storming off in a temper. He left at about nine, just as he says.'

'So his alibi was for the wrong time and he knew there was no point in lying about it as the restaurant would remember him. If Harper had given him an alibi, I would have been very suspicious of it. The fact that she doesn't rather tells in his favour — like she's sure he's got nothing to hide, nothing to do with the murder, anyway. And then there's another point.'

'What?'

'If he was really hoping to bed this girl Debbie last night, then he wasn't expecting to be able to go to Orion and kill Zac.'

'Could he have gone on the spur of the moment, after the girl walked out on him?' Morrie suggested. 'Say he'd heard a rumour about the hacking on FIX and decided since he wasn't going to get his end away after all he might as well chase it up for this paper of his. If he was in a bad mood, that might just have tipped him over the edge into killing Zac.'

'Why did he go out on a dinner date armed with a bread knife?' Bernie asked. 'I've heard of bondage but I'd call that very kinky.'

'Ah. Now you've got me there.'

Nick dropped Alex off and sprinted round to the bus station to get the last edition of the newspapers, scanning them all for up-to-date news of the Orion murder. There was very little that was new since the early edition. The only thing which gave him any comfort was the report that Superintendent Bernie Ackroyd of the Metropolitan Police was in charge of the case.

He smiled with affection at the grainy photograph of Bernie, looking like a Mafia godfather with his double-breasted suit and heavy-weight boxer's shoulders, staring bovinely at the camera.

He walked slowly back to his office where he found Shirley on the telephone.

Thank you,' she said as he walked in. She hung up. 'Aldershot, sir.'

'They've taken their time.'

'It was a while back and we couldn't give them any dates. They think very highly of your Corporal Edwards, though. He certainly had no black marks on his discipline record.'

'Did you ask about the boxing?'

'Seems he got literally knocked out in the finals of a fly-weight competition against another army unit. He had mild concussion and was off work for three days.'

'No after effects?'

'None noticed. But he gave it up after that.'

'Any word about his wife?'

'June Edwards. It seems that he was married when he joined up in 1975 and still married when he was demobbed in 1978.'

'Did you get a D.O.B?' Nick asked.

'October 1953.'

'So he was twenty-two when he joined up. He married very young.'

'I expect that's why it failed,' said Shirley, who had read the statistics.

'Let's call it a night, then,' Nick said.

'What's our next move?'

'Let's see. I've got some phials of fairly useless blood since I've nothing to test it against at present. I think all we have left to do is that reconstruction I was talking about. Maybe some passer-by can explain this discrepancy between the two descriptions.

'There's rain forecast again for tomorrow night.'

'Tomorrow it is then. Ten o'clock. North-east gate. Tell Carol. We'll stick her in a Hopbridge Comprehensive uniform – Susie Deacon must have one that'll fit her. Now, go home.'

Shirley decided to take a small detour on her way home.

'Come in, dear.' Elsie Parrish opened the door cautiously, then stood to one side to let Shirley into the narrow hall of the Parrishes' spruce little semi in Riverside Gardens. The corridor was further narrowed by cardboard boxes piled up against the right-hand wall. 'Nice of you to come.'

'I went to your flat and Joyce told me you were staying

here.' A reconstruction could come as a bit of a shock to the next-of-kin – suddenly confronted with a policewoman who looked like the victim. Shirley had come to forewarn the Parrishes. 'I said I'd see you again,' she reminded Elsie.

'Talk is cheap, though, and actions speak louder. I'm glad to see you. I've sent Tony and Barbara out for some air before bed.'

'Someone on the move?' Shirley asked, edging past the boxes.

'Only me.'

Shirley followed the old lady into the sitting room, knowing that she would elucidate when she was ready.

'I'm moving in,' she said finally, shifting a suitcase from the settee so that Shirley could sit down. 'They need me now to help look after Liz and ... well, they got worried at the idea of me stuck out on that Council estate, in a high-rise, without so much as a telephone to call for help. I told them I wasn't about to get raped but they're worried all the same. It's the first time crime has really touched our lives, you see – until last week it was something that happened to other people, something you read about in the papers. I've lived on that estate since they built it in the late fifties, most of my married life, and I've never felt threatened, not for a moment. Now, Tony's convinced if I stay there a second longer, I'll be burgled, mugged, murdered. I gave in. I can't bear to see him so afraid. That man has made him afraid.'

Shirley, remembering why it was she had joined the police force – to protect harmless people like these – was humbled and silent in the face of her failure to catch the Riverside Rapist, her failure to salvage anything of Elsie Parrish's fiercely-held independence.

'Is there room?' she asked at last, to purge the silence and the guilt. The house looked very small for four adults, surely they would be tripping over each other all the time.

'It'll be a bit of a squeeze,' Elsie agreed. 'The back bedroom's not really much more than a boxroom. But I've sold off my bits and pieces of furniture.' She spoke with more cheerfulness than Shirley could have called on in her situation.

'That's to say, the junk shop in Bridge Street took them

204

off my hands. And you wouldn't believe how little space the personal objects take up after sixty years, a few photos, a letter or two, Tony's old school reports — that's about it. It's daft the things you choose to keep. "We brought nothing into this world" — I remember Miss Barrington used to say that at Sunday school, when I was a girl — "and it is certain we can carry nothing out."'

'You won't be going out for a long time yet, though,' Shirley said, 'and you've still got Mr Parrish.' She pointed. Albert had been transplanted to a newer, and slightly larger, television set but he still had the twinkle in his eye. Elsie smiled.

'I've got the past, yes. About the future — I'm not so sure.'

'How is Liz?'

'A little better, perhaps. Or so I tell myself.'

'Where is she now?'

'Upstairs. Asleep. She sleeps a good deal at the moment.'

'Can I speak to her sometime.'

'So long as you don't expect her to speak to you, dear.'

'Has she still said nothing?'

'She speaks the odd word to me and her mum, nothing to her dad or to strangers.'

'No word about the man. No description? A face, a voice, clothes?'

'Nothing. The doctor says she's blotted it all out — that it's the only way she knows of coping.' Elsie touched Shirley's arm. 'You won't catch him until he does it again, will you, dear? Since Liz won't, can't, help you. If only there was something I could do.'

'He has done it again,' Shirley told her, breaking several of her personal rules. 'Or rather before — a couple of months ago. And an attempt just last night. We have descriptions now, and a means of pinning him down. You wouldn't believe what forensic science can do these days, Mrs Parrish.' She explained about the reconstruction scheduled for the following evening. 'We'll get him, I promise you.' She got up.

'I must go. I just dropped by, in case . . .'

205

'In case?'

'In case there was anything I could do.'

'You look tired, dear. Go home, to those who love you. Have a good night's sleep.'

Alison turned on to her left side, pulling the pillow well into her neck, hugging her knees to her chest. Her stomach felt doughy after the late-night pizza which Gerry, who had great faith in the soothing effect of starchy food, had coaxed into her.

'Carbohydrate is a great natural tranquilliser,' he had insisted, 'and so is a big glass of plonk. Have you never heard of comfort eating, woman?'

'Don't call me that,' Alison had protested. 'Zac used to call me that.'

Gerry had come banging on her door that evening, refusing to accept no for an answer. He'd had a few ripe things to say about Philip over dinner.

'Don't ask me what he thought he was doing. Getting both of us in there and not telling us. We could have put our heads together, and everyone knows that two heads are better than one. Especially two heads as efficient as ours.'

'So let's do it now,' Alison had said. 'Who is the hacker turned murderer?'

Gerry hesitated, then laughed. 'I feel a bit of a prat actually. Shall I tell you who my two prime suspects were?'

'Zac?' Alison had guessed.

'Zac and ... er ... you, Alison.'

They had both begun to giggle. 'I was supposed to have been away in Papua New Guinea,' she pointed out.

'"Supposed" being the operative word. You weren't exactly convincing.'

'No?'

'No. There are no deserts in PNG, Alison, let alone camels in them. That's Australia.'

'Oops.'

'Do your homework properly another time.'

*

206

After two minutes she lay on her stomach which eased the bloating feeling momentarily. But with her nose pressed into the pillow, she soon felt she could no longer breathe and no longer breathing was not something she cared to think about just now, thanks very much.

If only life was a horror video – then you could fast-forward through the scary bits.

She had only herself to blame: she had insisted on coming to London, looked on it as an adventure. And now, just when she wanted out, would have given anything to be safely back in her king-sized bed in Hope Cottage with Nick's soft breathing on the far side, now she was stuck. She had to wait until Bernie Ackroyd told her she could go.

She longed to be back in the Hop Valley with the smell of the sea in her nostrils when the wind blew from the north.

She smiled ruefully in the darkness. She had always lived by the creed that you could do whatever you wanted so long as you were prepared to pay the price. But sometimes the price was higher than you had budgeted for.

'Tell me about you and Phil?' she had demanded over dinner.

'Like what? Shall I draw you a diagram?'

Alison laughed and shook her head. 'I heard you took him for a ride a couple of years back and broke his heart.'

'Don't you hate drama queens?'

'I want to hear your side. Otherwise I shall be obliged to think badly of you.'

'Fair enough. It wasn't all one-sided. Phil and I went back quite a long way – to when he was starting up Orion. In fact it was I who suggested the name.' Alison looked a little blank. 'Orion the *Hunter*,' he said as though explaining something to a small, and not very bright, child.

'Oh! I never thought of that.'

'Phil wanted to call it "Huntsman Software" – of all the boring names.'

'You've got ten times the brains Phil's got, Gerry. How come you've let your life slip by while men like him grow rich and fat?'

'You sound like my old mum,' Gerry teased. He adopted

a whiny falsetto. '"Why can't you make something of your life, Gerard?" Because I want to have a good time, that's why, not work unless I absolutely have to. Lazy, shiftless, feckless – I've had all those hurled at me over the years. I bet he's not lazy, shiftless and feckless, is he?'

'Who?'

'The boyfriend you claimed not to have.'

'No. He isn't any of those things.'

'I want ...' Gerry said, 'I want someone else to do all the spade work and let me walk in and take the profits. Yes, that's what I want.'

'Never mind your philosophy of life. Get to the heartbreak.'

'Oh, Alison. I like a person to play hard to get. I enjoy the hunt as much as – better than – the kill, if you'll pardon the expression. Phil was so doggedly devoted. When a man turns himself into a doormat like that, it takes more than I've got not to wipe my feet on him. I despise anyone, man or woman, who just does as I tell them all the time.'

'And Phil did that?'

'In the end, you push them further and further just to see if there's a point where the worm will turn.'

'And is there?'

'If there is, I haven't found it. So I dumped him a couple of years back. It was that or start knocking him about. How can I put this? I wasn't going to let him turn me into a fascist by making himself a victim. Do you understand?'

She nodded. 'But you came back.'

'I ran into him by chance. I was down on my luck, out of money, needing a job. We drifted back into the same old one-sided relationship. I tried very hard to find somewhere else to live. Really.'

'And now?'

'Now? Who knows. I don't make plans beyond today. I dare say I shall stick around for a while. You?'

'I'm off home as soon as Ackroyd gives me the all-clear.'

'And the detective work?'

'Phil can do his own dirty detective work. Finding one dead body will last me for a long time, thanks.'

'I think you're very wise. You don't want to end up getting hurt yourself.'

She turned on her back and laid her arms loosely upon the quilt. She gave in and opened her eyes.

It is never really dark in London, however efficient your curtains, and Alison's landlord had seen no need for unnecessary extravagance. The mirrored dressing table, so innocuous in the daylight, reflected the door knobs of the wardrobe opposite as two unblinking eyes, just waiting for her to fall asleep, to drop her guard.

Alison had never seen herself as an imaginative woman; preferring the safer judgement of herself as pragmatic, realistic. In this she was mistaken. In just this way had her imagination troubled her in her childhood, in the shadowy Victorian vicarage which had been her home. Grownups forget the irrational fears of childhood – until such moments as these.

Twenty years ago her father would look into her room on his way to his own bed and, finding her wakeful and fearful, would sit for a moment holding her hand and smoothing back her tumble of red hair.

'"Thou shalt not be afraid for any terror by night,"' his quiet voice recited from his favourite psalm, '"nor for the arrow that flieth by day."'

'Thanks, Dad,' she whispered. She closed her eyes and the voice began to fade as she slipped into sleep. Her last conscious thought was that she could no longer make out if the voice which comforted her belonged to her long-dead father, or to Nick.

Chapter Twenty-Three

'So what've we got?' Bernie Ackroyd asked the next morning. He sat down on a table in the computer room where he and Morrie had set up temporary camp and began to swing his feet restlessly back and forward. He wanted to be out roaming the streets, asking questions.

Sergeant Morrison, who was sitting behind the table, shuffled the reports in front of him and began to address his boss's back, summing them up in the habitual monotone which frequently threatened to drive Ackroyd mad. It wasn't as if there was anything they hadn't already seen for themselves or surmised.

'He died from having his throat cut − '

'You amaze me.'

' − by,' Morrie persevered doggedly, 'a serrated knife, one with a jagged edge.'

'I know what serrated means.'

'Like a bread knife − sort you can buy at any kitchen shop, even a supermarket.'

'But not the sort of thing you'd carry about with you as a matter of course.'

'No.'

'So he came equipped, as we thought.' Bernie hurled the words back over his shoulder for Morrie to catch. 'As I said last night − Forster would hardly have gone out looking for a bit of spare with a bread knife up his jumper.'

'Wouldn't it be a bit conspicuous at the best of times?' Morrie murmured.

'It was a cold night, you can just zip a knife like that inside

210

your bomber jacket and have it out and ready for use in two seconds. The murderer came specially to kill Zac that night. So he will have bought the knife, new, a few days before, at a supermarket on the other side of London and he will have fed it straight down the nearest drain on his way out.'

'It wasn't all that sharp,' Morrie continued, finding nothing to disagree with in his boss's analysis. 'The wound wasn't what you'd call clean. Not neat, not clean and not particularly quick.'

'Wouldn't Zac have kicked up a bit of racket while all this was being done?' Bernie asked. 'Would you sit there and let someone hack at your throat without complaining, Morrie? As far as I can gather, this Zac was one of life's champion whingers.' Bernie's feet drummed against the side of the desk — a habit which frequently threatened to drive his sergeant mad.

'The computer room was soundproofed a few months ago,' Morrie explained, 'in response to complaints from the offices on the ground floor that the printer was disturbing them. Also it seems likely that the printer was still running when the . . . when his throat was cut.'

'Who says?'

'It was running when Cleary saw him in there at nine — he could just about make out the hum through the closed door.'

'But it wasn't running when Alison went in at nine-thirty.'

'It had quite simply run out of paper. People tended to leave a lot of listings to come out overnight, it seems, and Zac was usually in there until late so he would reload with paper when necessary.'

'Carry on.'

'The cut was made from left to right from behind.'

'Right-handed man.'

'Or woman.'

'Any of our little gang not right-handed?'

'Nope. They all are.' Morrie was very good at noticing little details like that. It was one of the reasons Bernie always asked for him on a case.

'Also,' Morrie continued, 'it was done from above.'

'So Zac was sitting down, at the operator's console, with his back to the murderer. It was someone he knew and trusted and had no reason to fear.' Bernie got up and turned to face Morrie, his arms folded. 'Just as we thought. It was someone he was willing to let into the building, someone he was willing to turn his back on.'

Morrie got up too, skirted his boss's large frame and sat down at the console. He faked a few taps at the keyboard. 'The most likely thing is that the murderer grabbed him by the hair.' Morrie seized his own hair and pulled his own head back. 'Pulled his head back and . . .' Morrie used his finger to give a convincing mime of someone drawing a knife blade across a yielding surface.

'Between nine-fifteen and nine-thirty.' Bernie Ackroyd paused to consider. 'He, or she, knew that Cleary was a man of regular habits and could be relied on to make his rounds at nine and be safely shut up in his cubby-hole again by quarter-past.'

'Which they would all have known.'

'Agreed. Fingerprints?'

'What do you think?'

'Everybody.'

'They all came in this room every day – all touched the door, the printer, even that terminal every working day.'

'And who's got an alibi?' Bernie paused then answered himself. 'Hunter, Walsh, both the MacAlistairs. Except that they're alibi-ing each other which doesn't wash with me when it's a question of husband and wife. Marks and Tatton are also alibi-ing each other and the same thing may apply in their case.'

'You think they're lovers?'

'I don't know. There's something curiously sexless about the Tatton girl, as if she gets her kicks elsewhere. Don't you think?'

Morrie wasn't prepared to offer an opinion. 'I've been married twenty years,' was all he said. 'How should I know?'

'Even if they're just mates . . . or what did Hunter call them? The Twins? They may still be sticking up for each other. They could be doing the hacking together. Who definitely hasn't got an alibi?'

'Alison Hope, Ruth Harper, Ruth Harper's pet journalist — allowing our closed circle to include nearest and dearest with sufficient knowhow. Oh, by the way.'

'What?'

'Hunter collared me late last night and asked when his staff could have access to this room again. Apparently we're holding up his work.'

'Tell him to fu — ' Bernie began. 'No, better still, I'll tell him myself.'

Nick made arrangements to reconstruct the rape of Elizabeth Parrish in Riverside Park that night. Carol was going to play the victim. Mrs Morecombe had agreed to wait in her shop with a light on as before and Carol would run out of the park and bang on her door at the requisite moment. Nick left for home at five o'clock.

Bernie Ackroyd was back in his office when Alison rang him from a call box in Moorgate station a few minutes later. He listened keenly to what she had to say.

'I like it as a theory,' he admitted. 'I like it just as much as I did when I first told it to myself earlier this afternoon.'

'You were already there.' Alison was glad she wasn't whistling in the dark. If Bernie Ackroyd had got there already, then her far-fetched theory wasn't so very far-fetched after all.

Bernie hesitated. His gut instinct was to trust her completely. 'It's just that, right from the start, all my witnesses have been telling me the same thing: that Clive Zacharzewski was Public Enemy Number One.'

'Yes, that was the puzzle. You'd expect him to be the killer rather than the victim.'

'And there's only one person, among all the witnesses I've spoken to, who had the sheer effrontery to commit this crime. Alas.'

'Yes.'

'Morrie and Rawlinson are checking up on it as we speak.

213

You go home now, girl. D'you hear? Don't take any risks. He's killed once ...'

'Okay,' Alison said, intending, as usual, to take no notice of the warning.

'How's things?' Nick asked as Susie answered the door to him shortly after nine-thirty. He'd waited until he could be certain she'd be back from visiting Bill in hospital. 'Sorry I haven't made it round before but things have been a bit tight.'

'Bill, of all people, understands that.' Susie took his coat and led him into the kitchen again. He could hear pop music pouring out of a radio in Sarah's room. How could anyone do their homework to that racket? He felt his joints creaking again. Maybe he should take up jogging to ward off middle age. Then again, maybe not. He could run when he needed to.

'Congrats, by the way.' She gave him a big hug. 'No one deserves a promotion more than you. Bill sends his love too.'

'Thanks.' Nick returned her hug. 'I can't stay long, I'm afraid. We're doing a reconstruction. Jog the memory of any witnesses, you know the sort of thing.'

'Bill's been furious not to be able to take part in the investigation,' Susie said. 'He's been following every word in the papers. I get such a telling-off if I haven't got the latest for him when I visit every day. What progress?'

'I wouldn't be exaggerating too much if I said none at all,' Nick admitted. 'I'm certainly nowhere near an arrest. But let's talk about Bill. He's on the mend, I take it.'

'He's recovering well from the operation ... physically.' Susie sat down and lowered her voice, fearing to let one of her daughters hear. 'But he's badly depressed, I think. There's no way the doctors are going to sign him fit for active duty for months yet. Even after he's convalesced, he's going to be stuck behind a desk for ages.'

'Oh, no!'

'Anyone would think you didn't like Sergeant Walpole.'

'I like her fine. But she's not Bill.'

'What a stick in the mud you are, Nick. Anyway, there are so many things he can't do and he's always been such an active

214

man. Even his beloved garden is going to be too strenuous for him for the foreseeable future. Alex was being wonderful, clearing up all the leaves, having bonfires, dead-heading ... He was a lovely boy, Nick. Nothing was too much trouble for him.'

'Why the past tense?' Nick asked. 'I know they'd had a bit of a row – '

'More than that. Sarah's ... "dumped him" is, I believe, the contemporary expression.'

'Ah.'

'She says she's too young to be serious about anyone and that "A" levels are going to take up most of her time over the next eighteen months.'

'Dear God!'

'I know.' Susie began to laugh. 'What sort of paragon have I brought into the world?'

'It would be music to most mother's ears.'

'There are other things than exams and careers, Nick. I want well-rounded children.'

'She has her tennis and her drama. She's about as well-rounded as a kid could hope to be.'

'Of course, she's absolutely right. All the same ... I was eighteen when I met Bill, you know.'

'Mmm, I know.'

'We were married a year later, in 1967. I suppose the swinging sixties were well underway up in London but they hadn't penetrated the Hop Valley. There's never been anyone else for either of us. I don't know what you're supposed to do when you meet Mr Right when you're still very young. Waiting changes the relationship but marrying young ... sometimes I think I should have had more experience before I settled down but – well, we've been so happy.'

Nick patted her hand affectionately. 'Why knock it?'

'Then we've had twenty years where young people seemed to do just as they liked without ever paying the price for it. Then suddenly, it's 1988, almost 1989, and monogamy's back in fashion – '

'Did it ever really go out?'

' – and my eldest daughter prefers swotting for exams and playing tennis and learning judo to furtive gropings behind the bike shed. As you say. I should be grateful but defying your parents is part of growing up, isn't it?'

'Sounds like that's what she is doing.'

'Good point. Bill, needless to say, is delighted although even he had to admit in the end that Alex was a likeable lad. Oh, I don't know, Nick. It's just . . . Sarah's so grown-up all of a sudden, so mature. The girls soon won't need me any more. I'm middle-aged, useless, redundant.'

'That's why you took up your nursing again, surely. I can't think of anything more useful than that. And Bill will always need you.'

'I know. I just feel so sorry for myself all of a sudden. You wait until your fortieth birthday – see how you feel.'

'Forty's hardly middle-aged these days.' Nick changed the subject to take her mind off things. 'Shirley tells me Sarah's anxious to take up real Judo.'

'She's asked for the kit for Christmas. What's it called? A *Judogi*?'

'Sorry, I tend to switch off when Shirley starts her lectures.'

'Tessa O'Shea, from the hospital, she's quite keen on these self-defence classes too. Judging by the number of times she comes into work with bruises after "walking into a door" or "tripping on the stairs", it's not a moment too soon.'

'She worries me, that girl.'

'Me too. I've known her since they were kids – her and Kevin. Their mother was a sister at the hospital when I was training – what? Twenty-three years ago? Tessa was such a solemn little girl, even then and . . . What is it?' Nick had been listening to her with increasing amazement and the look on his face now stopped her dead.

'Are you telling me that the O'Sheas are brother and sister?'

'Of course.'

'I assumed he was her husband! She led me to think so.' Hadn't she?'

'Mmm. Now I come to think of it she always introduces him by name, never as "my brother". They've always been very close, despite the violence. It's an unhealthy relationship, sick. I'd love to see

216

her out of it and settled with a nice boy of her own.'

'I think you'd better tell me all about it.'

'Their father left their mother while she was pregnant with Kevin and after that she started drinking – died of it in the end, about five years ago. Tessa was the only mother Kevin really had all his life. I can see her now, from the time she was about ten, running off after school to do the shopping and then going home to cook Kevin his dinner. She always seemed to want to fight his battles for him. And what thanks does she get for it? Her kid brother knocks her about.'

She paused to collect her thoughts. 'You remember that course I did on social psychology a couple of years back when I was planning to go back to work?'

Nick nodded. He remembered Bill's moaning about it, at least.

'They told me there that a baby animal, if it's shown no affection in the first five days of life, will *never* learn to show affection itself. It becomes, in effect, a sociopath.'

'And that applies to human animals too, I take it.'

'That's right.'

'And when a woman's husband walks out on her because she was pregnant, she's not going to lavish a lot of love on the newborn baby. Is that it?'

'Something like that.'

'But do they live as husband and wife, Tessa and Kevin?'

'I've never been able quite to work that out,' Susie said. 'And, to be honest, it's not something I care to delve into too deeply. What with my job and Bill's we see so much sadness and madness and ... downright badness, that I prefer to bury my head in the sand whenever I get the chance.'

'I know what you mean.'

Something had been lying buried, not in the sand, but in the shadows of Nick's mind for days. Now it burst into the sunlight.

'What time does the nightshift start at the hospital?'

'Ten pm. Why?'

That was it! Of course it did. Which was why Dave Edwards had been going off duty at ten the night

217

he and his balaclava had given Liz Parrish such a fright.

'So if you met a nurse coming in at the front door in her coat at midnight, what would you think she was doing?'

'I'd think she'd been over to one of the out-buildings, one of the portacabins,' Susie said, puzzled, 'and had put her coat on against the cold.'

'And if she took pains to tell you she was just coming on duty?'

'Then I'd think she was lying.'

The O'Sheas' house was in darkness when Nick arrived and there was no answer to his knock. He radioed in to get all beat constables and patrol cars looking out for the young man and asked for Tessa to be picked up at the hospital and brought in for questioning. Then he drove back to the park to call off the night's exercise.

Chapter Twenty-Four

Three hours earlier, up in London, there was only Alison and Gerry left in the office. Normality had been resumed at Orion, insofar as it ever could be, and Bernie Ackroyd had reluctantly allowed the computer room to be re-opened but no one else had felt inclined to linger.

Gerry looked set to make a night of it. Philip had called a staff meeting that afternoon and declared his intention of going ahead with Phase Three of FIX and Gerry, unlike Alison, genuinely wanted the job. He was hunched uncomfortably over his terminal, whistling the chorus of 'Waltzing Matilda'. A second chair stood next to his, piled high with computer print-out and manuals.

Alison was standing by the cupboard which housed the manuals, leafing through one without reading it. She hadn't done any work that afternoon but she had no intention of going home either.

Suddenly, the whistling had stopped and Gerry was behind her.

'I'm not sure what you're still doing here, Alison. Hanging round the office, I mean. You've not done a stroke of work all day.'

'You saw how grotty my bedsit is.' She put the manual back and turned to face him. He was standing much closer to her than was necessary for conversation. 'It's the sort of place women like Mary Lewis are found dead with an empty aspirin bottle beside them. I'd rather spend as little time there as possible until I can go home to Hope Cottage.'

'I have seen better gaffs,' he agreed.

Then his fingers were on her neck and, before she had time to react or to stop him, his lips closed over hers. But her mouth did not open to his hopeful tongue and he soon released her.

'I suppose the rich and famous Alison Hope is out of my league,' he said, turning away. He laughed without rancour and resumed his seat by the window.

'It's not that. My affections are already wholly engaged. Stick with Phil – he's probably richer than I am, anyway.'

'Ooh! That stung.'

'I meant what I said last night, Gerry. That you could have really made something of your life.'

'You're right. And it's too late now.'

At that moment the door opened. Alison would have had no difficulty in recognising the two men who came in as policemen even if she had not already met the shorter one – Bernie Ackroyd's sidekick, Morrison. Gerry glanced up and got up slowly and casually from his chair, smiling as if to welcome his visitors. Then Philip appeared silently in the doorway behind them, flustered and red in the face.

The two policemen were only halfway across the office when Philip blurted out, 'I'm sorry, Gerry. I had to tell them – '

Morrison turned savagely to silence him. 'I told you to stay in the car, Hunter!'

The other policeman said, 'Gerard Walsh, I am arresting you on suspicion of the murder of Clive Zacharzewski – '

Gerry pushed the spare chair towards them. The heavy weight of paper on it made it spin on its castors and it cannoned into the larger policeman who clutched his shin and cursed. Alison jumped instinctively out of the way of the missile and collided with Morrison who was now sprinting across the room. Gerry stepped nimbly on to his own chair and from there on to the windowsill.

He pushed the window open as far as it would go.

Morrison shouted, 'Don't let him!'

The two policeman rushed forward.

Alison yelled, 'Gerry! No!'

'Goodbye, Alison.'

He launched himself head first into the night air. Alison

220

and the two policemen held their breaths, waiting for the sound of impact. When it came, it was an anti-climax — a thud they would not have noticed had they not been listening for it. Philip came to stand a few feet behind them.

'I can't look,' he said in a hoarse whisper. 'They made me say he wasn't with me all that evening. That he went out for half an hour.'

'You're s-s-supposed to be close enough to t-t-touch someone you're arresting,' Alison said, 'then you c-could have stopped him.' She swayed and collapsed on to the same chair that Gerry had been occupying a few seconds — and a lifetime — ago.

'Get an ambulance!' Morrison told the other man. 'Bloody hell, what a balls up! What's Mr Ackroyd gonna say when he hears about this? He'll have us both out directing traffic tomorrow, Rawlinson.'

The man called Rawlinson muttered, 'It wasn't my fault', gave Philip a poisonous look and reached for the nearest telephone without further comment.

'They made me say it,' Philip repeated. 'They badgered me and badgered me until I couldn't think straight. It's not right.'

'But it's true though, isn't it?' Morrison snapped.

'Oh yes.' Philip looked bewildered at this irrelevance. 'It's true. He got blood on my black leather jacket,' he added indignantly.

Morrison gave a snort of disgust and turned his attention to Alison.

'Now, Alison love, you all right?' She didn't reply, just breathed a bit harder. 'Mr Ackroyd told you to go home, didn't he?' She nodded. 'You'll have to come along to the station with us, love, as a witness. And Mr Hunter too.' He glared at Philip. 'Mr Ackroyd will be wanting a long talk with Mr Hunter.'

'I don't have to come,' Alison said, finding her voice, 'assuming you're not arresting me, but I will.'

Morrie sat down next to her.

'Seem to know something about the law,' he remarked. 'Been arrested a lot, have you?'

'My . . . my fiancé's a policeman.' Like Ruth Harper

221

before her, she was stuck for what to call the man who shared her home and her life. Lovers, unlike husbands, had no official status.

'Yeah?' Morrie said. 'Which station?'

'Not in London.'

'We'll get you down to our nick, get you a nice hot cup of tea — just as soon as I can get things cleared up here.'

'Cleared up!' the constable echoed. 'We'll have to scrape him off the paving stones.'

'Shut up, Rawlinson.'

'Nick,' Alison said, hearing just one word of what Morrie had said. 'Yes, let's get to Nick.'

Morrie stared at her in surprise and Rawlinson mouthed, 'Shock,' and touched his forehead.

Nick caught a small sound behind him as he walked in at the north-eastern entrance to the park. He spun round, poised to fight. It was Paul Penruan.

'What the hell are you doing here?' Nick asked in relief. 'You're supposed to be ill.'

'I am,' he wheezed. 'Sally Ferris told me you'd all come down here to try to catch the rapist using Carol as bait.'

'Chinese whispers,' Nick said wearily. 'Now get out of here. You'll be no use to me with acute bronchitis.'

'I haven't come here to be any use to you. I've come to tell you that if any harm comes to Carol, Trevellyan, I'll break both your arms.'

'That will do,' Nick said coldly. 'In the first place remember who you're talking to. In the second place I'd break your neck before you got near me. In the third place Carol's a professional — she knows what she's doing and she knows how to take care of herself. In the fourth place this is a reconstruction, nothing more. And in the fifth place, I've just come to call it off.'

'Sorry, guv,' Paul muttered.

'So push off. That's an order.'

'No, I'm staying. If I'm not on duty, you can't give me orders.'

'Where is Carol anyway? Is she here? I told her and Shirley

222

to meet me by the entrance. I wish people would obey simple instructions.'

'She went wandering off over there with the Sarge to find the right spot — where the Parrish rape took place.'

Shirley appeared silently beside them as he spoke.

'Could you two make a bit more noise,' she said. 'If our rapist happened to be about he might not have heard you bellowing yet.'

'I'm in charge of sarcasm, Sergeant,' Nick told her. 'And we can all go home and get into some dry clothes and a hot bath. I know who — '

From a clump of trees, some fifty yards away, Carol Halsgrove began to scream.

Adrenalin poured from Nick's glands and pumped into his blood stream. He had forgotten that his feet were cold and that he'd had no supper.

There. He'd known he could still run when he needed to.

He reached the scene of the scream a good twenty seconds ahead of either Paul or Shirley and hurled himself at the black-clad figure who had hold of Carol. The rapist had learnt something from his fight with Ginny and although Carol was using every trick she knew, she was making no headway.

Nick and the rapist rolled over in the grass for a few seconds before the man jerked himself free and took to his heels in the direction of the water meadows. As Nick caught his breath, Shirley shot past him, following the rapist. Paul was on his knees by Carol with his arms round her.

'Carrie! Are you all right? Speak to me.'

'I can't speak, you great oaf, you're crushing me.'

'You stay here, Carol,' Nick said. 'Paul will stay with you.'

'Sir!' Carol protested, trying to get to her feet, looking very young and incongruous in a grey gymslip.

'Will someone please do as I tell them, just for once. Shirley and I can cope. Radio for help, Paul.' He hurtled off in pursuit of Shirley. Carol, her frozen terror passed, began to cry with relief as Paul picked up her radio.

223

'I like the outfit,' he said as he pressed the 'transmit' button. 'Hotel Victor from Penruan.'

Nick caught up with Shirley outside the hay shed, slithering to a halt on the wet grass.

'He's gone in there,' she said. 'What an idiot. We've got him cornered now.'

'Let's go in.'

'Pitchforks,' Shirley said. 'Scythes.'

'Wrong time of year,' Nick lied. He kicked open the shed door. There was no movement in the blackness.

'Police,' he called. 'We've got the place surrounded. You're under arrest. You might as well come quietly.'

'Reinforcements,' Shirley whispered. 'Where the hell is everyone?' She took out her radio.

'They're on their way,' Nick whispered back. 'You stay here. I'm going in.'

'You bloody stupid idiot —'

But Nick had already gone through the door.

The door swung to behind him leaving only the faintest crack of light from outside. But he was ready for that. He pulled a tiny but powerful torch out of his pocket and trained it on the stacks of hay in the far corner. It was the moment the rapist had been waiting for.

Frobisher had said the rapist was of below-average intelligence and Nick had expected him to make the mistake of retreating to the back of the shed, hiding there, hoping even for another exit. Instead the rapist was immediately behind the door. He kicked the torch out of Nick's hand and it flew up to the far end of the shed where its light played uselessly on the ceiling. Nick's reactions were fast and the next kick, which was intended for his stomach, caught him only on the thigh.

Even so, the ferocity of the blow caused him to stagger and lose his footing on the hanks of straw which served as a makeshift carpet for the shed. The rapist paused long enough to give him a vicious kick in the ribs before turning to the shed door to make his escape.

But something prevented the door from opening at once and he wrenched at it with all his force. It suddenly gave way and, unbalanced, he toppled backwards, narrowly

224

avoiding falling on Nick. Shirley Walpole stood there in the open doorway with such light as there was behind her.

The rapist lunged upwards at her. Nick started to haul himself to his feet, wincing, to go to her rescue. But before he could even make it to a standing position, Shirley had kicked the rapist smartly in the groin. As he slid back to the ground, moaning and clutching his injuries, she produced a pair of handcuffs and secured him to the door handle.

'Maximum efficiency, minimum effort,' she murmured happily. 'Now what have we here?' She retrieved Nick's torch, pulled away the balaclava and shone the light into the face of the rapist.

'Kevin O'Shea, I am arresting you on a charge of rape. You are not obliged to say anything but anything you say will be taken down and may be given in evidence.'

O'Shea, as was his habit, said nothing.

'What happened to the gentle art of Judo?' Nick asked, in amazement.

'There are times when a kick in the balls is just so much more satisfying.'

'Well done, Walpole!'

'Thank you, sir.' She held out her hand, helped him to his feet and dusted the worst of the dirty straw from him.

Chapter Twenty-Five

'Is there anyone I can ring for you, Alison?' DS Morrison asked. 'Mother, sister? This fiancé?'

'Him please.'

'What's his name?'

'Detective Chief Inspector Trevellyan, Hopbridge CID.'

Rawlinson cleared his throat.

'Ah,' Morrie said, 'Detective Chief Inspector. Um. Get him for me, will you, Rawlinson. I'll speak to him myself.'

When Nick and Shirley reached Nick's office the phone was ringing.

'Trevellyan,' Nick answered.

'Sir, Detective Sergeant Morrison, in London. I'm working on the Orion Software murder case.'

'Oh, yes?' Nick was still shaken and Morrison's words took a moment to register.

'I've got Alison Hope here. She asked me to ring you.'

'Alison? What's she doing there?'

'She was witness to a rather nasty incident when we tried to make an arrest at Orion's offices, sir.'

'What sort of incident, man?'

'A suicide. Fourth-floor window.'

'Dear God! Is she all right?'

'Just shocked and upset.'

'You won't be needing her for long, will you?'

'She's made a short statement. We're finished with her now.'

'I'll come and fetch her. Is she there? Can I talk to her?'

'Yes, sir.' Alison came to the phone.

'Nick?'

'Are you all right, my angel?'

'Nick, it was horrible. I never dreamt he'd do that.'

'Who? Never dreamt who would do that? Hunter?'

'Gerry, of course.'

'But I ... No, save it. I'm coming to get you and bring you home. But it'll take me at least three hours. I want you to sit tight now you've made your statement and wait for me, understood? Put Morrison back on.'

'Sir?'

'I'll be there in about three hours, Sergeant. I want you to take care of her until then.'

'Yes, sir. We'll get her a hot meal and find someone to keep her company.'

'Good, see you later.' Nick hung up and said:

'You're on your own, Shirley.'

Nick climbed into Alison's Jaguar without stopping to change and headed east, disappointing the Thames Valley police by driving the performance car at a steady seventy along the M4. He reached Hammersmith flyover at about one o'clock, turned south at Earls Court and made his way easily along the empty embankment to Blackfriars where he turned north again into the City of London.

He parked outside the police station just after one-thirty, went in and gave his name at the desk. Morrison and a constable he introduced as Rawlinson appeared almost instantly. The three men shook hands.

'You didn't get your man then,' Nick said with sympathy.

'We got bits of him,' Rawlinson put in cheerfully. Morrison glared at him.

'Not exactly the best night's work we've ever done,' he agreed. 'Miss Hope's in one of the rest rooms, sir. She's still a bit shaken but I think she'll bounce back.'

'No question.'

'More than Walsh did,' Rawlinson interspersed again. 'Bounce, I mean.'

227

'One more word, Rawlinson,' Morrison said quietly, 'just one more word.'

'Sarge!'

'About this private detective work she was doing in that place, sir — ' Morrison began, shaking his head.

'No good looking at me like that,' Nick told him. 'I'm not her keeper, unfortunately. She's got a mind of her own. I think she's learnt her lesson now though, don't you?'

'Let's hope so. This way. Er . . . sir?'

'Yes?'

'Do you know you've got straw in your hair?'

'It's an old West Country custom,' Nick told him, removing the offending debris. Morrison looked as if he believed him.

Alison jumped up as soon as she saw Nick and flung her arms round him. She didn't cry but he could feel her breath very hot and fast against his neck as she strove to control herself in front of the other policemen.

'Come on,' he said. 'Time to go home. Say goodbye to the nice sergeant.'

Just as they reached the front door, a voice hailed them. It was Bernie Ackroyd who was just starting to get into his stride in his interview with Philip Hunter.

'Nick! They only just told me you were here.'

'Bernie, you old bastard.' They embraced.

'You in charge of this mad woman?' Bernie asked.

'In a sense.'

'Well try and keep her under control, can't you?'

'I'll try.'

'You're not rushing off? You've got to come round and see Linda and the kids. Just let me polish off Hunter and we'll hop in a taxi.'

'Bernie,' Nick said patiently, 'it's after one o'clock in the morning and Alison needs to get home and sleep for a week.'

'Oh yeah.' Bernie looked crestfallen. He stopped barring their way. 'Keep in touch, now.'

'I will.'

'You treat this boy right, Alison.'

'I will,' she said.'

*

'He'd been getting more violent.' Tessa sat still and straight on the chair in the interview room, her hands folded neatly in her lap. 'There'd always been that wild streak in him but it was becoming more difficult to hide the bruises. More difficult to lie them away.'

'Why didn't you report him?' Shirley burst out. You had to keep your temper in the interview room, stay in control, but the woman's calm was getting on her nerves.

Tessa looked at her in incomprehension. 'He's my brother. I had to protect him.'

'You knew he was the Riverside Rapist?'

She nodded. 'The first time — it must have been the middle of October. I was at home that night. He came in, covered in mud, all keyed up, excited. I'd never seen him so . . . alive. He told me what he'd done — poured it all out, every detail.'

'And you didn't go to the police!'

'I told you. He's my brother. He was less violent after that. For a little while. He was quiet, docile, pottering about the house and garden, keeping out of trouble.'

'So that was a lot better for you?' Shirley broke in contemptuously. Tessa nodded silent assent.

'Then about three weeks later, he started to get rough again. There was that night your boss saw us — the Chief Inspector, Mr Trevellyan — when he clouted me one in the middle of the Market Square. I thought we were in trouble there. It had got bad again then. I realised he was ready to break out — to do it again.

'The night of the second rape I was at work at the hospital. I left home at nine-thirty and Kevin walked with me as far as the off-licence on the corner. I knew that drink made him worse. Mum used to drink, you know, after Dad left. She used to say he'd left because of Kevin, because he didn't want the responsibility of another child, that one was bad enough. She was always telling us that.

'They brought the little Parrish girl in at about half-past ten. It almost broke my heart to see her — '

'And yet you still didn't go to the police.'

'I told you . . . Then Sister sent me over to the stores for something and as I was coming back in the front door I saw your boss. I knew he was police. I knew he was there about

229

the rape. So I stopped and spoke to him. Mentioned that I was just coming on duty. Then when he came round asking about Kev's alibi, I told him he'd been with me at the time, been at home until I went out, just before midnight, long after she'd been brought in.

'I joined your self-defence classes. I thought you might let something slip – so I'd know if the police were getting close. Besides ...'

'You might need to defend yourself one of those days?'

'Mmm.'

'But you didn't alibi him the third time?'

'I didn't know about it. She fought him off and she didn't come to the hospital. I hadn't expected him to break out again so soon. It was like he was getting the taste for it.

'Do you realise what you've done?' Shirley asked in disgust. 'If you'd turned him in when he did the first rape, you'd have saved Liz Parrish and her family. You said yourself the sight of her almost broke your heart. Your stinking brother has ruined their lives. How many other lives would you have let him destroy before you saw the light?'

'He was all I had,' Tessa said. 'I was all he had. It was my duty to protect him.'

'WDS Walpole ending interview at eleven-fifteen.' Shirley clicked off the tape recorder. 'I'm going to charge you with aiding and abetting a rape,' she said angrily. It was the most serious charge she could bring, more serious than assisting an offender or obstructing the police, and harder to prove. But she was going to make it stick.

Nick settled Alison in the passenger seat of the Jaguar reclining it as far as it would go, and wrapped a rug round her.

'You've had a shock,' he said. 'Sit quietly and don't talk unless you want to. I want to hear all about it, but we have a lifetime ahead of us for that.'

He got into the driver's seat and turned the car back towards the Embankment. 'We'll be home in no time.'

'I didn't know you knew Bernie Ackroyd,' Alison said twenty minutes later, as they joined the M4.

'Policing's a small world. We've been meeting at conferences and on training courses for years. He's older than I am, of course, outranked me long ago. He's one of the best coppers there is.'

'Yes. I could tell.'

'If he'd been there tonight, no way would your mate have been allowed to leave us all with egg on our faces.'

'Is that all his suicide means to you? An embarrassment for the police?'

'I didn't know the man,' Nick said, not unkindly, 'and I can't afford to be sentimental.'

'He doesn't seem your type. Ackroyd.'

Nick laughed. No. Bernie – the rough, rabble-rousing, womanising Bernie who'd left school at fifteen – was not his type.

'They say opposites attract,' he said.

Somewhere outside Swindon she said, 'I'm ready to talk about it.'

'I'm listening.'

She recounted the events of the last few days.

'I almost forgot – before he jumped he said, "Goodbye Alison".'

'Not "Goodbye, Philip?"'

'No. "Alison". I was the one who shopped him to Ackroyd – although Ackroyd had already worked it out for himself, of course – and I was the person he chose to say goodbye to. Do you think he realised that it was me?'

Nick gave a grunt which might have meant anything then said: 'What about this electrified terminal? That must have been him.' He shuddered. If he'd known about that incident at the time . . .

'Dear God, Alison – '

'It was Gerry who saved me,' she interrupted. 'He wasn't out to harm me, just to frighten me off – that's all. I expect he thought I'd panic and get the next train home.'

'He didn't know you then, or he'd have realised it would have the opposite effect. He didn't know what a stubborn, pig-headed, little – '

'All right, all right. You've made your point.'

'You liked Gerry Walsh.'

'I liked him. I liked him a lot.'

'Dearest ...'

'I know. I'm a lousy judge of character. Don't say it. But I liked him and he liked me.'

And yet she could hear still one of the last things he'd ever said to her, at their dinner the previous evening when she'd told him she was going home as soon as she could.

'You don't want to end up getting hurt yourself.'

The remark, which had seemed innocuous at the time – an expression of his concern, if anything – now took on the shadow of a threat.

Nick turned the car off the M4 outside Bristol and began to head south along the M5. Beside him, Alison began to cry quietly. It was something she rarely did and never in front of any witness but him. He reached his left hand over and squeezed her knee. Then, more practically, he took out his handkerchief and passed it to her.

Nick had no objection to people crying – he had been known to shed a tear himself: when Elizabeth Taylor fell off The Pie and they disqualified her from the Grand National on a technicality; or when Humphrey Bogart told Ingrid Bergman that the problems of two little people didn't amount to a hill of beans in this crazy world. He happened to disagree with Bogart on that point.

Alison, on the other hand, saw tears as an admission of weakness.

'I was just thinking,' she said through the thick cotton. 'Just before the police arrived, he was whistling "Waltzing Matilda". He was always doing that.'

'So?' Nick looked puzzled. 'The result of too much time spent working in Australia, I imagine.'

'Remember what happens to the Jolly Swagman when the police arrive?'

Nick ran through the lyric in his mind. 'I see,' he said slowly. '"You'll never take me alive, said he".'

They were both silent for a while then Nick said: 'Well, my angel, at least you got your hacker. Your mission could be said to have been wholly successful.'

'Gerry Walsh wasn't the hacker.'

Nick considered this. 'Too hard for me, Holmes.'

232

'We all jumped to the same conclusion when the murder happened — me, Phil, Bernie Ackroyd — that Clive Zac had rumbled the hacker and got himself killed as a result. It was the other way round. Zac was the hacker. Gerry was on to him almost at once — long before I was.'

'How, I wonder?'

'He was always the most obvious suspect, almost too obvious. That's why his murder was so baffling. It seems that Gerry had already worked out who I was by the morning of the "accident" with my terminal. I'm not sure how, but he said something later about my boyfriend and Mary Lewis wasn't supposed to have a boyfriend. It was the day after your visit — I think he must have seen us together that morning. Maybe heard you call me by a different name.'

'Bugger it! Did I forget? So Walsh decided to frighten you off for some reason. But how did that help?'

'Zac's reaction to the "accident". He said something like "This is all very puzzling" as if to say that he was the criminal round here so why should anyone else try to kill me. I mean, no one in their senses could have believed it had been an accident. Zac certainly didn't.'

'So then Walsh was sure who the hacker was? Why didn't he go to Philip?'

'Gerry was short of cash. He'd spent all the money he'd earned in Australia enjoying himself in the States. He decided it was a nice piece of action, killed Zac and planned to take over where Zac had left off. I like to think he didn't go in there with the intention of killing him. To blackmail him, perhaps, or just ask for a share of the takings. My guess is that Zac wouldn't play ball and had underestimated how far Gerry would go.'

A little voice reminded her that Gerry had gone to the computer room that night armed with a bread knife, which didn't quite fit in with her theory.

'He had a lot of nerve, this Walsh.' Nick spoke with grudging respect. 'I almost wish I'd met him.'

'Gerry wasn't within five thousand miles of London when the hacking started, remember? He didn't even know FIX existed. Why in the world would anyone have suspected him?'

'And how did you work all this out?'

'It was something he said to me the other night, the night after the murder. How his ideal set-up was to have someone else do all the spade work; how Phil was infatuated with him and would jump through hoops if he told him to. I thought about it today and suddenly it all fitted. Phil had given him a false alibi. I rang Ackroyd but Ackroyd knew. He'd already sent his men round to interrogate Phil until he retracted.'

'What a mess! Bernie will charge him, if I know Bernie. He'll probably go to jail. Why do people do these things?'

The question was really rhetorical but Alison answered him anyway.

'Love. Infatuation. Lust. Whatever you want to call it. Something very close to love, I think. There was something oddly lovable about Gerry.'

'If Philip had been a woman, cohabiting with Gerry, his alibi would have been viewed with extreme scepticism right from the start.' Nick tutted in disgust. 'But Bernie seems to have accepted at face value Philip's talk of Walsh just being a mate he was putting up for a few nights. Bernie always did have a bit of a blind spot about gays — as if he doesn't really believe they exist.'

'Phil presumably realised that Gerry had killed Zac but thought he'd done it for *his* sake — to rid him of his hacker in the quickest and most final way. Or chose to think that.'

'Not just a woman's prerogative then, that sort of stupidity,' Nick said thoughtfully.

'Come again?'

'I'll explain tomorrow. Philip's paid a high price for getting rid of his hacker.'

'He's a broken man.'

'So are you by the look of you. A broken woman rather. How fortunate that I'm not the sort of man who says "I told you so".'

'I'm just exhausted, that's all. I've been a bloody nuisance, haven't I?'

'Just like always. Promise me you won't ever change.'

Just outside Taunton she asked: 'What is it that makes some people able to kill for money, or for the most trivial

234

of reasons, when you and I and most people couldn't kill anyone for any reason.'

'I might be able to — to save my own life, or to protect you, or anyone else who was vulnerable. I think you could too. But to answer your question: the best way I can put it is that they just seem to have a little piece missing, a restraining bolt that the rest of us have. They have a little wire loose somewhere in the circuitry.'

'Don't talk about loose wires.' She yawned and sat up. 'Are we nearly home?'

'Soon. Then I'm going to run you a bath and put you to bed.'

'What time is it?'

'Just after four.'

Nick ran a hot, foamy bath for Alison.

'Clothes off,' he said. She handed them to him.

'Stick them outside the door. Mary Lewis's clothes are going in the bin first thing.'

'Good riddance! How long will it take for your hair to grow back to its real colour?'

'Oh, the dye will wash out in a few weeks.'

She got into the bath and lay back with a sigh. Nick sat on the surround by her head and soaped and massaged her shoulders. She peered up at him through the steam.

'You were right, Nick. You always are. It's infuriating.'

'I can see that it would be.'

'I didn't ask what was happening about your rapist.'

'We arrested him tonight.'

'What? When?'

'About half an hour before Sergeant Morrison rang.'

'Does that mean you should have been down at the station this evening questioning him?'

'Shirley will cope perfectly well. It was her arrest and a good one too. He put up quite a fight.'

'You said she'd be no good in a scrap.'

'There you are then. I am sometimes wrong.'

'You didn't get hurt, did you?'

'A few bruises.' He fetched her a clean bath sheet. 'Here,

235

wrap yourself up warm. I'm going to make you some hot milk and then you're going to sleep.'

'I'd rather have a glass of brandy,' she said sleepily.

'No chance.'

Chapter Twenty-Six

'Hold on a minute!'

Nick leafed through Tessa's statement again. 'Where's the bit where she mentions the first rape? There!' reading it quickly. 'I thought so. She says the first rape took place in the middle of October. Pauline Taylor was raped a month before that.'

'By a tall, thin man,' Shirley agreed, 'and not a short, stocky man. You mean there are two rapists on the loose in the valley after all?'

'Are there?' Nick asked. 'I wonder ... I wonder if that is what I mean.'

'You think Tessa may not have known about the first rape, Pauline's rape?' Shirley asked, puzzled. 'That she might not have been in when he got home that time? That he might have had time to clean himself up before she got home?'

'What I mean is that I want to talk to Pauline Taylor myself.' Nick got up.

'She's always refused to speak to anyone but a woman officer,' Shirley reminded him.

'I know.'

Was that because she thought a woman officer would be more sympathetic, or because she would be more gullible?

Pauline, confronted with Nick's soft brown eyes which seemed to her to pierce through to her guilty soul, broke down at once under his questioning.

'I knew my dad would kill me when he found out I was pregnant,' she sobbed. 'I had no money for a private

237

abortion – no way of getting any. I didn't dare tell him. Then that girl was raped and everyone was talking about it and I realised that if I said I'd been raped too, that might be a way out of it. I thought you might fix up for me to have an abortion without telling my parents.'

She looked up at Shirley Walpole through tearful eyes. 'Or if they had to be told that someone else would do the telling, tell him it wasn't my fault. Stand up for me. Like you did.'

Shirley stared stonily back at her. She did not trust herself to speak.

'Pauline,' Nick said, 'you gave Sergeant Walpole a description of the alleged rapist which conflicted with other information we had, which could so easily have misled us, stopped us picking up the real rapist before he could rape again, resulted perhaps in our suspecting an innocent man. Can't you see what a terrible thing you did?'

'I know, I know, but nothing could be worse than him,' she gestured at Taylor, 'if he knew the truth. I was desperate.'

'Who's the child's father?' Nick asked. 'Couldn't he have helped?'

'I don't know.' Nick looked at her in despair. 'I really didn't know his name.'

It was just as he'd said to Susie last week, Nick realised. This plain little thing, who'd never been shown a moment's affection by anyone, let alone had a boyfriend, was easy prey to the first man to kiss her and pet her and call her his sweetheart.

'Will I still be able to have the operation?' Pauline asked.

Nick shrugged. He'd had four hours' sleep and was too tired even to think through the moral implications of any of it.

'I believed you.' Shirley found her voice at last. It was a cold and angry voice and Pauline shrank away from her in fear. 'I believed you, befriended you. And you made a bloody fool out of me.'

She turned and walked out of the room, brushing aside Mr Taylor who had stayed strangely subdued throughout the interview. Nick heard the front door slam. He stood up.

'You'll be hearing from us if we decide to prosecute,' he told Taylor. Mr Taylor made no reply but stood staring at his daughter almost without expression. His silence spoke more than any words could do. Nick was glad to leave the hateful house and catch up with Shirley who was sitting on a bench by the bus stop, waiting for him.

'She didn't make a fool of me,' she said as Nick joined her. 'I made a fool of myself.'

'Utter crap, Walpole.' Nick sat down next to her and took her hand.

'I was so pleased with myself, interviewing her on my own, cutting you out, asking all the right questions. And I forgot to ask myself the one fundamental question that any detective starts with: is this witness telling me the truth?'

'I forgot to ask some pretty basic questions myself, come to that. It was natural for you to believe her; just as it never occurred to me to doubt Tessa's apparently throwaway remark that she was just starting her shift. Pauline's story fitted in with the rape we already knew about.'

'I wanted to believe her, you mean.' She avoided his eye. 'I've done nothing but make a bloody fool of myself since I got here.'

'That's right,' he agreed. 'Like when you set up the classes for those girls on your own initiative, so giving Ginny the means to fight the rapist off – '

'Having led her to risk entering the park at night in the first place,' Shirley broke in crossly.

'Like when you sensibly told me not to go into that shed while I behaved like the most hot-headed rookie instead of waiting for reinforcements. I'd have screamed blue murder at any constable who did the same and you didn't utter a word of reproach.'

'It's the sort of crazy brave thing you do though, isn't it?' she said, looking up at him. 'Like when you saved Alison's life.'

'Ah. You heard about that?'

'Carol told me when I first arrived. She was so proud of you.'

'Like when you came in after me to save me from a beating I richly deserved,' Nick continued. 'Like when you

239

arrested O'Shea. Yeah. You've done nothing but make a tit of yourself from start to finish, Walpole.'

Shirley smiled at him at last and they both began to laugh. Things weren't so bad: O'Shea was off the streets; life was getting back to normal. They could afford to laugh again.

'I never asked how Alison was,' Shirley said.

'She'll be fine after a good long sleep. She's very resilient. She's a fighter, a survivor, just like you. Just the sort of person I like to have around me.'

'Does that mean you won't be asking for me to be replaced?'

'No way! I'm not going to break in yet another new sergeant. Come on. We can't sit here all day holding hands. People will talk.' She pulled her hand away from his as if he were burning her. 'I don't make friends easily, Walpole, and I want you for my friend.'

'You got it,' she said in her best Cagney and Lacey accent. They got up and began to walk back to their police car.

'Who was the girl who got raped in the middle of October, then?' Shirley asked suddenly.

'We shall probably never know. Unless she's prepared to come forward now we've arrested him. I suspect she did what Pauline claimed to do — went home, had a hot bath and washed away the dirtiness, explained her muddy skirt by a fall in the rain ... and is trying her damnest to forget it.'

'But she never will forget it. She'll be stuck with it, perhaps for the rest of her life.'

'Perhaps. Or she may genuinely be able to put it behind her.'

'She's probably just a kid, though. He liked them young — in school or Guides uniforms.'

Nick, for once, elected to drive, letting Shirley relax in the passenger seat.

'Nick?'

'Yeah?'

'Would you have been taken in by Pauline?'

'Possibly not. There was something very glib about her statement, all that talk about feeling worthless. Oh, it's the sort of thing rape victims say, all right, but she'd got it off too fluently, too pat. She'd got it from a magazine article or a book. I should have picked that up from her statement from the first.'

'I should have picked it up from *her*.'

'We've been through all that, Walpole. Let's not start again. Anyway, I'm great at being wise after the event. I have a gold medal in hindsight.'

'But you would have known!'

'Which is precisely why she asked for a woman, someone who would naturally empathise and take her side. A man is always that tiny bit more sceptical – he's seen the infinite vagaries of human sexual behaviour from the other side. Remember too, that I've more years' service than you have, and am two ranks higher. Don't try to run before you can walk.'

'You won't be recommending me for promotion this year,' Shirley said with a sigh. 'I don't blame you.'

'I most certainly shall.'

She glowed with pleasure and sat in happy silence for a while before remarking, 'She got the bit about the balaclava right. Lucky guess, I suppose.'

'Not exactly. She daren't risk describing his face, we might have asked for a photofit or an identity parade. That would have been taking the whole charade too far. She had to say she hadn't seen his face, so a hood or balaclava was the most logical thing.'

As they drew up outside the station she said, 'What will we do about the Taylor girl? Will we prosecute?'

Nick thought back to the blank, loveless face of Mr Taylor in his bleak sitting room; to the despair he had last seen in Pauline's eyes.

'I think she'll have punishment enough,' he said.

241

Postscriptum

The London Stock Market duly crashed on the 25th of November 1988, following disastrous trade figures. Jennifer Tatton and William Marks, who had transacted further carefully researched sales within that account, made an overall profit of almost seventy thousand pounds with which they continue successfully to speculate.

Philip Hunter is on bail awaiting trial on charges of Assisting an Offender, contrary to Section 4 of the Criminal Law Act 1967 and Obstructing a Constable in the Execution of his Duty, contrary to Section 51(3) of the Police Act 1964. He is breezily optimistic about a non-custodial sentence. He is having Jennifer hurriedly trained to take Zac's place as Orion Software's Technical Support wizard so, given Jennifer's eclectic moral code, it may not be long before he finds himself back at Square One.

Philip and Alison have, by unspoken agreement, let their friendship lapse.

Phase Three of FIX has been shelved indefinitely owing to the lack of reliable freelance programmers, and Ruth Harper's contract has not been renewed following the piece about the FIX hacking which appeared in *Computing Tomorrow* under Carl Forster's byline. She is temporarily unemployed and her roots are beginning to show.

Nick persuaded Shirley that she would never get a conviction of aiding and abetting against Tessa O'Shea and she is on bail awaiting trial on the same charges as Philip. She has resigned from her job at the hospital and does not care whether she gets a custodial sentence or not. Kevin O'Shea is on remand and, after psychiatric tests, is being held in a secure mental hospital.

Pauline Taylor ran away from home on the day following her visit from Nick and Shirley, taking the meagre contents of her father's wallet with her. Her whereabouts are at present unknown.

Elizabeth Parrish, her parents and grandmother are slowly piecing their lives back together, knowing that they will have to relive the ordeal if O'Shea ever comes to trial; and that things will never be the same again.

Alex Porter has found himself a new girlfriend.